The Life and Death of Libby Morgan

A Novel

Lauren Lee Mann

Cover design and interior formatting by the author.

Published by **Crick & Ember Press**, an imprint of **Crick & Ember Publishing LLC**
First Edition, 2025

ISBN: 9798999426710

Printed and distributed by Kindle Direct Publishing

Contents

For my dad, the first man who showed me what devotion looks like, whose quiet grit lives in every line of Big Al.

For the creatives who were told they were "too much," and the later-in-life ADHDers who finally heard the music beneath the static. You weren't wrong. You were never broken. Just misnamed.

And for younger Lauren, who wrote in margins, online journals, blogs, who built whole worlds from spiral notebooks and silence. It's nice to see you again.

Prologue

Liv

Backstage smells like ozone and perfume. The air is hazy with sweatproof powder, glitter mist, and dry shampoo that costs more than rent. Techs with headsets bark cues over the thrum of house music bleeding through the walls. A lighting rig hisses above, recalibrating for one final sweep. At craft services, a bottle of rosé pops open—sharp enough to make two interns' flinch.

Everything is in motion. The machine is alive.

A stylist tugs at the hem of a gold dress. A hair tech double-checks the curl pattern from behind, fingers flying. Someone laughs too loudly, drunk already, probably, but no one pauses to care. The countdown to live is on.

And in the center of it all: Libby Morgan.

She moves like liquid spotlight, parting the chaos with her presence alone. She doesn't need to speak loudly. The air around her adjusts. People lean in. Laugh on cue. She offers air kisses, cracks a joke about the humidity, tosses back vitamin water laced with something no one questions.

No one ever questions Libby.

And somewhere inside her... I watch it happen.

They keep saying she has a show tonight. They mean me, I guess. But they don't see me. They see her.

Libby.

She's the one they dress and paint and shine up like glass. The one they trust with the live mic, the sparkle, and the gold that hugs just enough to remind people she's still relevant. Still perfect.

They don't ask how I am. They ask what time she's on.

I watch her in the mirror, the way her lashes lift, the smile that stretches without effort. Her voice: bright, crisp, and poised. She talks to the crew, laughs with the stylist, kisses the air on both sides of Sterling Vale's face.

She's good at this.

Libby never flinches. Libby never forgets a line. Libby doesn't need sleep or food or truth.

I sit inside her like a ghost. I used to fight to get out. Now, most days, I just... observe.

Sterling leans down. His cologne hits before his voice. Amber, citrus, and the cold steel scent of control.

"You're gonna kill it tonight, sweetheart."

His hand brushes the small of my back. He slides the pill into my palm like always. It's practiced. Ritualistic. A quiet transaction no one around us seems to notice.

A smooth oval. The color of chalk. The taste of obedience.

I don't answer.

Libby smiles. Libby takes it with a sip of lukewarm champagne. Libby winks and sways to the beat of the track warming up in her earpiece.

Inside, Liv screams.

Sterling Vale. My maker and my mirage.

There was a time when I admired him— genuinely. He saw me when no one else did. Plucked me from obscurity and polished me until I sparkled beneath the lights. He spoke in prophecy. Painted the future like gospel.

He said, *"This is how we protect Olivia."*

But what he meant was, *"This is how we make Libby too valuable to kill."*

I loved him once; in the way a child might love the fire that warms her hands before it scorches her skin.

He built Libby with brilliance. Precision. Artistry. And he buried me beneath every version of her he sold.

I want to vomit. I want to bolt. I want to tear the dress from my skin and scream until it echoes down the halls. But I smile. I take the pill. Because she always does.

Backstage hums like a machine. The lights are too hot. The air too tight. I can feel the sweat beginning to bead at my spine beneath the bodice. The sequins scrape. The lashes itch. The sound tech is tightening the pack at my waist.

Libby grins.

Liv disappears.

The countdown starts. Ten. Nine. Eight.

I feel the air tightening in my chest, like a corset around the part of me still trying to breathe. My heartbeat isn't mine. My thoughts aren't mine. The lights flicker against my skin like flames.

The audience claps. She waves, graceful, timed, adored.

I scream behind her ribs. Just once. It doesn't make it out.

The music starts.

I don't know what will happen next. Not really. One second, we smiled, her voice sugar-sweet on cue. And then, I say it. Or she does. Or maybe we both do.

"I'm so tired."

Just that.

Two seconds of live broadcast. Enough to end everything. Or begin it. The room doesn't gasp. It holds its breath. The director cuts to commercial.

I feel Libby cracking. Just a little. Just enough.

Maybe this time... I can claw my way out.

Albert Reed didn't believe in DVRs or cable news.

He believed in coffee at 5 a.m., Philadelphia sports, and turning off the damn television when the world got too loud.

He was retired, technically. But he still showed up at The Crick four nights a week, wiping down glasses, fixing the cooler when it buzzed too loud, arguing with Tucker about which team had the worst bullpen in the NL East. He said it was to help out. Truth was, it kept his hands busy. Kept the ghosts quiet.

Most nights, it worked.

But tonight, he couldn't sleep.

His body felt off, like something was pressing down on his chest, low and steady. Like a summer storm you can feel in your joints before it ever touches the sky.

Marianne had gone to bed hours ago. So, he sat in the worn leather recliner in the den, a blanket over his lap and a cold beer sweating in his hand.

The TV flickered soft light across the room. A summer special. Some pop show. Big smiles. Bright sets. Glitter. Something he'd usually flip past without a second thought.

Except his daughter was on screen.

Or someone who wore her face like a costume.

He watched her glide across the stage in a gold dress, his little girl who used to sing to the goats behind the barn, now wrapped in diamonds and makeup, eyes wide and hollow.

The crowd cheered. The lights flashed.

"That's not her," he said to no one. Not for the first time.

Then she stopped.

4

No music. No smile. Just her mouth parting like she was about to say something important.

"I'm so tired."

Two seconds of silence.

Then static. Commercial. The sound of the ocean crashing, trying to cover up a crisis.

He didn't move. Just stared at the empty screen.

Big Al had seen a lot of things. Wrecks on I-95. Fights in bars. Loss, you don't come back from.

But nothing hit him like that silence.

He knew two things in that moment: That wasn't Libby Morgan breaking down on stage. That was Liv. And she needed to come home.

He reached for his phone and scrolled past managers, publicists, and agency contacts.

He called Dorian.

"She's not okay," Al said, voice firm, heart racing. "I don't care what the press says. I want her home."

"She'll fight it," Dorian replied quietly. "You know she will."

"Let her," he said. "Let her kick and scream. I'm still her father. And I'm bringing her back."

Chapter 1: The Sound She Didn't Make

Dorian

Dorian didn't watch the broadcast. He didn't need to.

He'd seen this moment play out in his dreams—always glamorized, always tragic. His rescue was theatrical: late, defiant, cinematic. He'd sweep in on a white horse with diamond-studded reins and a playlist to match. Whisper some lyrics that unlocked the door to who she used to be. Carry her back to herself.

But dreams didn't have sirens. Or Narcan.

He parked outside the high-rise and slipped past security with a pass they forgot he still had. No one stopped him. Sterling never thought to revoke it. Dorian was legacy here. Ghost and guardian.

He stepped off the elevator and into the penthouse. And immediately, he knew.

This wasn't Libby's space anymore. Not entirely. The place was massive—vaulted ceilings, polished stone, glass swallowing the skyline—but the bones didn't matter. It was the skin of the space that told the story.

Soft earth tones. Cream throws over deep chairs. A bamboo fountain in the corner, trickling like the creek behind her childhood home. Plants everywhere—ivy, rosemary, snake grass—like she'd tried to root something. Stay grounded, even as the world spun her off-axis.

Crystals on the sill. A stack of poetry books beside the couch. A broken guitar pick under the kitchen island. A mug with half-dried tea leaves and a lipstick smear she never bothered to wipe away.

This wasn't curated for guests. It was hers. Liv's chaos. Soft and searching. Untamed. Trying.

And in that chaos... silence. Not peace. Stillness. No music. No phone buzz. Just quiet— the kind that follows something loud and shattering.

And then he saw it.

The piano. Grand. Ebony. Its lid open. Its keys barely touched. A half-finished glass of champagne rested on the edge. Libby's drink.

But the room... the feel of it... was all Liv.

A single note hummed, low C. Pressed and held. Dorian crossed the room like a breath held too long.

She was draped across the keys. One arm limp. One hand slack in her lap. Face turned toward the light, hair undone, lips parted. No makeup. No persona. No walls. Just Liv.

He dropped to his knees.

Her chest barely moved. A rise. A fall. Then nothing. Then again.

He pressed two fingers to her neck.

There it was. A pulse. Faint. Thready. Like a wire fraying.

He knew that rhythm—the fragile thread before the break. Maybe she'd hovered. Maybe she'd already decided not to come back.

But he wasn't giving her that choice. Not tonight.

He dropped his bag. Fumbled the zipper. Pulled the kit. Uncapped the nasal spray. One spray in her right nostril. He counted.

One one-thousand. Two one-thousand. Three—

She jerked. A gasp, sharp, shallow, stunned. Her chest hitched. Then fell. Then rose again.

Still unconscious. But breathing.

He lowered his forehead to hers.

"Not today," he whispered. "Not you. Not yet."

She was pale. Skin clammy. Lips tinged just barely. But she was here.

She left the door unlocked.

That was all the permission he needed.

He reached for his phone. "She's breathing," he told Al. "I got to her in time."

Silence. Then Al said, "Bring her home."

That was the moment Dorian stopped waiting for permission. He moved on instinct, grief and love braided like rope in his chest.

He made one call to a doctor he trusted—a woman with no social media presence and a track record of helping the invisible stay alive. Then another, to his assistant, encrypted and discreet.

They booked the jet. Cleared a private medical transport. He asked for full detox prep. Soft linens. Warm lighting. No cameras. Nothing sterile. Nothing that would feel like punishment.

He packed her bags in silence, pausing once to stare at a photograph of the two of them, laughing, caught mid-harmony in a tiny studio from the old days.

He put it in her bag.

By the time the EMTs arrived, she was stable enough to move. He never left her side. Through the elevator. Through the lobby. Into the car.

She didn't wake. Not fully. But her hand curled once around his fingers, just enough to say: *I'm still here.*

He tightened his grip.

"I know," he whispered. "I've been here the whole time."

What he didn't say—what he'd never say aloud—was that he'd watched her disappear for months. Her posts grew stranger. Her captions sounded like strangers had written them. He watched interviews where her eyes sparkled too brightly, her laugh a half-second too late.

He called. She didn't answer. He showed up to rehearsals only to find she'd left early. He sent flowers. Voicemails. Her favorite records, reissued on vinyl.

Nothing.

And still—he stayed close. Orbiting. Because he loved her.

Not like a crush. Not like a phase.

He loved her like breath. Like marrow. Like losing her would mean losing himself.

Olivia Reed, *Liv*. She was his best friend.

He hadn't saved her. Not really.

She left the door unlocked.

That's all it took.

But he'd walked through it.

And now—he'd bring her home.

Memory: Liv

The silence she keeps for herself.

The air smelled like honeysuckle and warm stone.

Liv lay back in the tall grass where the creek curved wide behind the old pasture, just beyond the barn. It was late afternoon, and the light softened everything it touched. The air buzzed low with crickets. The goats made the occasional sound like they were gossiping in the distance, but mostly, there was quiet.

Sweet, sticky quiet.

The kind you didn't get in a house full of weekend chores and Phillies games looping from the den. The kind you couldn't buy or bottle. The kind that made time hold its breath.

She was seventeen. Barefoot. Skin freckled and kissed with sweat. Her guitar rested forgotten against a tree. Her notebook lay open beside her, a few lyrics scribbled and crossed out in looping blue ink.

Tucker's arm was beneath her neck. The other draped across her ribs, his hand rising and falling with her breath. He tapped his fingers there, slow and steady, like she was his metronome.

"You're always hummin' something," she whispered, eyes closed.

"You're always writin' it down," he murmured, his voice brushing against her hair.

She smiled without needing to see him. The inside of her lids glowed orange from the sun. His shirt smelled like cut grass and the faint tang of motor oil. His breath warmed her temple. His chest was solid against her back, his presence effortless but anchoring.

He made everything feel quiet.

Not just the air. Not just the crickets and the breeze and the soft babble of the creek. He quieted the chaos inside her. The questions. The climb. The pressure to prove and polish and perform.

Tucker didn't ask her to be anything but here.

He ran his thumb along the curve of her side, and her whole body sighed beneath his touch. His hair caught the light—dark, a little unruly, and gently blown by the breeze. She opened her eyes and turned her head just enough to see his profile. His lips, slightly parted, bitten from thought, looked darker in the sun, almost red.

She wanted to press her mouth to his. To taste the shade of stillness he gave her. To live in it.

He caught her watching and smiled with that small, knowing grin—the one that said *I see you* without saying a word. He kissed her forehead, then let his lips rest there like punctuation.

This was it.

Not a dream. Not a goal. Just this.

The way he held her like something precious, not impressive. The way he didn't speak of tomorrow. The way he made her feel like the only girl in the whole goddamn world.

Years later.

When it got dark.

When the pills dulled her edges.

When Sterling raised his voice.

When the audience demanded more.

When the lights blinded—

Liv would come back here.

To this patch of grass. To this moment. To Tucker's arms. To the silence.

She'd replay it like a song only she could hear. Because Libby couldn't find this place. Only Liv could.

And Liv had buried it deep enough to be safe.

And now, drifting somewhere between the edge of death and the call back to earth, that memory wrapped around her like armor. The light of that day shimmered beneath her lids. She clutched it tighter than breath.

Somewhere distant, she felt a body—hers—jolt under a spray of something cold. She wasn't in the creek. She wasn't in the field.

But for one more heartbeat... she stayed there. Just a little longer.

Where love had no audience. Where quiet was enough. Where she was enough.

Then the darkness began to lift.

And the world came back in pieces.

Chapter 2: The Ceiling Fan Spins Backward

Liv

The ceiling is beige.
And spinning.
Not fast. Not slow. Just enough to make her—me—feel like I'm floating. Like I'm dreaming. Like I'm seventeen again, just back from the crick, barefoot and burned by the sun, and Tucker is downstairs talking baseball with Big Al, and I can still smell hay through the open window.

There's music somewhere. Faint. A note held long enough to hurt. Maybe the piano. Maybe just my pulse.

I blink. It takes a second to register that my lashes aren't glued on. That my face feels... naked. My tongue is thick. My mouth, dry.

"Olivia?" a voice whispers. Not stage-whispered like fans. Real. Raw.

I turn my head. The room slides sideways. But I see a blur of flannel. A silhouette in the doorway. The shape of a mother.

"No," I croak, barely audible. "No, no, no, no."

It rushes in like cold water. The show. The lights. The champagne. The damn pill. Dorian's voice saying something soft. Gloves. Needles. Darkness. And now this.

I'm home. In my childhood bed. With the soft, faded comforter I thought my mother had thrown out. My guitar case—not Libby's bedazzled one, but mine—propped in the corner. A dusty trophy shelf still bearing a 1999 Garnet Valley Talent Show ribbon.

My chest tightens.
Not from fear.
From shame.

Because this version of me was never supposed to come back here. Liv, the girl who sang barefoot and kissed one boy under the stars, was welcome. But this... this hollowed-out mess who can't perform without being medicated, who flatlined in a goddamn penthouse suite...

This woman was never supposed to let her parents see her like this.

"Where's Dorian?" I whispered, teeth clenched.

"Downstairs," Mom answers. Calm. Measured. Like I'm not breaking in front of her.

"I swear to God, if you all staged some kind of—" I sit up too fast. My stomach lurches. My hands shake.

I'm not detoxed. But I'm awake now. And everything hurts.

"We didn't stage anything," Dad says, stepping into view.

"You nearly died," Mom adds.

"You want to scream at someone?" Dad crosses his arms. "Scream at me. I'm the one who told Dorian to bring you home."

"You had no right," I rasp.

"I had every right," he says, voice low. "You're still my little girl. Even when you don't want to be."

Silence.

Except the ceiling fan.

Still spinning.

Still backward.

I don't storm out. I walk. Barefoot, like always. The wooden floor cool against my heels. The screen door creaks, and I wince at how loud it sounds. But no one follows.

The air is thicker here. Sweeter. The summer heat wraps around my skin like memory.

The back steps are chipped in the same place they always were. The path is overgrown but not forgotten. I follow it with muscle memory, not thought.

There used to be acres beyond this fence. Fields. Trees. Horses that didn't belong to anyone and old tractors rusting like art. Now it's neighborhoods, vinyl-sided houses with trimmed hedges and HOA rules about garden heights. A high school that is twice the size it was when I left. A Target where the pumpkin patch used to be.

But this strip of land—this crooked, fragrant mess—is still ours.

The garden.

Wild. Colorful. True.

Poppies. Coneflowers. Black-eyed Susans. Lavender stalks that hum under the weight of bees. It's all still here. A riot of color growing in confident, chaotic rows. No pruning. No pretense. Just life doing what it does.

A few weeks of nonstop rain had overfed everything. Then, like the sky had run out of patience, the temperature jumped from sixty to a hundred overnight. The kind of heat that scorched your lungs. The kind that felt personal.

I kneel at the edge, palm grazing the petals.

"You're still here," I whisper to the blossoms. "You waited."

A gust of wind lifts my hair. I close my eyes.

And for a moment, I hear music.

Not the produced, auto-tuned nonsense they make Libby sing.

Real music. From the inside out.

I feel her stir—the persona. The polish. The defense mechanism.

Libby.

They can't see you like this. Get up. Smile. You're a star.

No, I say, quietly but aloud. *You're a cage.*

You'll ruin everything if you stay here.
I already did.
Don't let him see you weak.
And just like that, I feel him before I see him.
Dorian.

His footsteps are slow. Careful. Like he knows this isn't a place to interrupt—only enter.

"You look like a ghost," he says gently, sitting on the low stone wall beside me.

"I feel like one."

He picks a daisy and hands it to me. I don't take it.

"She's loud today," he adds, not needing to name her.

"She's terrified."

"Of what?"

"Of me coming back to life."

Silence again. The wind stirs the lavender. The world doesn't end.

"I missed you," he says.

"You were the only one who never stopped calling me Liv."

"Because Libby never returned my calls," he smiles, soft.

Finally, I take the flower. Hold it like it might root something inside me.

For the first time in months—maybe years—I don't feel numb.

Not safe.

Not healed.

But real.

And that's more dangerous to Libby than anything.

I don't know how long I sit there. The garden folds around me like a cocoon—warm, fragrant, buzzing with life that doesn't need approval or applause.

The bees don't care what awards I've won. The daisies don't know what I've done to deserve this silence.

They just keep blooming.

I lean back against the stones, head tilted toward the sky. The sun spills across my face. I let it.

Dorian doesn't speak again. He just... stays. Like he always does.

Unmoving. Unjudging. Present.

It makes me ache in places I've long numbed out.

I run my fingers through the soil. Let the dirt gather beneath my nails. I used to do this before every school recital—dig until I hit something solid. Something unpolished and mine.

"I used to think this place was magic," I murmur. "Like, if I wrote something here, it would come true."

"Maybe it did," Dorian says softly.

"If that's true," I sigh, "I wasted my wishes on becoming someone I can't survive being."

The wind shifts. The peace holds for one more moment.

But deep down, I feel it coming. The burn. The breaking. The withdrawal.

My skin already itches in anticipation. My muscles twitch beneath the calm. My mouth is dry again—not just for water. For numbness. For silence. For pills I can't have anymore.

"I'm not ready for this," I whisper.

"No one ever is," he replies. "But you're not alone. Not this time."

I press my hands against my thighs to stop them from trembling. The garden blurs as tears threaten, but I won't let them fall.

"You can't tell anyone I'm here," I say, voice raw. "Not even your mom. Not yet. No managers, no label, no rehab press release. No press. Period."

16

"I already wiped your socials," he nods. "Told Sterling you were in Switzerland. He bought it."

"How?"

"Because I sent a photo of a mountain and a handwritten thank-you note from Libby Morgan."

I let out something close to a laugh.

It hurts.

And still, it holds... this peace.

But beneath it, we know:

Tomorrow might bring the hallucinations.

The vomiting.

The rage.

The night she tries to leave barefoot and sobbing, just to feel in control.

But for now—just this.

The garden. The friend. The flower in her hand.

The hum of bees like a lullaby.

The sun, too bright but honest.

The dirt beneath her nails, still warm from the day.

And the quietest truth of all:

She is still here.

For now, that is enough.

Chapter 3: The Body Remembers

Detox doesn't come with sleep. Just flashes—like lightning behind closed eyes. Then pain. Then noise. Then shame. And then the crawl.

I don't know what day it is. Day Two. Day Three. Day Ten. Time isn't linear in here. It's a loop of nausea and heat and screams that sound too animal to be mine.

My body is a traitor. My skin—soaked and shaking. My bones—humming like wires about to snap. Everything inside me wants out.

The world shrinks to tile. To my knees. To the retching.

I clutch the porcelain like an anchor and heave nothing but bile and air until my throat is raw and my ribs ache like they've been kicked from the inside. I'm not a person anymore. I'm a wound. A body on fire. A scream folded into skin.

"It hurts," I sob. "God, it hurts."

"I know, baby." Mom's voice, behind me. One hand on my back. The other holding my hair. Her presence is steady. Soft. Unmoving. The only thing not spinning.

I shove her away. Hard. Anger flares before I can stop it.

"You don't know!" I spit. "You don't know what it's like to be ripped out of your own goddamn body!"

She doesn't flinch. She stays.

"You let them take me," I scream. "You let me disappear. You smiled for cameras when I needed you to see me!"

"I didn't know how to reach you," she whispers, voice cracking.

"You didn't try!"

The silence that follows isn't peace. It's defeat.

I retch again. Hard enough to see stars.

When I wake, I'm not sure I ever slept. The bed is soaked. Sweat clings to my skin like shame. The sheets are twisted on the floor. I can smell myself, and I hate it. I hate me.

Dorian sits at the edge of the bed. His hands clasped. His eyes red. Like he's been praying. Maybe he has.

"Why didn't you stop me?" I rasp.

"I tried," he says, voice thin. "But I wasn't brave enough to lose you over it."

"You watched me disappear."

"I didn't know what to do... So, I wrote songs about you, Liv. I just... didn't have the guts to sing them out loud."

"You were my best friend," I whisper, more broken now than angry. "And you let them destroy me."

"You were already slipping," he says. "I thought if I stood still, maybe you'd come back."

The door creaks. Big Al walks in, slower than usual. He carries a cold washcloth and a bucket. He doesn't say a word. He doesn't have to.

His shoulders slump—not in exhaustion, but grief. The kind only a father knows. The kind that says *I was supposed to protect you. And I didn't.*

"You always fixed things," I whisper.

"I failed," he answers, no hesitation. "You were slipping through my hands and I just... thought I had more time."

He kneels. Places the washcloth on my forehead. His hands tremble.

It undoes me.

"I didn't want this life," I cry. "I just wanted to make you proud."

"You did," he chokes out. "Even when you were gone. Even when you were Libby. You were still mine."

I scream again that night.

Not just from pain. From grief. From rage. From the hollow where my voice used to live.

I scream at God. At them. At me.

And no one leaves.

They stay.

They hold my head.

They clean me up when I soil the sheets.

They whisper lullabies I forgot they knew.

They don't ask me to be better.

Just to breathe.

But between the breaths—

The ghosts arrive.

Sleep doesn't come. Not really. Only dark pulses. Twilight hallucinations. And nightmares so sharp I wake in pieces.

I see Jax's fists again. Not raised. Not at first. Just clenched. Threatening. Like thunder before the strike.

I see the bruise he left high on my ribs. The way he screamed about betrayal when I said no to a red carpet. The apology he texted with a diamond bracelet. The apology he didn't give the night he shoved me hard enough that my wrist cracked against the counter.

I see Elliot's back as he walks away. Suitcase in hand. The silence he weaponized. The way he used calm to kill my spark.

I see Sterling—grinning, arm around my waist—whispering into my hair about what songs the label wants. How he called me marketable, not magical. How he said sexy, not sacred. How he'd laugh when I cried, because it "wasn't good for the brand."

I see myself. A thousand selves. Each one a version I carved to survive.

Libby smiling through red carpet questions about Jax's arrest.

Libby singing into a mic with ribs taped from the bruising.

Libby on set with a makeup artist covering a black eye and calling it "eye shadow fallout."

It hits like truth.

It is harder than any detox pain.

Because now—I can feel it.

All of it.

The shame. The regret. The betrayal of every time I stayed. The memory of every time I left someone good because chaos felt more familiar.

I remember the man I loved who walked away to protect me.

Tucker, with his shaking hands and goodbye eyes.

I remember the call I never returned from Dorian.

The fans I lied to.

The lyrics I changed to make them less "depressing."

The pills I took with champagne and silence.

My life was a storm.

And I called it normal.

Now I lie in bed, soaked in sweat and sin and the absence of all my coping mechanisms. And there is nothing between me and the truth.

No veil.

No glitter.

No Libby.

Just Liv.

And she is gutted.

I want to peel my skin off just to quiet the memories.

I want to run until I disappear again.

I want to not want.

But I do.

I want to live. Even when it hurts.

I don't remember when the pain starts to change. It doesn't stop. It doesn't fade.

It... dulls. Like a blade losing its edge.

I stop vomiting. I start crying instead.

Hours. Days.

And then—

One morning, I woke up.

And it's quiet.

Not numb.

Not peaceful.

Just quiet.

My skin is still tender.

My throat, raw.

My thoughts, jagged.

But I'm here.

Not dead.

Not Libby.

Just Liv.

Scarred.

Shaken.

Alive.

Chapter 4: Rooms With No Names

I didn't want a circle of folding chairs.
I didn't want to sit in a church basement with weak coffee and fluorescent lighting while strangers whispered *"one day at a time"* like it was enough to stitch a soul back together.
I didn't want any of it.
But Dorian made a call.
And two days later, they showed up.
Rey.
They weren't what I expected. Not clinical. Not over-eager. Just... still.
They moved through the house like the floorboards knew them. Like the walls relaxed.
No clipboard. No business cards.
Linen shirt. Clean sneakers.
Cropped hair like they'd stopped chasing perfection and started choosing breath.
"Heard you're trying to kill a ghost," they said, setting their bag by the kitchen table.
"More like... bury one without killing myself in the process," I said.
"Same thing," they replied. "Trust me."
We don't sit in circles.
We don't hold hands or say mantras.
We sit.
We breathe.
Sometimes in the kitchen.
Sometimes on the porch.
Once, lying flat on our backs in the garden until the sky turned orange.
We don't rush.
They ask a question.
I deflect.
They wait.
Sometimes I talk.

Sometimes I cry.

Sometimes I close my eyes and try to remember who I was before applause became oxygen.

Rey doesn't ask me to let Libby go. They ask me what parts of her kept me alive.

"She's not the villain," they say. "She's the wall you built when the world wouldn't stop throwing bricks."

"What if I need her?" I whisper.

"Then we don't tear her down. We invite her to rest."

Rey never talks about themselves unless I ask. But when I do, it's never small talk.

They tell me about the year they lost their voice—not metaphorically, literally.

A throat surgery gone wrong. Months of silence.

They say that's when they learned what pain sounds like when it has no language.

They tell me about learning to listen before they learned to heal.

That silence taught them everything therapy school didn't.

Sometimes they hum.

Not a melody, not exactly.

Just presence—vibrating in the air between us like a tuning fork looking for resonance.

Their stillness isn't passive.

It's weighted.

Like they're holding space open for something sacred.

I start to trust it.

Start to crave it.

Not just the quiet, but the being seen in it.

In the quiet hours between sessions, I go outside.

The garden holds me better than the bed does.

I sit in the dirt, hands resting in the soil, feeling its pulse.

The lavender hums. The wind moves in long exhales.

The poppies don't ask who I am.

I see the old path to the creek. I don't walk it. Not yet. But I remember it.

I let the silence settle over my skin.

It doesn't numb.

It doesn't sting.

It just is.

Inside, I drift.

Past the dusty piano.

Past the notebooks.

Past the old Gibson guitar that leans in the corner like it remembers things I don't.

I don't write.

I don't play.

Not yet.

But sometimes, in between breaths... I hear a melody.

Not in the room. Not from the past.

Somewhere just outside of language.

A note held long enough to hurt.

A chord that hasn't found its resolve.

It hums behind my ribs. Faint. But present.

Maybe it's memory.

Maybe it's music.

But it's mine.

And for now, that's enough.

The kitchen smelled like coffee and fried onions.

A strange comfort.

The kind of smell that clings to a place, not just a moment.

I padded in barefoot, hoodie swallowed around my shoulders, eyes still sticky from sleep or crying—I wasn't sure which.

Big Al stood at the stove like he had every Sunday of my childhood.

Pan in one hand. Spatula in the other.

He didn't look up.

"You want toast or eggs?" he asked.

"Neither."

"Toast it is."

I sank into the chair at the table, the one closest to the window.

The sunlight pooled across the faded wood, and for a second, I pretended we were normal.

Pretended I was just tired from school, not from breaking apart in detox.

Pretended I was still a daughter and not a washed-up myth.

Pretended he was still just my dad, not someone I'd hurt a thousand different ways.

"You don't have to play babysitter, you know," I muttered.

Al flipped the toast without flinching. "I'm not."

"You have a life. A job. Friends. Better things to do."

He snorted. "I work at a bar, Liv."

I blinked. "Wait. What?"

"Yeah," he said, pouring coffee into a mug. "That kid Tucker—you remember him?"

My throat tightened. "Barely."

"He opened a place. Local joint. Real nice. Live music on Thursdays. Trivia on Tuesdays. And a jukebox that never works right."

He set the mug in front of me.

Not fancy.

Just hot and full.

"Tuck lets me help behind the bar. Fixes up some old cars with me too. We keep each other busy."

I stared at the steam curling from the rim. "Tucker lets you work for him?"

Al raised a brow. "He doesn't 'let' me. I let him think he does."

I almost smiled. Almost.

"I didn't know," I said quietly. "I didn't know you guys stayed close."

"He came around after you left."

"Out of guilt?"

"Out of grief," he said, sitting across from me. "And love. The same kind that kept me watching every award show you ever skipped. The same kind that made me call Dorian when I saw you on TV saying you were tired."

I looked down at my chipped nail polish. My pulse beat against my ribs like it didn't know where to land.

"He gets to have a relationship with you," I said, the bitterness sneaking out before I could stop it. "And I don't."

Al didn't answer right away.

He let the silence breathe.

"He showed up," he said eventually. "Even when he didn't know how to fix anything."

I flinched.

"You can be angry, Liv. Hell, be jealous if it helps. But don't forget—he lost you too."

That hit deeper than I was ready for.

"I ruin things," I whispered.

"No," he said firmly. "You're just not done figuring out how to hold them."

He reached across the table and covered my hand with his.

His fingers were rough. Familiar.

"You're not a ruin. You're my kid. And you're home. That's all that matters."

I didn't cry.

But I felt something break and settle inside me.

The toast popped.

He buttered it without asking.

Chapter 5: Everything in Its Place

Tucker

The smell of fresh coffee, floor cleaner, and wood polish meant the bar had been properly opened.

Tucker Hayes walked the floor like a man inspecting a runway. Every table had a story. Every barstool a familiar lean.

He wasn't the kind of owner who stayed behind an office door counting profits. He walked the floor. Washed the taps. Fixed the jukebox when it skipped. The Crick wasn't just his bar. It was him.

It sat right on the Bethel-Chichester line, tucked back just far enough from the highway to feel hidden, but close enough to pull in crowds from Route 322 and the Concord jughandle sprawl.

Plenty of parking. No one stumbled in by accident.

He'd made damn sure it was still technically Bethel Township. He was a Garnet Valley Jaguar. Still had the old letterman jacket in the back closet to prove it. The Chichester Eagles might've had the tougher name, but he liked to remind people: Jaguars didn't fly. They stalked. They struck.

That said, he was a Philly boy. He bled green. Cursed refs like it was prayer. Al had told him once that Tucker cried the day the Eagles won the Super Bowl. And it wasn't wrong.

Inventory order? Done before sunrise. Flyers for next month's open mic? Hung neatly on the community board. Brewery collabs? Rotating tap list kept it fresh. Local vineyards for the wine crowd. One small-batch whiskey from a Delaware County distiller that he swore by.

Everything had its place.

It had taken ten years and a busted shoulder to build this life. Over twenty-two years since the dream of Phillies pinstripes turned into torn ligaments and a classroom at Delco Community. Ten years of leaning into something real. Something his hands could hold.

Now, it worked. The business. The rhythm. Life.

Mondays were slow—bookkeeping, supplier calls, and cleaning kegs. Tuesdays were prep. Wednesdays picked up. Thursdays meant local bands and Open Mics. Fridays and Saturdays? Packed. Sundays? Eagles. All day. Even during the offseason, they found a way to talk draft picks and camp rumors.

Tucker's friends could talk Birds in their sleep.

And through it all, Big Al held court. He was the unofficial mayor of The Crick. Bartender. Bouncer. Philosopher. The guy with a story for every beer poured.

"In '89, we were down by two, ninth inning, bases loaded..."

"You ever hear of a love song so sad it bent the jukebox?"

"My daughter wrote better lyrics at sixteen than half these Grammy hacks now."

Tucker grinned every time Al said that last one.

But this week? Al wasn't there. Wasn't at the bar. Wasn't answering his phone. Wasn't even under the hood of the Impala they'd been rebuilding in the garage.

Three days turned to four and then eight. Tucker told himself it was probably something minor. Flu. A leak in the basement. Maybe the garden needed retiling.

But today was Monday. Routine day. And Big Al didn't miss routine.

So, Tucker closed the books early, let his assistant manager take over, and drove roads he hadn't touched in months—not since Christmas.

Al usually came to him. The bar. The garage. The side lot behind Tucker's place where the Impala waited, half-restored like some slow-motion resurrection.

It was an unspoken rule: Tucker didn't go to the Reed place. Too many ghosts. Too much memory.

But Al was quiet now. And Al's silence always meant something was wrong.

The wind caught in the window crack, carrying honeysuckles and earth, Bethel scents that hadn't changed in decades. And still, somehow, everything felt different.

He passed the old gas station where Liv used to grab grape soda after softball. The bend in the road where he taught her to drive stick. The dip in the hill that always made her laugh like they'd gone airborne.

He didn't mean to think of her. But Al always meant Liv. They were a matched set.

She was the music.

Al was the mechanic.

One taught him how to fix what broke.

The other broke him open.

He slowed at the curve near the old train tracks, let his hand fall to the center console where an old CD case still lived, burned years ago, black Sharpie scribbled across the top: "Garage Demos – L.R."

He hadn't played it in years. But he hadn't thrown it out either.

The closer he got to the Reed property, the tighter his chest felt. Not fear. Not even anticipation. Something older. Memory.

The driveway looked the same. The porch still leaned slightly to the left.

He parked, engine off, just as the wind picked up. He didn't walk up the front porch, maybe it was instinct. Maybe something else pulled him.

He walked around the side of the house, past the barn, toward the old garden path. Wildflowers spilled over the stones like they always had. Nothing manicured. Just color. Life. Time.

And then—

Music. A single note. Soft. Familiar. Piano.

He turned the corner and stopped cold.

Through the screen door, the light filtered across the hardwood and onto a woman at the bench. Hair loose. Shoulders slouched. Barefoot. Pressing keys like she wasn't sure they'd respond.

He knew that shape. That posture. That soul.

She was different. Smaller somehow. Faded around the edges.

But it was her. Liv.

She looked up. Their eyes met.

No words. Not yet. But everything else said:

You came back.

You stayed.

I never stopped listening.

Chapter 6: When You Let Go First

Memory: Liv

It was late spring, the kind of night where the road still steamed from a passing storm and the air carried the scent of grass clippings, wet asphalt, and lilac. The kind of night that made the whole world feel like it might bloom again, if you just held your breath and believed hard enough.

Liv did.

She believed in everything that night.

In the way Tucker's truck rumbled like a lullaby on idle. In the low thrum of her demo CD playing, quiet, intimate, unfinished.

In the future she'd mapped out so carefully it scared her.

They were parked near the crick. Windows down. Engine off.

The world soft around the edges.

She leaned into the seat, one leg curled beneath her, still damp from their walk through the field. Her hair smelled like rain. Her heart beat a little faster every time she looked at him, like it had every day since seventh grade.

Tucker was her safe place. Her storm shelter. Her home.

But something felt off tonight.

He hadn't touched her hand since they left the pasture.

He hadn't sung along to track four, her favorite.

His hands gripped the steering wheel, thumbs tapping a rhythm that didn't match the music. His jaw clenched, released. Clenched again.

She was about to ask what was wrong when he finally spoke.

"I think we should take a break."

The words landed like a punch.

At first, she didn't move.

Didn't blink.

The CD kept spinning, the scratch of a guitar solo leaking from old speakers like a wound.

"A break?" she said, voice small.

"Yeah. I just..." He swallowed. "I need to figure some stuff out."

He didn't look at her. Just stared at the windshield like it held a better future he didn't know how to claim.

"Tuck," she said softly, "we've been together since middle school. What do you need to figure out?"

"You're leaving."

Her heart squeezed.

"You're heading to New York, and you're gonna work with Sterling, and, and you're gonna become someone. I can feel it. Everyone can."

She smiled, just a little. Because she wanted that. Not just the becoming. But the part where he said it like a prophecy.

"I want you to come with me."

He flinched.

"I want you to hang out at the studio," she pushed on, voice rising. "I want to explore the city with you. God, Tuck, we could defer college, live off my advance, let me be your sugar mama," she teased, trying to pull him back to her with laughter.

But he didn't laugh.

"I don't belong in that world," he said. "Not like you do."

"That world is nothing without you in it," she whispered. "I don't want to do this without you."

He finally turned toward her, and his eyes were already wet.

"You think I don't want to go?" he said, voice breaking. "You think I don't want to stay up all night eating street food and sleeping on a floor mattress in some sixth-floor walk-up and watching you blow the roof off every studio you walk into?"

"Then why are you ending this?"

"Because I can't be the reason you don't."

Her breath hitched.

"I love you, Liv. But I can't be the anchor that holds you back when you were meant to fly."

"You're not an anchor," she snapped. "You're the only reason I ever believed I could."

Silence. Just the creak of the truck cooling down.

The faint hum of frogs near the waterline.

"I'm broken," he said. "I don't know who I am without baseball. Without a plan. And you, you already shine so bright it hurts to look at you."

"I never asked you to have it all figured out," she said. "I just asked you to be with me."

He looked down at his hands.

"You were never small, Liv. But if you stay for me... maybe you will be."

And just like that, he handed her freedom like it was mercy.

She didn't cry. Not yet.

She sat in his truck and watched the boy she loved set fire to everything they'd built, just to keep from holding her back.

He thought it was kind.

But Liv would carry the scorch marks for the rest of her life.

The world remembers it differently.

They say Liv Morgan left a small-town boy behind to chase fame.

But Liv remembers the truth:

She had a plan for them to be forever.

And he let go first.

Chapter 7: Nice to See You, Too

Liv

Before I open the door, I see him. Tucker Hayes. All 6'2" of him is broader than I remembered but still lean in the way he always was. A man now, not just the boy who carved our names into the barn siding with his house key and said forever like it was a fact, not a hope.

His hair is longer. Thicker. Pushed back with just enough defiance to suggest he doesn't really style it, just runs a hand through it and lets it do what it wants. I used to tease him for that. Used to love it.

I want to touch it now. God help me, I want to bury my hands in it, pull him close by the collar of that faded Henley and taste every year we lost.

His beard is trimmed close, coarse, darker than his hair. It makes the sharp cut of his jawline look even more unforgiving. His lips, though soft. Slightly parted. Red like he's been biting them, nervous.

His eyes sweep the porch. Not frantic. Just... scanning. Alert. Watchful. That's the thing about Tucker—he never missed much. Not even now. Not even me.

There's a dimple in his cheek that only shows when he's thinking hard. It's there now.

And his scent, though the wind barely carries it, I know it. Woodsmoke. Citrus. Motor oil and something warmer beneath it all. Like pine needles drying on a dashboard. Like memory itself.

It hits me like hunger. My body flinches. Just the smallest tremor. But I feel it all the way to my spine.

Because for a moment, just a moment, it feels like being seventeen again. Like climbing into his passenger seat with wet hair and bare feet, like stealing kisses under floodlights and building futures out of midnight drives.

I am not that girl anymore. But God, I remember how she felt. And the man standing on my porch? He's a reminder of everything I lost. Everything I loved. Everything I might still want... if I were someone new. Someone whole.

I open the screen door before he can knock.

He freezes.

So, do I.

He wasn't coming for me. That's obvious from the way his eyes flicker, not just surprised, but blindsided.

"I was... checking on your dad," he says, voice slower than usual. "He hasn't been at the bar. Won't answer his phone. Thought maybe the garden fell on him or something."

"Nope," I say, trying to keep my voice light. "Still vertical."

The look he gives me says you were not what I expected to find.

"Hey, Tuck."

"Hey, Liv."

His name is heavier in my mouth than I meant it to be. He shifts on his feet; hands stuffed in the pockets of his jeans. I cross my arms over my chest. Not defensive, just trying to keep my body still. It's been twitchy all day. The kind of skin-crawling discomfort they don't put in rehab brochures.

"You, uh... want to come in?" I ask, then instantly regret it.

He shakes his head slightly. "Just wanted to make sure Big Al wasn't dying."

"He's not," I say. "Well, he says he's not. You know him. Could be actively having a stroke and still trying to finish the oil change on the Buick."

"You look..." he trails off, then stops himself. Smart man.

I raise an eyebrow. "Go ahead. Say it."

"I was gonna say 'alive.' But it felt a little dark."

"It is dark," I say. "You should've seen me before Dorian drugged me and smuggled me out of LA."

That earns the faintest smile. I press my fingers to my ribs, trying to settle the tremble in my hands.

"Kidnapping's not usually part of recovery," he says, and he's either oddly perceptive or at least keeps up on social media.

"Yeah, well. Apparently Narcan and NDA nurses were cheaper than rehab PR."

He doesn't laugh, but the corner of his mouth lifts.

"Your secret's safe with me."

"Not really a secret if you just found me sweating through a flannel on my parents' porch."

He glances behind me, toward the house. "So... this is real."

"Unfortunately."

Another pause. Longer this time. He looks like he's deciding whether to stay or run.

I lean against the doorframe, arms still tight across my body. "I'm not good company right now, Tuck."

"Didn't come for company," he says. "Came for Al. Found you instead."

My stomach flinches, even though it's the truth. Especially because it's the truth.

"Lucky you."

"Not sure that's the word I'd use."

38

Silence again. But it's louder this time. The kind that hums.

I glanced toward the swing. The cushion's sun faded. A coffee mug still sits on the table beside it. Mine from this morning, half-full. I haven't touched it since the anxiety hit around noon.

"Wanna sit?" I ask, pointing to the swing. "If I stay standing, I might start shaking again, and I'd like to preserve a shred of dignity in front of you."

He nods. "Yeah. Alright."

We walked to the porch swing. Not quite shoulder to shoulder. Not quite apart. But something is shifting.

It's not Libby who sits beside him this time. It's me. Liv. Raw. Ruined. Unvarnished.

He leans back, resting one arm along the swing's top rail like he used to do when we'd drive nowhere with the windows down.

I pull my knees up and wrap my arms around them. Feel the tremble slow.

"Garden still looks good," he says. "Mom's been out there every day."

He nods, eyes on the trees now, the light catching in his lashes.

"You're really here," he says, more to himself than to me.

I want to answer. But I'm not sure I am. So, I stay quiet. And the silence doesn't ask anything of me. Not yet.

Chapter 8: Should We Be Listening?

Dorian

From the kitchen window, the view was cinematic. Porch swing. Golden-hour lighting. Tucker Hayes sitting rigid like he was bracing for impact. Liv curled into herself like the breeze might peel her skin back if it tried hard enough.

Dorian sipped his tea.

"They're not saying anything," he noted.

"It's all in body language," Marianne said, leaning over his shoulder with a mug of her own. "See that knee twitch? That's her trying not to run."

"And he keeps scratching the back of his neck," Dorian added. "That's Tucker's version of screaming into a pillow. Or he still has that tapeworm from sixth grade."

"You two are worse than me and my book club."

"You are the book club."

"Exactly."

They both laughed, soft enough not to carry through the screen.

The sun bent low over the garden, casting long shadows through the back trees. A breeze rustled the leaves, gentle as a sigh. Inside, the kitchen smelled faintly of rosemary and something sweet— like Marianne had baked earlier and tried to distract herself with the simplicity of flour and heat.

"So," Marianne said, straightening up, "how bad was it, really?"

"On a scale of one to full-blown intervention jet flight?" Dorian's voice softened. "It was bad."

"I thought so."

"She flatlined for eleven seconds."

Marianne's breath caught.

"Jesus."

"She hates it when I say it out loud."

"I hate that it has to be said at all."

They watched the swing creak back and forth, both unmoving on it. It looked like a scene from an old film—silent, suspended, drenched in golden sorrow.

"I'm still mad at her," Marianne admitted.

"Good. That means you're still here."

"I never left."

"No," Dorian said, glancing at her. "You didn't. But she did."

They stood shoulder to shoulder, the kind of closeness forged by time and loss and the shared ache of loving someone who didn't always want to be loved.

Then:

"What do you think they're saying?" Marianne asked.

"Something painfully awkward."

"He probably said she looked tired."

"She probably told him she detoxed in flannel and cried on the piano bench."

"Do you think they've hugged yet?"

"If they have, it was stiff and short, and no one inhaled."

Marianne chuckled, the kind that comes out like a sigh. Her eyes stayed on Liv.

"I used to think they'd be the ones," she said.

"They still might be."

"Too much damage."

"Or," Dorian said, finishing his tea, "enough scars to recognize each other now."

"What if she runs again?" she asked suddenly, voice breaking.

"Then I'll go get her again."

"And if she dies this time?"

Dorian didn't blink.

"Then we bury her right next to Libby Morgan and never let the world speak her name again."

Marianne turned to him, eyes glassy.

"You really love her."

"I always did. But not like he does."

"No one does," she whispered.

Outside, Liv shifted. Tucker leaned just slightly toward her. It was nothing dramatic. But it was real.

Dorian and Marianne stood, breath held like two kids watching a wild animal move closer to the edge of the woods. Hope and fear braided into one long, quiet moment.

"Okay," Dorian said finally, "I think they might've just made it through the first thirty seconds without exploding."

"Miracles do happen."

They didn't look away. Not yet. Not while it still mattered.

Chapter 9: This Feels Like Yesterday and a Lifetime Ago

Liv

The swing groans under us, same way it always did. We don't look at each other. That would make it real. We both stare forward like two strangers sharing a park bench, waiting for different buses.

I pick at my fingernails. My leg bounces again. I try to hold it down with my hand, but it just twitches harder, like my body's airing the inside of my brain. I want stillness. I want silence. But my skin is a riot and my nerves are short-circuiting.

"So," he says finally, "you're home."

"Apparently."

"Is it permanent?"

"Is anything?"

He nods; lips pressed into a line.

I glanced sideways. He's still got that profile. Strong jaw. Soft eyes. The kind of face that used to make me feel safe before it made me feel abandoned. And now, here it is again. Familiar and foreign.

You don't get to look like that, I think. Not when I'm like this. Not when my stomach's still a war zone and my head feels like it's been fogged over by ghosts.

"You run this whole big life," I say. "Bar owner. Community hero. Probably got a street named after you in Media."

"Just a beer named after me," he says. "Tuck's Red Ale. Goes great with wings and heartbreak."

I let out a small laugh. It hurts. I let it hurt. Because at least it's not numb.

He watches me out of the corner of his eye but doesn't say anything. Doesn't push.

"You look tired," he says before catching himself. "Not in a bad way. Just, like you've been through it."

"You mean like I died and got rebooted in my childhood bedroom? Yeah."

A pause. I rest my forehead on my hand. Sweat beads at my hairline. My shirt clings to my back. I can still taste metal in my mouth from the meds. Still feel the echoes of the night sweats and the rage dreams.

"I'm detoxing," I say bluntly. "My body is pissed the fuck off."

"I figured."

"You always were good at reading between the lines."

"You used to sing between them."

That almost undoes me.

A thousand nights rush in at once. Me on the floor of our old rehearsal space. Him on a milk crate with a notebook, humming harmony. Our knees touching. Our hearts are not yet broken.

The swing creaks again. I focus on the sound. Try to anchor myself in the rhythm of something that isn't my thoughts.

Tucker shifts beside me, arms resting on his knees. His body heat grazes my shoulder and it's like being held without touch.

And there it is. That hunger. Not just for food or peace or clarity—but for him. For his hands. For the weight of them on my waist. For the way his mouth would slant just before he kissed me. For the sound he made when I used to trace the line of his collarbone with my fingertips.

I close my eyes. Try to will it away.

Because I'm not ready. Not for touch. Not for him. Not even for myself.

But I remember it. I feel it in my hips and my throat and every part of me that still wants to be claimed by something that isn't pain.

"Tucker..."

"Yeah?"

"I didn't leave you. You let go first."

He looks at me. Really looks. And I see it. Regret. Still fresh. Like he's been polishing it for years just to keep it from fading.

"I know," he says.

That's all. Not an excuse. Not a fix. Just the truth, finally spoken.

The sun drops lower behind the trees. The porch swing keeps groaning. And for the first time since I came home, the air doesn't feel like it's pressing me into the ground.

We sat in silence. Not healed. Not whole. But facing the same direction.

Chapter 10: The Ones Who Knew Me

Liv

It had been three days since the porch. The silence between us had stretched long, but not bitter. More like a question waiting to be asked.

I found myself in the garden at sunrise, hands still stained with dirt from yesterday's weeding. The world was quiet in that way it only is before 7 a.m., before texts and talk shows and reminders of who they think I am.

I sat on the porch steps, coffee cooling beside me, and tried to remember the last time I'd written something for no one. No label. No charts. No expectations. Just me.

And I thought of Dorian. Of where we began. Of what we built before it got named and managers and monetization plans. Of the church of almost.

It started in Dorian's parents' basement. Cement floors, low ceilings, walls lined with old Christmas decorations and canned beans. The kind of place that smelled like damp cardboard and possibility. The kind of place where you could be bad at something before you got good. Where no one listened unless you invited them to. Where no one tried to make you into anything.

He had a four-track recorder and a borrowed mic that sparked when you tilted it wrong. I brought my notebook and a guitar with a crack near the neck that buzzed if I strummed too hard.

We called it the church of almost. We lit candles when the mood struck. We whispered harmonies late into the night. We wrote songs we were too afraid to sing in daylight. And we were good. Not polished. Not performative. But true.

There's one night I always return to. I was sixteen. Dorian had just come out to me. Quietly. Casually. Like it was no big deal. Like I was the only person in the world he trusted with that version of himself.

We'd just finished a song, one of those raw, aching things we never released. I was lying on the rug, stomach down, fingers curled in the fringe. He sat cross-legged, plucking chords that didn't go anywhere.

"You think we'll make it?" I asked.

"Define 'make it," he said, tuning the G string until it sang.

"Enough to live on music. To be heard. To be whole."

He didn't answer right away. Just kept playing.

"I think we already made it," he said. "We're making it right now. This is the part they'll never understand."

And he was right. The world came later, with its contracts and lighting rigs and vocal coaches who told me how to breathe like someone else. But that night? That was mine.

When we started Jag Records, it wasn't a brand. It was a promise. To stay true. To stay weird. To stay free.

We made our first logo with a Sharpie on Dorian's mom's receipt pad. The name came from a lyric I wrote in his kitchen: "just a jagged little hymn in a broken gospel town."

He said, "Jag. That's it."

I said, "Jag sounds like a car crash."

He said, "Exactly."

"Everyone will think we named it after the school mascot, you know that right?" Freakin' Jaguars.

Years later, when Libby was on magazine covers and Jag had a team of interns who'd never set foot in a basement, I'd still dream of that room. The green light on the recorder blinking. Dorian's laugh when I hit the wrong note and kept going. The silence after we finished something real. No audience. No autotune. Just the ones who knew me.

Dorian

He still had the old recordings. Not on a hard drive. Not in the cloud. On CDs. Labeled in Liv's handwriting, half-cursive, all sharp edges.
"Basement Hymns – Vol. 1"
"Olivia"– Try #4"
"Don't Erase This One"
He kept them in a shoebox under his bed. Not for nostalgia. For proof. Proof that once upon a time, they made music that didn't beg for approval.

When he couldn't sleep, on tour, in green rooms, in luxury hotels that felt like prisons, he'd play them on an old Sony Discman, wiping and blowing off the dust when it got dirty.

There was one song, in particular, that undid him. Liv called it "Blood in the Ink." Unreleased. Unmastered. Just her voice and a guitar so out of tune it felt intentional.

She sang like she was confessing to God and didn't care if He answered.

He'd never forget the way she looked after they recorded it. Barefoot, mascara smudged, eyes wide and wet. Like the song had taken something from her, and given her something back.

"Burn it," she said.

"No," he said.

She didn't fight him. She trusted him.

That was the difference. Before the fame. Before Sterling. Before Libby. Back then, Olivia

Reed still believed she could be seen without being consumed.

Liv

But even then, when the candles burned low, and we lived in our own world in that basement, Dorian knew we'd need more than magic to protect what we made.

He became the face of Jag. The frontman. The recruiter. The soul that lured other misfits into our orbit. He could speak both languages: the tender code of artists, and the sharp syllables of contracts and clauses. He built the team, mentored the talent, sat across desks from executives twice his age and made them blink first.

I stayed behind the curtain. A co-founder. A ghostwriter. A shadow in the credits. Not because I didn't care, because I couldn't risk anyone knowing Olivia Reed still existed. By then, I was Libby Morgan, property of Empire Nine, locked in a glittering cage I'd helped design.

Jag Records never held my name on its artist roster. But when Dorian drew up the paperwork for our partnership, back when we thought "partnership" just meant trust and tacos and sharing headphones, he'd included a clause I forgot even existed.

"All original work created under the Jag Records imprint, whether written, produced, or performed, shall be jointly owned by Olivia Reed and Dorian West, regardless of external affiliations or stage persona."

Legal protection, disguised as love. Because he knew.

He knew one day; the machine might come to claim what it didn't birth. That Sterling might twist his smile into ownership. Those contracts inked in red carpet lighting had a way of turning art into collateral.

And he knew I wouldn't remember. Not when the lights hit. Not when the voice changed. Not when I became Libby Morgan so completely, I forgot what I'd already protected.

But Dorian remembered.

Jag was ours. No matter what the world thought they bought.

Chapter 11: Noah and the Quiet Years

Prompt: Write about someone who loved you well.

Rey gave me this prompt last week. I didn't touch it. I told them I was busy. That I needed to organize my vitamin pill box or alphabetize the spices or call the insurance company about something I made up. Anything but sit in that question.

Because when someone asks you to write about love, your brain doesn't go to easy ones. It doesn't go to the grand gestures or the headlines. It doesn't go to the men who burned bright and left you in ash. It goes to the one who stayed quiet.

So today, when the house was empty and the sun hit the old pine table just right, I opened my notebook, and I wrote:

Noah Michael smelled like cedar and ink and patience. He loved me like you'd love a fragile thing you believed could still fly.

We met in a studio we weren't supposed to be in. I was fresh off a press tour, hollowed out by smiling. He was there tuning a piano that didn't belong to him. Looked up, nodded once, and kept working. Like I was anyone. Like I was just a girl.

He didn't care about Libby. He barely recognized her. When I told him I wrote songs no one would ever hear, he said, "Play me one." No fanfare. No seduction. Just curiosity.

He made me laugh when I forgot how. Slipped jokes in where silence threatened to swallow me.

He dried my eyes without making it dramatic. Just handed me tissues and said, "You don't owe me the clean version."

I told him about Tucker one night, how loving someone so young made every other love feel like a translation. Noah didn't flinch. He didn't compete. He just listened. Then kissed my wrist like it was sacred and said, "I'm not trying to erase anyone. I'm just here now."

His family loved art and effort and second helpings. They read poetry out loud and argued about brush technique. They welcomed me like I'd always been theirs, offered me wine and advice and winter scarves hand-knitted in soft wool. It was the only holiday I didn't feel like I was performing.

We got married at the courthouse with coffee stains on the paperwork. I wore a dress that didn't zip all the way. He forgot his tie. We laughed the whole drive home. And for a while, we were... good. Quietly, wonderfully good.

We'd lie on the floor with guitars and red wine, writing songs that only existed between us. He'd stop mid-verse to read me Neruda or dog-ear a page in a book he thought I'd like. He once told me, "You don't have to sound perfect to be powerful." He never needed me to sparkle. Just to be.

He was the first person who asked about Olivia and didn't flinch when she answered. But I did. I flinched every time the world called, every time Sterling dangled applause like oxygen.

And Noah... he didn't fight it. Didn't yell. Didn't plead. He just... stepped aside.

There was one night, though, when he tried. I was packing for a red eye to London. Another surprise performance. Another contract I hadn't read. He stood in the doorway, arms crossed, eyes heavy. "You don't have to go," he said.

"I do."

"You don't want to."

"I don't know what I want." He stepped forward, took the passport from my hand, and held it like a question. "Then stay," he said, quietly. "Stay, and we'll figure it out."

I kissed him goodbye an hour later.

Maybe I needed someone to fight for me. Maybe he thought letting me choose was love. Maybe we both mistook silence for support when it was really surrender.

I think if he'd slammed a door, I would've stayed. If I'd cried harder, he might've followed. But we thinned. Like mist in the morning sun.

I found one of his letters not too long ago, tucked into a book I haven't opened in years: "I know you think you're choosing your art over me. But I think you're choosing your performance over yourself. And that's a grief I can't carry for both of us."

I didn't understand it then. I do now.

We could've been more. If we'd fought harder.

I write his name slowly. *Noah*. Not a wound. Not a regret. Just a soft place I once got to rest.

And I remember our last morning. It was almost sunrise. We didn't sleep. The bottle of red on the counter was down to the sediment, but we poured it anyway into mismatched mugs because the good glasses were packed. The apartment was half-boxed. My boots are by the door. His records are already gone.

We sat on the floor. Quiet. Spent. The kind of quiet that follows the last "I love you" you'll ever say to someone out loud. We knew it was ending. Not with fury. Not with blame. Just the slow exhale of something that had already decided to leave the room.

But that morning... we made love like people who didn't believe in endings. Like people who needed to memorize each other, bone by bone. It wasn't desperate. It wasn't performative. It was devotion. One last offering.

After, he pulled the blanket around us and whispered, "I hope whoever's next gets to see you like this."

I kissed his temple. Held his hand. I didn't say it, but I thought it:

No one gets to see me like this.

Because even in that moment, even with his body wrapped around mine and his breath soft against my hair... I drifted. Back to the crick. To a truck that smelled like motor oil and mint gum. To a boy who kissed me like he believed it would save us both.

Every love after Tucker was a translation. Beautiful, but not fluent. And Noah... God, Noah tried. He loved me well. Better than most. Better than I deserved, maybe.

But love without presence is like singing to an empty room. Eventually, you go quiet.

I left the journal on the kitchen table without meaning to. Closed. No name. Just the leather cover and the frayed ribbon tucked between the pages.

Dorian walked in, humming something half-finished. A new hook, probably. He stopped when he saw it. Tilted his head.

"You writin' again?" he asked, not pushing.

I nodded.

"About anything good?"

"About Noah," I said—surprising both of us.

He set his coffee down, didn't speak right away. Just gave me that look—the one that says *you don't have to perform here.*

"Good," he said finally. "You never really got to grieve him."

I traced the stitching on my journal. "It wasn't that he hurt me. We just let each other go."

Dorian exhaled slowly. "Maybe that's the worst kind of goodbye."

I didn't answer.

We just sat there, in the stillness.
The quiet years echoing louder than any applause ever had.

Chapter 12: The Safe House

Life has a funny way of reminding you of your past, when your mind is already heavy. It was the end of the 6 o'clock news. The part after the politics and the weather, when the anchors soften their voices and say things like, "And finally tonight, a story about love."

I was folding towels in the living room. The good kind, fluffy, mismatched, probably older than me. My parents never upgraded what still worked. Marianne was humming in the kitchen. Big Al had fallen asleep with the recliner half-raised. I was about to turn the volume down when I heard the name.

"Elliot Shaw, the private equity executive turned philanthropic strategist..."

I froze. The screen shifted to a crisp image of Elliot in a navy suit, smiling that quiet, calculated smile. Standing next to a woman who looked like she'd been photoshopped into real life, blonde, elegant, too young by half. She wore a gown that didn't wrinkle and a gaze that didn't wander. They were posed in front of a marble rotunda, accepting some humanitarian award.

"The couple met during a clean water summit in Geneva and plan to expand their foundation's reach into under-resourced rural communities across the U.S."

I stared at the screen like it might blink first. Not because I still loved him. I didn't. Not because I missed him. I hadn't in years. But because he looked exactly like the man I married, and somehow more himself. As if being with her allowed him to inhabit his full design. Logical. Disciplined. World-improving.

I watched them smile for the camera. It was the first time I realized that Elliot Shaw had never belonged to me.

He used to write our weekly meal plan on a whiteboard. Color-coded by protein. Breakfast, lunch, and dinner. He even added water goals and a reminder to "pause between bites for mindful digestion."

I told him once it felt like we were preparing for a cleanse that never ended. He smiled like that was the point.

In the early days, I found comfort in it. The predictability. The clean angles of his life. No glitter, no headlines, no high heels in the hallway at 3 a.m. Just Elliot in a pressed Oxford shirt, slicing cucumbers with surgical precision while asking if I'd taken my supplements.

He didn't love chaos, and I was chaos pretending to be cured.

But I didn't marry him by accident. Elliot wasn't a Libby choice. He was the first choice I made as Liv. After the second overdose, quiet, buried, pre-social media. I needed something that didn't burn.

I needed someone who didn't look at me like a song, or a brand, or a thing to fix. He didn't know how to hold me emotionally, but he never mishandled my body. He never raised his voice. He never demanded I perform. He simply offered structure.

And for a time, that was enough.

We had rituals. Quiet ones. A Friday night calendar sync. Morning smoothies made with clinical precision. Soft jazz on Sundays while he reorganized the spice rack alphabetically. He taught me how to iron pillowcases. How to keep receipts in a labeled file. How to respond to emails with grace instead of urgency.

I once woke up from a panic attack, gasping in the linen closet, and he simply sat beside me, handed me a room-temperature bottle of water, and said, "We'll review your triggers later. Let's just breathe right now."

I mistook his stillness for safety. And maybe, for a while, it was. I convinced myself love could be assembled—structured like a room. If everything had its place, maybe I wouldn't come undone again.

But what I needed was connection. What Elliot offered was control.

I was—had always been—chaos in motion. And chaos does not want to be contained. It wants to be seen.

Dorian

Outside, the garden hummed in late summer stillness. Dorian stood by the trellis, fingers wrapped around a chipped coffee mug he wasn't drinking from. The moonlight scattered across the greenhouse glass, soft and broken, like them.

He hadn't meant to overhear the news. But he saw Liv freeze. Watching her jaw set, her shoulders still. The kind of silence that didn't ask for comfort, just space.

He stayed in the garden. Not because he didn't care. Because he cared so deeply, it scared him sometimes.

She was his twin flame. Not in the romantic sense, though they'd blurred those lines in their twenties, high on creation and codependence, but in the way their souls mirrored each other's frequencies.

They burned hot. They built worlds. They broke each other open. And no matter how many times they drifted, something magnetic always pulled them back. It was a knowing he carried in his marrow. Even when she disappeared for weeks. Even when her name became a headline. Even when she didn't call.

He watched from the wings. Made sure her name stayed protected. Sent flowers under fake names. Called Noah when the shadows got long. Tracked set lists and sleepless flights. Because if anything ever truly happened to her, he'd feel it before the world knew.

He closed his eyes, breathing in rosemary and soil and the ache of almost-lost things. He'd spent a lifetime navigating in-betweens. Half Black, half Asian. Too much of both. Never enough of either. Queer in a world that always wanted a label. But he'd never needed one.

He loved who he loved. And he'd loved Liv in ways no language could hold. They didn't always make sense. But they always made music. And when they had a break, those gaps between albums, between calls, between breakdowns. It hollowed him.

Because he wasn't just her producer or writing partner. He wasn't just her best friend. He was her echo. And if she ever stopped singing, he wasn't sure who he'd be without her voice to harmonize against.

He whispered to the sky like it was a stage light.

"Let her stay."

Chapter 13: The Show We Don't Talk About

Liv

Rey doesn't ask what I thought of the segment. They wait.

The office smells like sage and old paper. Not my mom's scent, not really, but something between eras. Marianne's books are still on the shelves. Rey added a weighted blanket and two new degrees. The air is still learning how to hold both of them.

"I didn't feel anything," I say. Then I adjust my sleeves, because I'm lying.

Rey doesn't push. They just tilt their head, like they're waiting for the real sentence.

"He looked happy," I say finally.

"And it felt like a betrayal."

Rey nods.

"But not of him," I add. "Of me."

They write something down, slowly, deliberately, like the words need time to arrive.

I stare at the floor. The pattern in the rug starts to blur.

"Elliot was the first man who never hurt me," I whisper. "But I still left."

Rey says, gently: "Sometimes safety doesn't mean sanctuary."

That is when the memory starts to climb out of me.

Not of Elliot. Not of the whiteboards or the water goals or the silence that used to feel like stability.

But of the first man who made me feel *chosen*.

The last man who made me feel afraid.

Rey asked me to name the moment it changed.

I told them I did not know. But that was not true.

It changed the night he punched the mirror instead of me. And then blamed the glass for being in the way.

Jax Holloway did not walk into the room. He claimed it. He was all jawline and swagger and stage heat, an influencer before that word meant anything. He had twelve million followers and one focus: domination. Of the screen. Of the scene. Of me.

The first time we met, he kissed my cheek like he already owned the rest of me.

The first time we slept together, I felt like I was dissolving. Not in love, just in attention. His was nuclear. He made you feel like being seen was the same as being chosen. And I was *starving* to be *chosen*.

"I need someone who gets it," he told me that first night in Miami. "All these bitches wanna be famous. You are famous."

He said it like worship. But what he really meant was:

I want someone who already has power so I can take it from her.

In the beginning, Jax was all champagne and spotlights. He brought me on stage to sing one line in his song, just to watch the crowd scream my name instead of his. He said it turned him on.

He booked us joint press interviews and whispered "power couple" like it was a spell. Sent flowers the size of furniture. Called paparazzi before our date nights so we could "control the narrative."

I thought it was strategic. I thought we were partners.

I didn't realize he was curating a cage.

It started with shoves. Not in anger, playful, he said. Too much wine. A misunderstanding. A bad night.

He was *sorry*.

Then came the yelling. Then the slamming doors. Then the wall behind my shoulder splintering. Then the bruise that showed up in a photo and got cropped out by management. Then the push that knocked me backward onto marble tile. Then the silence after.

He cried harder than I did the first time he hit me.

"I can't lose you," he said, curled at my feet, hands shaking. "You're the only thing in this world that makes sense."

I told him I was okay.

Because I believed it would go away.

Because I thought I was strong enough to fix him.

Because I didn't want the world to know that the woman who sold out stadiums could not walk through her own front door without bracing for impact.

"I think you provoke me," he said once, after a show I performed half-drugged and half-dead.

"You wear clothes like that and expect me to share you with the world."

"You post pictures like that and wonder why I'm angry."

"You say you love me, but you let them own you."

He told me he wanted to be my world. But what he meant was: he wanted to be the cage.

Rey's office, my mom's office, is still safe and too bright.

I sit on their couch and try to name the color of fear. It's not red. Not black. It's the gray of a dressing room right before the knock on the door. It's the sound of his voice in my ear, whispering

62

Smile, baby, they are watching. It is the silence I learned to wear like armor.

There was a night, I don't remember which city, when he knocked me unconscious. I woke up to him sobbing, clutching my body like a child with a broken toy.

"I didn't mean to," he kept saying. "I love you so much it hurts."

It did. It hurt for years. It hurt in my sleep. In my ribs. In my silence.

I never reported him. Because they told me the show must go on. Because they said a scandal would ruin the brand. Because Libby Morgan wasn't supposed to bruise.

Rey asks me again to name the moment it changed.

I tell them it never changed. It just ended.

And even then, not because I escaped. But because one night, the cameras caught it. And the world finally believed what I hadn't dared to say out loud.

I sit in Marianne's old study, now Rey's temporary office, long after the session ends.

Not crying. Not breathing quite right. Just holding still. Like if I move too fast, the past might catch me again.

When I finally open the door, the house smells like rosemary and rain. Marianne's baking something she calls a "grief cake." No occasion, just instinct.

She doesn't ask how it went. She doesn't ask at all.

She just dries her hands on a dish towel, crosses the room, and wraps me in her arms.

Not tight. Not gentle.

Just enough.

The way only a mother can, when she doesn't need to know the story to understand the ache.

And for the first time since I said his name out loud, I let myself lean.

Marianne's arms stay around me just long enough to say what words can't. Not a question. Not a fix. Just presence.

When she lets go, she presses a kiss to my hair and hands me a slice of the grief cake.

"Still warm," she says.

Then she goes back to the kitchen like nothing happened.

I take the plate. I go upstairs.

Not because I'm hungry.

Because I need to be somewhere I can fall apart without anyone watching.

My childhood room doesn't look the same, but the bones are still mine. Faded paint on the closet door. A sticker from a long-lost notebook, curled at the corner of the window frame. The scent of lavender sachets and a girl I haven't met in years.

I sit on the edge of the bed and place the cake on the nightstand. Uneaten. Too sweet for this ache.

I think about Jax. About the first night. About the last. About the thousand slivers of myself I handed him, thinking if I gave enough, maybe he'd finally stop breaking them.

Rey said naming the pain is part of the process.

But now that I've said it out loud—his name, the bruises, the silence—I'm not sure what to do with the echo it left.

It doesn't roar.

It hums.

A low, constant vibration behind my ribs.

A reminder that survival has its own soundtrack.

And I've been humming it for years.

I lie back; arms folded across my stomach like I'm holding myself together.

And maybe I am.

Maybe that's the first real thing I've done in a long time.

Chapter 14: When the Cameras Stopped

It had been nearly two months since I disappeared.

No public statement. No official rehab check-in. No cryptic Instagram captions or burner tweets. Just me, a stack of blank journals, and a body relearning how to feel safe inside itself.

Some mornings I'd sit in the greenhouse with my knees to my chest, scrawling half-sentences on seed packet backs, phrases that spilled out before I could name them. Not songs yet. Just fragments. Echoes. Proof I hadn't gone silent.

I hadn't touched a phone. Hadn't looked at a screen.

Dorian and his manager handled everything else—canceled the tour, paused Jag's press machine, kept the wolves from sniffing too close.

No one knew where I was. Not yet.

Then the email came.

Subject: Seeking Statement: Libby Morgan: The Rise and Ruin – A Netflix Docuseries

I was in the kitchen, helping Dorian re-pot a basil plant that kept leaning toward the window like it was trying to escape.

He read it first. Didn't say a word. Just handed me the phone, lips pressed into a line.

It took a moment to register the words.

I set the phone down like it might explode.

"They want us to talk about the greatest hits," I said. "The overdoses. The breakdown. Jax."

Dorian didn't look up. Just pressed the soil in with his thumbs.

"They always do," he said. "They wait until the blood's dry."

The cameras didn't start rolling because I collapsed. They started because someone caught it.

Security footage. A hotel hallway. Jax's arm on mine. My body folding like something already broken. A blur. A choke. A scream swallowed by bad lighting and worse timing.

That clip played on repeat for weeks.

But the real show didn't start until Sterling Vale walked into frame.

Sterling Vale was the kind of man who never walked—he arrived. He didn't just speak, he declared. Words were weapons in his mouth, always aimed, always lethal. Six foot three, manicured hands, suits that whispered money and control. He smelled like leather-bound contracts and faint cologne with a predator's undertone.

He discovered me at a showcase for unsigned acts when I was barely nineteen. He didn't smile, didn't clap. He just pointed.

"You," he said from the shadows. "You're not a singer. You're a commodity."

And I thought it was a compliment.

I was too young to know the difference between admiration and acquisition.

Sterling didn't flatter. He forecasted. Predicted the future and then made it law. When he said I'd headline Madison Square Garden, I did. When he said I'd win awards, I smiled on red carpets with borrowed diamonds in my ears.

He built Libby like a skyscraper—glass, dazzling, impossible to ignore—and buried Olivia Reed somewhere beneath the foundation.

But he said all the right things. That was his genius.

"This is how we protect Olivia."

"This is how we make sure the real you survives the noise."

"This is just packaging, baby. You stay sacred."

He said it with a voice like velvet and barbed wire. The kind that could lull you into a lullaby while stealing your name.

Sterling Vale didn't just create Libby. He colonized her.

He knew how to kiss the wound and call it branding. How to cradle my chin in a meeting and later grip my wrist just hard enough to remind me where the power lived.

We weren't public. We weren't private.

We were curated.

He curated me.

He slipped Ambien into my tea before interviews and told me it was "for the edge."

He left pills by the sink with sticky notes shaped like hearts.

He reworked lyrics, reworked tour dates, reworked my damn sleep schedule, all in the name of optimization.

He was a maestro of manipulation.

The kind that made you say thank you as he tightened the noose.

The kind that held your face during a panic attack and whispered, "This is the price of legend."

And I paid it.

I paid it with my body, my voice, my name.

Because when someone tells you that your pain is proof of greatness, you start to believe suffering is part of the contract.

He never yelled.

He didn't have to.

His silence was its own form of violence. His praise always conditional.

"You've got five years to make forever," he once told me.

Five years of sold-out tours, brand deals, and sleepless nights.

Five years of interviews scripted by PR reps who'd never even heard my music.

Five years of losing myself in Libby Morgan's wardrobe while Olivia quietly faded from the mirror.

When the video leaked—the one that showed Jax's hand and my body going limp—Sterling didn't ask if I was okay.

He asked if we could obtain the rights.

He spun a press release before I'd even seen the footage.

Said I was on a wellness retreat. Spiritual recovery. An artistic sabbatical.

"Silence is power," he told me.

But what he meant was: Silence protects the investment.

I remember sitting in his office one last time.

Glass walls. Framed awards. Air too cold. Everything too perfect.

My name etched in platinum above the fireplace, like a ghost wearing jewelry.

He sat across from me, legs crossed, eyes sharp.

"You're trending," he said. "Pain sells. Let's frame it right."

That's when I realized:

I was never the artist.

I was the product.

And Sterling Vale was just the man who dressed the coffin.

I didn't reply to the email.

Not because I had nothing to say.

But because when I do speak, it won't be for clicks.

It won't be for Netflix.

It won't be his version.

It'll be mine.

Unfiltered.

Unforgiven.

And finally, free.

Chapter 15: Back Where I Left Me

I wanted Booth's Corner. God, I wanted The Sale. It was always packed; sticky floors, loud voices, and stands selling everything from homemade pickles to knockoff perfume. Fresh Amish produce sat beside deep-fried everything. Craft booths elbowed against variety stalls hawking neon socks and off-brand electronics. The air reeked of vinegar, grease, and something floral that didn't belong.

Unlicensed Eagles gear overflowed like treasure—hats, hoodies, baby onesies with crooked stitching. I didn't want any of it. I just wanted to see some kid hold up their first gold chain in the mirror, wide-eyed, too proud to care if it turned their neck green by Monday.

But I can't walk into a crowd like that. Not yet. Not when people still think I'm in Switzerland doing chakra therapy and drinking mountain rain through glass straws.

So I start smaller.

Dorian takes me out early. Real early. The kind of morning where the air still feels forgiving, and the shadows make everything look soft around the edges.

We head toward Glen Mills, back roads first. No highway. Windows down. The smell of wet leaves and earth still clings to the tires from last night's rain.

"I'm not going in anywhere," I warn him.

"Wouldn't dream of it," he says, too casually. "We're just driving. Maybe a drive through. Maybe a roadside stand. Maybe a detour past what used to be Granite Run Mall."

My groan is automatic. "That place used to mean something."

Now it's all glass storefronts and corporate lighting. A lifestyle center. No more photo booth or old-man Santa in a threadbare red suit. No more prom dress racks or CD shops with posters of whoever we used to be.

I didn't cry when my marriages ended. But seeing Granite Run turned into a luxury pedestrian plaza? That almost broke me.

The hospital I was born in, Riddle, rises out of the trees like a spaceship now. More wings. More glass. More parking decks. It used to be small enough that the nurses called your mom by her first name. Now it has valet.

"You okay?" Dorian asks, catching the way I'm staring out the window.

"I just..." I pause. "I think I thought coming back would put everything in rewind. Like the trees would remember me."

"They probably do," he says gently. "They're just too polite to say anything."

I grew up in Bethel Township, a patchwork of wooded lots and winding roads, where the stars still shone through the trees at night. But weekends and holidays, that was Marcus Hook. My grandparents' rowhome wedged tight with stories and stoops, Blackbeard legends, old ships, and the sweet burn of refinery in the air. The kind of place people called undesirable until they were invited in and fed.

322 used to be a sleepy, cracked-lane highway. Now it's widened, relentless. It cut through neighborhoods like an unforgiving blade—homes gone, trees leveled, memories rerouted.

You can still smell the river sometimes, though. A mix of salt, diesel, and decades. In Garnet Valley, it's more nature—damp moss, honeysuckle, the sweet rot of overripe figs in summer. But in the Hook? It's layered. It's history.

And food? The best cheesesteaks don't come from Philly—at least not to Delco natives. They come from tucked-away joints like Di Costanza's in Linwood or New English in Marcus Hook, where the inside-outs are greasy miracles and nobody asks for your order twice.

If you *do* go into Philly, you skip Pat's and Geno's. That's tourist lore. Real ones hit Angelo's, Dalessandro's, or Jim's Roast Beef. And if you are lucky enough to carve out a day, you make the pilgrimage to Reading Terminal. Because South Philly to the bottom lip of PA—down into Delaware—that's where American food lives. Not hoity. Not toity. Just real damn good.

And Eagles fans? We *bleed* green. When the Birds took the Super Bowl in the 2017 season— first time ever—beating the Patriots, the whole region lit up like it was redemption itself. Jason Kelce, our mummer-hearted center, now retired into Delco life, gave that speech, and the city roared. My grandfather, George, cried. Said it was the first Super Bowl he ever lived to see. He passed a few months later, quiet, with a worn Eagles cap on the nightstand.

And then—like lightning striking twice—we did it again. February 9, 2025. Knockout game against the Chiefs. This place *erupted*. We were America's new team. A country united.

We stopped at a diner instead of a drive through. Not that anyone would recognize me. It's one of those places with linoleum scrubbed into translucency and servers who call you "honey" without making it feel performative.

"I'll just have water," I say when the waitress comes.

She gives me a long look. "You want what now?"

"Water," I repeat, instinctively flattening the vowel. Libby Morgan had trained that out of me, years of media coaching turned my native tongue into something polished and vaguely Californian.

"You mean *wooder*?" she smirks.

Dorian nearly chokes on his coffee.

"Yeah," I sigh, smiling despite myself. "Just a glass of *wooder*."

Fall's creeping in. You can feel it even in the heat, the way the air starts to hesitate. The farm stands are already putting out pumpkins like it's a race. It's August. No one buys gourds in flip-flops. And Linvilla's probably got the hay bales stacked like scaffolding, ready to convince someone it's sweater weather while they are still sweating through their tank top.

I want to go. But not yet. The thought of being seen, recognized, posted, it makes my stomach twist. I'm not ready for selfies and whispered looks and people asking if I'm her.

So, for now, I wave at Linvilla Orchards from the car window like an old friend I am not ready to hug.

But one day soon, I will go. I will walk through the apple trees. I will eat something fried and too sweet. I will buy cider even though I don't drink it. Because it is still home. Changed. Shined up. Grown past what I remember. But home.

We drove past Temple Road twice before Dorian made the turn. "This it?" I ask.

"Yep."

"It looks like a paper supply warehouse."

"That's the idea."

The building's unmarked. No logos. No signs. Just a long, sun-faded stretch of cinderblock with a loading dock and a keypad entry. You would never guess it housed one of Jag Records' most sacred side-projects, a private writing room, demo booth, and studio lounge built inside what used to be a discount carpet showroom.

It's perfect.

"Why do I feel like I'm about to meet my handler in a CIA safehouse?" I ask.

"Because I'm driving a twenty-year-old truck with a cracked Eagles bumper sticker and blackout tints," Dorian says, patting the dash of Big Al's beloved Chevy. "We're nothing if not discreet."

"Discreet smells like beer and brake fluid," I mutter, rolling down the window to breathe.

He grins. "Welcome home."

Inside, the room is quiet, cool, and lined with soundproofing foam and thrift store furniture. There is a lava lamp on one table and a record player with exactly three vinyls on the shelf, D'Angelo, Fiona Apple, and some unreleased live Jag acoustic sessions. It smells like coffee grounds and old wood. Like someone has been creating here, not just existing.

And then, I hear her. Sadie Bell. She is sitting cross-legged on the floor in cutoff jeans and a Widener sweatshirt two sizes too big, hair piled in a messy bun, humming to herself while flipping through a dog-eared notebook.

She looks up when I enter but does not jump to her feet or start fan-girling. Just lifts her chin like she has been expecting me.

"Hey," she says. "I figured you were a myth."

"I am," I reply. "Mostly."

She smirks and offers a fist bump. I laugh.

"I know who you are," I add. "We Zoomed twice. You made fun of my mug collection."

"You had a #1 Grammy Godmother coffee cup," she grins. "I stand by my roast."

She's quick. Sharp. No pretense. And real.

I hand her a folded paper, worn soft at the edges. "Found this in a lyric book from... years ago. I don't think I ever sang it aloud."

She opens it. Reads silently. Then again, slower.

"This is beautiful," she says.

"It's a mess."

"Yeah," she nods. "That's what makes it beautiful."

She picks up her guitar without asking. Strums something soft. Humble. Something that doesn't try to impress.

And for the first time in a long time, I don't feel the need to perform.

I just sat on the floor beside her. Back to the beginning. Back to the basement. Only this time, it's not Dorian's. It's ours.

I murmur the first line, without meaning to: "I disappeared before I died..."

Sadie nods, adds gently, reverently: "...but I'm still here, and so's the sky."

We look at each other. Not like artist to muse, or mentor to ingénue. But like two ghosts who realized they are still warm.

Chapter 16: The Quiet in Between

Most mornings, I needed my hands to move before my mind caught up. I swept the porch. Refilled the bird feeders. Picked dead leaves from Marianne's herb pots with slow, steady fingers. There was something sacred in the silence of small chores, something that made my heart beat a little slower, like it remembered how to live inside a body not constantly bracing for impact.

The porch still smelled like pine sap and weathered wood. The kind of scent that soaked into your skin. The bird chatter changed with the hour—sharp chirps near dawn, lazy coos by mid-morning, like even they had circadian rhythms. I dug my fingers into the dirt of the herb pots, the soil cool and slightly damp, and felt a grounding I hadn't known I needed. Letting the soil cling under my fingernails felt like proof that I existed—here, not there. Liv, not Libby. A body in motion, not performance. A spirit relearning presence.

The hose had a new nozzle. I didn't ask who brought it. I watered the garden in spirals, watching the sun climb the side of the barn like it had somewhere to be. My knees ached. My wrists were sore. But it felt good to move, without purpose, without show. Just movement.

The grief didn't scream anymore. It didn't roar or claw or sob. It just... hovered. Like fog, low and familiar.

Sometimes, I hummed. Barely-there threads of melody escaped when I thought I was alone, small sounds caught between memory and muscle. I never finished anything. Didn't dare call it writing. But I kept a journal open on the kitchen counter, and sometimes a lyric landed like a leaf falling without rush.

I wasn't sure if the music was coming back. But I knew I was listening.

Tucker had started showing up more. Not in grand gestures. Not with questions or demands or some sitcom-style moment of reconciliation. He'd just... be there. Sometimes in the garage with Big Al, pretending not to overhear when I sang quietly from the porch swing. Sometimes at the kitchen table, flipping through the local paper like it was still 2003. Once, I caught him bringing a new hose for the garden, even though I hadn't said the old one had cracked.

He never stayed long. But he didn't rush off either.

It was awkward, in the way only old friends with unfinished history can be. We never said the big things. Never mentioned the years we'd lost or the song I'd written that was secretly about him. We did not talk about the night I left, the fame, the overdoses. Instead, we talked about tomatoes. Or the weather. Or how the Eagles better not choke this season after last year's unbelievable win in the Super Bowl. We existed in the quiet in between.

I found him in the shed one morning, reorganizing my dad's tools like it was a normal thing to do on a Tuesday. "You don't work here, you know," I said, arms crossed.

He didn't turn around. "Al lets me use the lift. I pay him in Sixers tickets and cheesesteaks."

"You're a con artist."

"I'm a Jaguar," he corrected with a grin. "We know how to negotiate."

I snorted and walked back toward the house, but I didn't go inside. I sat on the steps instead, waiting. He joined me ten minutes later, wiping grease off his hands with a shop rag like it was a ritual.

We sat in silence. The good kind. The kind where no one expects anything but presence.

"Do you remember that summer we built the stage by the barn?" I asked suddenly.

Tucker smiled, slow and soft. "You mean you built the stage while I got splinters and Al yelled about stolen lumber?"

"It had lights. And a fog machine."

"Which you broke trying to make it look like Wembley."

"I was dramatic."

"You are dramatic."

I nudged his knee with mine. He didn't flinch. There was something sacred in the way we avoided saying the wrong thing. Something tender in the fact that he didn't ask if I was okay. Because he knew I wasn't. But I was here. That was enough, for now.

"Bench is still broken," Tucker said after a while, nodding toward the sagging wood near the edge of the garden.

"It's been broken since prom," I replied.

"I offered to fix it back then."

"You offered to burn it and say it collapsed under the weight of my emotional baggage."

He grinned. "I stand by that plan."

We did not talk about the night it *actually* broke. Late spring. Too warm for jackets, too reckless to be sober. We had left his truck at a friend's to sneak around the property like kids with secrets, giddy and tipsy and in love with the idea of being in love. The stars were too bright. The air too thick with honeysuckle. We crashed onto that bench like it was built to hold our heat, our hunger. It wasn't. The wood cracked beneath us mid-kiss, splintering like a firework. We laughed so hard we cried. And then we kissed again, in the grass. Because logic had nothing on that kind of gravity.

But fifteen minutes later, we were knee-deep in spiderwebs and rusted nails, doing what Delco kids do best, making it work with what we had.

Tucker held up a splintered board like it had personally offended him. "I think this one's older than Wawa."

"Nothing is older than Wawa."

"Maybe Booth's Corner."

"The Sale," I corrected automatically.

And he gave me a look like he'd just caught a glimpse of the girl I used to be. He didn't say anything. Just handed me the drill.

We worked like that, mostly quiet, sometimes laughing, always careful. He didn't flinch when I struggled with the heavier end. Did not try to take over. Just matched me, step by step.

As we worked, I studied him. Tucker the man was quieter. More contained. Not dulled, but refined. Like time had sanded down the sharpness, left behind someone slower to speak, quicker to listen. He still had the same hands. Same smirk. But his silences carried weight now. Even after everything, after the walking away, the heartbreak, the silence... I found myself curious. Not about who he'd been. But who he was now. And who I might be, beside him.

When we finally sat down on the patched-up bench, it creaked like a warning. But it held.

"You gonna put on a show?" he teased, nodding toward the garden like it was a stage.

"Only if you're serving dollar wings and domestic drafts."

"Libby Morgan, humble queen of the hoagie special."

"Liv Morgan," I corrected, "Reed."

He looked at me, long and steady. Then said, "Yeah. That's what I meant."

Big Al

79

From the kitchen window, Big Al watched them. Liv and Tucker. Not talking about the past. Not pushing into the future. Just... being.

Her bare foot nudging a loose stone. Tucker scratching at his beard like he was thinking too hard. The bench held. It wasn't much. But it held.

Marianne came up behind him, resting a hand on his back. "You spying, old man?"

"Just supervising."

"You didn't blink for five straight minutes."

He grunted, shifting his weight like he could carry the ache if he moved just right.

"She looks better," Marianne said gently.

"She looks like my girl," he murmured.

She let the words hang in the air. His only girl. His miracle. His kid who used to make up songs about squirrels and tomato vines and cry when they stepped on worms after the rain.

He remembered the day they built that bench. And the day it cracked. But before all that—before Tucker, before Libby Morgan—he remembered Liv at age six, in polka dot leggings and a sunflower shirt, barefoot in the dirt. He'd sit on that bench with her giant Minnie Mouse in his lap like a plush VIP, while she performed. She'd sing made-up songs to the butterflies. Recite poems that made no sense. Twirl until she fell down. And he'd clap like she was center stage at the Met. Because to him, she was. She always had been. An ingénue, before he knew what that word meant.

He'd nearly lost her. Not just to the overdose. But to the noise. The mask. The damn machine that stole her voice and sold it back to her dressed in rhinestones.

He didn't know if this peace would last. Didn't trust that it could.

But for now, this moment, this cracked bench, this old friend beside her, he let himself hope.

Marianne leaned her head against his shoulder. "You're allowed to be happy."

"I am," he said. "Just scared to death of it."

Chapter 17: Strangers at the Wawa

Liv

I knew something was up when Dorian asked if I still had Big Al's old cooler.

"Why?"

"Because we're picking up VIPs," he said, too casually. "And they need a place to stash contraband."

"What kind of contraband?"

"Snacks. Wigs. Possibly emotional baggage. Hard to say."

They landed at New Castle Airport like it was a covert military operation.

Ari Monroe burst out first, dressed in head-to-toe neon pink camo. A matching mullet wig flopped around their shoulders, and sunglasses the size of my future bad decisions swallowed half their face.

"Why does the sky feel like it's pressing on me?" Ari groaned when they were in the car. "And why did that airport smell like lukewarm gumbo and shame?"

"It's Delaware," Pax muttered, adjusting a fake mustache and hauling a tote bag that said Sadie Sink for President.

"Hey," I said as the highway unspooled ahead of us, "a former president used to land at that airport personally."

"And we've been in Pennsylvania for ten minutes," Pax added.

"I don't believe in state lines," Ari declared, flipping open the cooler like it owed them money.

Inside, Dorian had stocked Wawa iced tea, Tastykakes, and Italian hoagies.

Ari gasped. "Okay. I take it back. I believe in this."

Back at the house, they didn't stop moving. Ari touched everything. "Is this vintage or just poorly lit?" they asked, pausing at the hallway's floral wallpaper like it might answer.

Pax made coffee, reorganized the spice rack, and found my old box of concert lanyards, then cried over it in the laundry room for six unapologetic minutes.

Dorian just smiled. "Chaos is the healing."

It was absurd. And perfect. The only people in the world who ever saw Liv and did not try to sell her for parts.

Maybe that's why my inner circle had always been made up of people who didn't care about the mask, only the pulse underneath.

And Eli. The quiet in the storm. I missed him more than I'd ever let myself admit.

The first time I saw Eli was at a church basement meeting in LA, the kind you weren't supposed to talk about. I hadn't planned to be there—I was hiding from a press tour hangover and ducked into the nearest building when a fan started chasing me for a selfie.

He was speaking when I came in. Tall. Still. Steady. He didn't use notes. He didn't cry. He just told the truth. How he'd driven drunk. How he'd killed the only two people he'd ever truly loved. His wife. His daughter. He said he kept the grief like a sacred object—not to punish himself, but to remember. To honor. To never forget what recklessness could take.

I stayed in the back, frozen. Then I came back the next week. And the next. Eventually, he sat next to me. Didn't speak. Just nodded. And that was enough.

He was a retired jazz musician, once a name whispered with reverence in smoky clubs. But he'd walked away after the crash. Never touched a trumpet again. Until the night he asked me to sing something—anything. He hummed. I followed. And something opened. He became the calm to my chaos. The one who never asked for more than presence. The longest clean stretch I ever had began with him.

I really wish he was here right now. We needed someone to balance the chaos.

They made noise. They took up space. They reminded me what it felt like to be known.

Ari insisted we go out "undercover." I refused. They insisted harder.

Next thing I knew, I was in a curly red wig and oversized sunglasses that made me look like a washed-up cartoon detective. Pax wore a Best Aunt Ever hoodie and a pair of Crocs. Dorian donned a fake ponytail and introduced himself as "Larry."

We went to Wawa. I could've listed half a dozen local spots we *should've* gone to, but they were obsessed with the cultural rite of passage and wanted to experience it for themselves.

Ari took thirty photos of the touchscreen ordering system. Pax had a spiritual experience in front of the mac and cheese. Dorian threatened to disown us all when Ari tried to order a cappuccino with almond milk, and no lid.

"Hey, wait! They have oat milk too," Ari added.

But Dorian was making that face he makes when he's one nerve away from losing it, so I jumped in to defend my bestie.

"Act normal," I hissed.

"This is normal," Ari said, sweeping a silk robe behind them like a magician about to reveal a trick no one asked for.

Back at the house, we sat in a loose circle on the porch and passed around stories like communion. Bare feet. Open wounds. Unfiltered breath.

No Libby. No labels. No one performing.

Pax stretched out on the step, cigarette flickering in rhythm with their pulse. They spoke softly, like they were still somewhere else.

"I loved her so much I stopped painting," they said suddenly. "Like if I created anything that wasn't about her, it meant I'd moved on." They laughed once—short, sharp. "Turns out grief doesn't care if you stay loyal. It just keeps eating."

Ari nodded like they knew that exact flavor.

"First time I burned out," they said, voice unusually quiet, "I was in Paris. Had a line debuting at Fashion Week, a loft full of rented models, and a nosebleed that wouldn't stop for twelve hours. My assistant thought I was dying. I kinda hoped I was."

They sipped from a wine glass that had held three different things already that night. Mostly different Wawa drinks, "I stayed anyway. I finished the damn show. Then I threw up on a Versace intern and went to rehab."

Pax snorted. "Iconic."

"I'm nothing if not memorable," Ari said, grinning, but their eyes didn't sparkle. Not really.

Dorian just listened, knees pulled to his chest, a quiet rhythm in his fingertips like he was tapping out a melody only he could hear. He didn't share a story. He didn't need to. His eyes held enough.

I didn't say much. Not until the night folded in around us and the stars made everything feel honest. And even then—it wasn't a statement. It was a breath.

We were halfway through arguing about the best Wawa hoagie combo (Ari was wrong, obviously, Italian everything sweet, with extra oil was the way to go) when the gravel shifted in the driveway.

Not a screech. Not a blast of music or engine roar. Just the steady crunch of tires moving slowly.

I stood. Dorian already knew.

"He made it," he said softly.

The car door creaked open. And there he was.

Eli Wynn. Tall. Lean. Dressed in dark linen and denim. Hat tipped low. No smile. Just eyes that carried lifetimes and a walk like jazz, measured, sure, a little bit sad.

"Liv," he said, arms open.

I didn't run to him. I just walked. Straight into the space that always felt like permission.

He held me like I was glass and iron at the same time.

The porch went quiet.

Ari blinked. "He's... cool."

Pax whispered, "He's giving Miles Davis if Miles Davis did grief counseling."

"That's Eli," Dorian said. "Don't try to understand him. Just breathe near him."

Eli tipped his hat to them all. "Y'all got enough volume to raise the dead out here."

"You bring the sermon?" Ari asked.

"I bring the silence," he said.

Later, I found him talking to Big Al over coffee in the garage. No raised voices. No instructions. Just men who've seen enough to know when not to speak.

Al offered him a beer. Eli shook his head. "Thirty years dry."

Al nodded once. No questions. Just respect. They talked about classic cars. Fishing lines. The ache in your knees when the weather changes.

But when I passed through the room, Eli glanced over and said, just loud enough for me to hear: "You look lighter."

"I'm not," I said.

He smiled, small and true. "You will be."

It was after midnight. Big Al had already bowed out, muttering something about "the only drum circle I care about being the one at Franklin Field."

Marianne kissed my cheek and handed me her tea. "Don't let them keep you up too late."

I nodded, knowing full well it was already too late. But that was kind of the point.

The lights were dimmed in the living room. Pillows scattered. Guitars and notebooks open like altars. Ari had turned the old lamp into a spotlight using sheer scarves, and Pax was balancing a bowl of popcorn on their head like it was a crown.

That's when the door opened again. Tucker stepped in.

Worn Phillies cap. Hoodie with the sleeves pushed up. Hands still smelling faintly of citrus cleaner and hops.

He looked at the scene like he had stumbled into a cult.

"What the hell is this?"

"A séance," Ari announced. "We're summoning Liv's voice."

Pax added, "Also, we're slightly buzzed on Tastykakes and existential dread."

Tucker glanced at me. I shrugged. "Welcome to my inner circle."

Ari, naturally, zeroed in.

"And who is this fine man of blue-collar mystery?"

"Tucker Hayes," he said, offering a hand, a half-smile already playing at his lips. "Mechanic. Bartender. Keeper of secrets and questionable decisions."

Ari took it with theatrical flair. "Ari Monroe. They/them. Gender deity, fashion demigod, occasional chaos engine."

Tucker blinked. "The... they... them. Got it. Deity?"

"Close enough," Pax said, already entertained.

Tucker paused, nodded slowly, then added, "Well. Honored to be in divine company."

Ari grinned. "You are a fast learner, Tucker Hayes. I like you."

"Don't say that too loud," he said, leaning in just a little toward me. "She might get jealous."

I rolled my eyes, but it pulled something warm through my ribs anyway.

He settled in on the edge of the couch, not trying to dominate the space, just present. Observant. Laughing in the right places. Watching Ari's hands as they gestured through a story. Glancing at Pax with that subtle, big-brother curiosity. And every so often... looking at me.

Not with pressure. Not with pity. Just watching. The way someone looks at a fire they used to know. The kind you shouldn't touch twice. But still remember the heat of.

I picked up the old acoustic. Fingers uncertain, trembling just enough to remind me I hadn't done this in a long time.

No makeup. No lighting cues. No retakes. Just breath.

I strummed a soft E minor. A hush fell.

Then I sang. "If I disappear before I die..."

My voice was slow, frayed at the edges, worn like denim washed too many times.

And then, like a thread stitched through the quiet, Sadie's old lyric rose up from somewhere deeper: "...but I'm still here, and so's the sky."

The room stilled. Even Ari and Pax, mid-banter windup, fell silent.

Tucker's eyes held mine, no judgment. Just recognition. That quiet kind you only get from someone who knew you before.

Eli leaned forward, voice gentle, anchoring. "That's enough."

And for a breath, the world fell away.

I closed my eyes as the last chord died.

In the silence, I felt them again: Tucker, the friend I forgot. Dorian, the one who stayed. Ari and Pax, bright lights with nowhere to be but here. Eli, the stillness I didn't know I needed.

For once, I wasn't singing to prove anything. Just to say: I'm still here.

I looked around that cocoon of mismatched souls.

"We have work to do," I whispered.

No stage. No cameras. No spotlight, except the warm glow of friendship and truth.

Just us. Together. Starting again.

Chapter 18: The Notes Between

The old upright had been returned, but it still hummed slightly off when the air got too damp.

I pressed one key. Then another. Nothing followed. I closed the lid.

In the days after the Wawa run, and the way Tucker said my name like it wasn't breakable, my inner circle had grown bold. Dorian played old stems in the kitchen. Ari left sketchbooks on the table next to lyric fragments I hadn't touched since L.A. Sadie slipped her earbuds into my hand and whispered, "This is what I listen to when I write. In case it helps."

It didn't. Not at first. The page stayed blank. The piano stayed closed. But something inside me shifted, small. Like a breath catching on the edge of a lyric.

A hunger. Not for fame. Not for applause. For connection. For the girl who used to hum into a tape recorder on the barn roof. Who carved song titles into her Converse and whispered harmonies into creek water.

I couldn't force it. Every time I tried, my hands stilled. So, I got up. Wandered the house. Ate a slice of leftover lemon bread. Ate another. Snacked on almonds. Then crackers. Then more lemon bread. It wasn't about hunger. It was about having something to do.

I sat back at the piano. Touched one key. Let it ring. Then another. This time, a note followed. Then a phrase. Then a hum that didn't feel like Libby. I didn't feel like anyone but Liv.

Something was different this time. I didn't write it down. Not yet. I wasn't ready to claim it. I wasn't writing for a label. Or a deadline. Or a room full of suits deciding whether my voice fit this season's market.

I was writing because the ache had finally made space for language. Because the words showed up uninvited, honest, and whole. Because something inside me was ready to be seen. Not as Libby. But as Liv.

So, I stayed at the bench. Feet bare. Shoulders loose. One hand on the keys, the other curled around a chipped mug full of nothing. And for the first time in a long time, I didn't feel like I had to prove anything. I just... played.

The living room had the scent of lemon bread and soil. Warmth from the sun spilled in through the screen door, draping gold across the hardwood. I'd left it open to hear the birds—a morning orchestra of finches and wrens, darting in the trees like gossiping neighbors.

When I finally stepped outside, the air was just cool enough to wake my skin. Dirt clung under my nails, and the scent of basil and earth followed me like a song I hadn't finished. Every time my hands sank into the soil, something inside me unclenched.

Somewhere between the piano bench and the garden path, I started to hum. Nothing dramatic. Just a melody that stuck around long enough to be annoying. It came in waves, usually while I was deadheading lavender or trying to untangle hose from trellis.

I didn't even realize I was doing it until Ari caught me mid-hum over the tomato beds.

"Well, well, well," they said, crouching beside a pot of wilting parsley, dramatic as ever. "What's that I hear? Could it be? A melody? From the one and only Libby-frickin'-Morgan?"

I rolled my eyes and turned my back. "It's not Libby. And it's nothing."

"Sounds like a chorus to me," Ari said. "Gritty. Sad. Very comeback docuseries core."

I flipped a garden glove at them.

Dorian wasn't much better. He caught me writing a line on a seed packet and started humming the Jaws theme under his breath. "You're one sprouting verse away from a bridge," he warned. "And I'm telling you now, if you pretend like this is just for you, I will leak it to Sadie."

I threw the seed packet at his forehead. He caught it. Read it. Then paused. "You wrote this?"

He sounded almost... reverent.

I shrugged. "It's not finished."

"Doesn't have to be," he said, slipping it into his back pocket like a prayer. "Just don't forget you still can."

That night, Dorian stayed up late mixing stems from old demos, laying them gently beneath the new phrases I didn't want to admit were forming. His headphones were cracked. His tea was cold. But he hummed under his breath with a concentration so full of love I couldn't look away.

"I'm not ready," I told him from the doorway.

"You don't have to be," he replied, eyes still on the waveform. "Just don't forget the sound of your own voice."

Ari raided the attic and came down covered in dust and triumph, holding up an old jacket I used to wear in middle school—fringed denim, scribbled with lyrics in glitter pen.

"This?" they said. "This is art. This is origin story couture."

They hung it in the hallway, right next to the sketchpad filled with abstract versions of me: one in profile, eyes closed; one mid-scream, surrounded by roses and razor blades.

"You're allowed to be every version," Ari whispered when they caught me staring.

"I don't know how."

"That's okay. I do."

That night, after everyone had drifted to their corners of the house, I found Eli in the garden, watering the hydrangeas by moonlight. His movements were slow, deliberate. Like everything he did was a ritual.

"You can feel it again, can't you?" he asked without looking up.

"Feel what?"

"The part of you that's been asleep."

I nodded, even though he couldn't see it.

He handed me the hose. "Then let it wake up slow."

We watered in silence. The moonlight spilled across the soil like a benediction.

The next afternoon, I found my mother in the sunroom, half-hidden behind a stack of poetry books. She was curled sideways in the antique rocking chair, legs tucked beneath her like she'd never outgrown the habit. One hand held a cracked-spine copy of *The Dream of a Common Language* while the other absentmindedly traced the rim of her teacup.

"Adrienne Rich?" I asked, stepping over a pair of socks Sadie had abandoned like breadcrumbs across the floor.

Marianne looked up and smiled—not surprised, but soft, like she'd been expecting me.

"She found me again this morning," she said. "I think she always knows when I'm aching for an old truth."

I sat beside her on the window seat, the cushion faded but familiar beneath me. Light poured in like it was blessing the room.

"When I was ten," I said, "I found that book on your nightstand and tried to read it like it was a spellbook."

She laughed. "In a way, it is."

"I didn't understand half of it," I confessed. "But the rhythms... they stuck."

Marianne closed the book and reached for a second stack beside her. "I kept some of yours. From middle school. Tucked between the real poets, hoping you'd someday find your way back."

She handed me a tattered folder—stickered, smudged, the corner bent where I used to dog-ear pages like secrets.

Inside were my old poems. Scrawled in glitter pens and blocky loops. Poems about horses and heartbreak and the moon. One about Tucker's eyes, written when I was thirteen and aching in a way I hadn't had language for yet.

"They're awful," I said, laughing through my embarrassment.

"They're honest," she replied. "Which is better."

We spent the next hour reading. Her favorites. My favorites. Swapping lines like recipes passed between generations of women who knew how to keep stories alive.

She read me Mary Oliver like a prayer. I read her a new piece I hadn't told anyone about—half-formed, messy, scribbled in the margin of a gardening catalog.

She didn't critique it. Didn't even blink.

She just said, "That line? That one about your voice being a weather pattern? That's Liv. That's the Liv I've missed."

I hadn't realized how much I needed to hear it. Not from a producer. Not from a fan. But from the woman who first taught me that metaphors could be doorways, that language could be a form of rescue.

"I thought you wanted me to stop writing," I whispered.

Marianne shook her head, gentle but firm. "I never wanted you to stop. I just didn't want it to consume you."

There was a silence between us then. Not heavy. Not strained. Just full of everything we hadn't said across too many years.

She reached into the bottom of the pile and pulled out a cloth-bound journal. I recognized it instantly—the deep plum color, the velvet spine worn down from her thumb.

"I've been writing, too," she said.

I blinked. "You have?"

She nodded, handing it to me. "Don't read it all. Just this page."

She flipped it to a poem titled "When the Birds Return."

It was about me.

About the day I came home. The light in my eyes she was afraid to trust. The tremble in my voice when I asked if the lavender had survived the frost.

I read it twice, then closed the journal and pressed it to my chest.

"You never stopped seeing me," I said.

"Not once."

I leaned into her shoulder like I used to when I was little. Let the quiet stretch.

"Will you read to me?" I asked.

She didn't answer right away. Just picked up the Rich again and began where she'd left off.

The words wrapped around us like a lullaby. Safe. Known.

And for the first time in years, I let myself be the daughter. Not the star. Not the headline. Just Liv.

Just her girl.

Sadie didn't say much. But she was always near. Reading. Playing. Humming just loud enough for me to hear when I needed it, quiet enough to disappear when I didn't.

We sat at the edge of the creek, legs stretched long over the rocks, the water cool against our ankles. The sun had dipped just enough to cast everything in amber.

Sadie leaned back on her elbows beside me, hair still damp and wild from a swim upstream. It clung to her back in waves the color of late-summer wheat, light brown, streaked through by the sun. No styling. No effort. Just who she was.

She wore a collage of bracelets, some friendship-style, others rough leather, woven metal, threadbare cloth. Her fingers were bare, calloused. The kind that spoke of late nights with a guitar and a life lived without apology. She looked like someone no one could edit.

"I was seeing this guy last year," she said suddenly, tossing a pebble into the water. "Said I was too much. Too weird. Too tall, too loud. Said it like it was a compliment but wanted me smaller."

My chest tightened.

"What'd you do?" I asked.

She looked over at me with a smirk, but her eyes were steady. "Told him I don't crop my edges to fit his screen."

I laughed, startled and grateful.

Sadie went back to watching the water, as if it held secrets only, she could understand.

"You're brave," I said.

"I'm stubborn," she replied. "Maybe the same thing."

I studied her for a long moment. She was eighteen, but already full of stories. Not just the ones she told, ones she carried in her bones. Her presence made you slow down, like listening to a favorite song in a quiet room.

"You scare me a little," I admitted.

She turned, curious. "Why?"

"Because I see the parts of me I left behind. And the parts I wish I'd protected better."

Sadie didn't flinch. "That's the trick, though. You didn't lose them. They just got buried."

The way she said it, like it was already decided, already forgiven, made my throat tighten.

She pulled a gum wrapper from her pocket, flattened it, and handed it to me. Lyrics scrawled in sharp loops. Not polished, but true.

"You write like someone who already knows what she's surviving," I said.

Sadie shrugged. "Don't we all?"

I held the paper gently. "Can I keep this?"

"Nope," she said, grinning. "But I'll write another."

We sat in silence, the creek moving slowly around our feet. I didn't say thank you. I didn't have to. She knew.

And maybe that's what made me feel safest with her. Not the music. Not the honesty. But the way she saw me and didn't flinch. Like whatever was left of me was still worth saving.

Chapter 19: The Crick

Earlier that evening, I sat on the porch with Dorian, our legs tucked under an old quilt Marianne had draped across the swing. The sky was a watercolor bleed of dusk. Crickets had just started tuning up.

I hadn't meant to say anything. But somewhere between my second glass of lemon balm tea and the way the breeze curled around my ankles, it slipped out.

"I haven't seen Tucker today."

Dorian didn't flinch. Just sipped and nodded. "He's probably at The Crick. Open mic night."

I blinked. "They do that?"

He laughed, low and easy. "Every Tuesday. Place fills up by seven. Teens, college kids, people pretending they're not in their forties. Tucker makes it work. It's licensed as a restaurant, so underage kids come for the nachos and a chance to sing like their future depends on it."

"He still that strict?"

"Won't even let a sip go unverified. Last week a guy tried to sneak his little cousin a cider and Tuck practically turned into Judge Judy."

I could see it. That line he walked so carefully—protector, not tyrant. Watchful, not paranoid. Still himself.

Something pinched behind my ribs. Not pain. Not exactly. A catch. A stitch. Like missing something that never quite belonged to you in the first place.

"You ever go?" I asked.

Dorian swirled his tea and tilted his head. "A few times. Met Sadie there. She was sixteen. Hair like a prairie girl, boots like she'd borrowed them from a punk rocker. Got up onstage with this weird little banjo-uke hybrid and sang a mash-up of Joni

Mitchell and Fiona Apple. Half the room didn't know what to make of her."

I raised a brow. "And you?"

"I knew. Instantly. That kid was fire and folklore. Raw. No polish, no pretense. Just this... certainty. Like she was born knowing who she was."

His voice softened, like he was remembering a constellation, not a kid.

"You should see her now," he added. "Owns that room like it's her birthright."

I looked out at the darkening trees, the porchlight catching moths in ritual flight. I thought of Libby. Of what it used to feel like to belong on a stage, not just command it. Of Sadie stepping into that light without armor.

Think you're ready? I asked myself.

No, I answered.

But maybe I could watch someone who was.

I shifted on the swing. Dorian noticed.

"You're waiting for him," he said gently.

I shook my head, too fast. "I just noticed he wasn't around. That's all."

He didn't argue. Just raised an eyebrow that said everything.

"You know you don't have to make him the villain to make yourself the hero," he added.

"He's not a villain," I whispered. "But he let me fall. And I don't know how to stop needing someone who proved I couldn't trust them to catch me."

Dorian leaned back, legs outstretched, face tilted toward the stars just beginning to emerge. "Then maybe tonight isn't about him. Maybe it's about you seeing the stage again and remembering that you still want it."

"Even if I do... what does that change?"

He looked at me. "It means you're alive again."

We didn't go in through the front. Too risky. Too loud. Too much.

Dorian parked two blocks down and we walked. Hood up. Wig low. I looked like a failed college poet trying to dodge loan collectors.

The summer air clung to my skin.

You could smell the bar before you saw it— beer, fryer grease, cologne, and old gravel soaked in memory.

The Crick. Not The Creek, obviously. Not in Delco. Here, we drop vowels and pretenses. Crick rhymes with stick. It feels like a challenge.

It was the name we gave the water that sliced behind our childhood homes, muddy, loud, never quite clean, but always ours. We drank warm beer on its banks. Kissed boys who didn't know what to do with their hands. Dared each other off rocks. Came home with bruises and songs.

The Crick isn't just a bar. It's a living scrapbook.

Every stool, every chalkboard special, every groove in the floorboards holds a piece of someone's coming-of-age.

And tonight, mine was trying to slip back in without being seen.

We slipped through the side gate. The back door creaked like it recognized me, though I'd never been here before.

Inside, the light was gold and low. The kind of warm that flatters even bad decisions.

Guitars were being tuned on the tiny stage. Open mic night, like always.

Dorian squeezed my arm. A check-in. I nodded.

We hovered near the kitchen door. I kept my head down, eyes darting, from the bar to the stage to the exit sign.

Tucker was working. Of course he was.

He moved like the bar was his body, fluid, efficient, in sync. One hand pouring a pint, the other steadying someone's shoulder mid-laugh. He smiled without reaching for it. His laugh lines deeper now. A little silver in his beard. No effort, all ease.

I watched a girl lean in. Her hand on his arm. Tossed her hair, laughed like a dare. He didn't lean in. But he didn't pull away either.

My jaw clenched. Just slightly. Enough to remind me I had nerves left to hit.

He turned then, wiped down the counter, glanced toward the kitchen. Did he see me? I wasn't sure. But he stood straighter. Eyes sharper.

My stomach curled. Not with jealousy, exactly. More like grief. Like I was watching someone light candles in a house I used to live in.

The bar was exactly him, oak and mahogany, worn but cared for. The kind of place that tried to be craft but stayed loyal to Yuengling and wings. Local sports flags, but Edison bulbs over the taps. Hipster-adjacent without selling out.

I hated how much I liked it.

A server passed with a tray of IPAs. The scent hit me like a challenge, hops, malt, memory. My mouth watered.

Dorian's hand was on my back, steady. "Breathe," he whispered.

I did.

Music started.

A girl I didn't recognize stepped to the mic. Early twenties, maybe. Wide eyes. Nervous hands. She strummed three hesitant chords and sang.

It wasn't polished. But it was true. Her voice cracked. Her gaze dropped between lines. She didn't apologize.

I remembered being her. Before. Before glitter. Before pills. Before applause cost something.

The room clapped. Soft. Real. Not polite, present. Worse, somehow.

I couldn't stay. Dorian was already moving.

We slipped out the way we came. Into the dark. Into the silence.

I didn't cry until we got to the car.

"I miss it," I said. Voice breaking.

"I know," Dorian replied.

"Not the fame. Not the shows. Just... the singing. The being heard."

He didn't answer. He didn't need to.

The stage was calling. But this time, I'd decide how to answer.

We were nearly to the car when I heard footsteps.

"Liv."

Tucker's voice. Low. Familiar. Too much.

I turned. Hoodie up. Moonlight catching his profile like a photograph I'd hidden too long.

"You weren't gonna say anything?" he asked.

"I didn't want to make a scene," I said. Too clipped. Too defensive.

"Would've been nice to know you were there."

"Would it?"

He blinked, like I'd cut too close. Dorian's keys jingled. Then silence. He stepped away. God bless him.

Tucker looked tired. Not work-tired. Us-tired.

"You don't get to ghost a whole life," he said. "Then hover like it still owes you something."

My chest burned. "I'm not hovering. I'm surviving."

"In a hoodie and a wig? At the back door?"

"I'm not ready," I snapped. "You think I want to be recognized? I can barely breathe in there without wanting a drink or a disguise."

His jaw flexed. "Then why come?"

"Because I miss it," I said. "Not the crowd. Not the chaos. The truth. Someone singing like it matters."

"So, sing," he said. "God knows you used to."

"Don't you dare."

"Dare what?"

"Talk to me like you believed in me. Like you didn't walk away and watch me vanish."

His eyes met mine again. That careful, deliberate Tucker patience. But it was cracking around the edges.

He was always steady. Always the anchor. But now—his hands were in fists. His shoulders tight. He kept blinking like he didn't trust what might come out if he let the silence stretch too long.

And I saw it. Not just anger. But grief. The kind that lives in a man who stayed silent too long.

"You think I didn't fight?" he said, voice low. "You think I just walked away?"

I didn't answer. The words caught in my throat, sharp as glass.

"I came to L.A. once. You never knew. I waited outside Jag Records for an hour, hoping to see you or Dorian. You were on a billboard across the street. I was scared if I saw you again, I wouldn't leave. So, I did. I got in my car and drove home."

I stared.

"You were right there," he said. "But you were already gone."

My breath caught. The ache widened.

"You let me disappear."

"You disappeared before I ever let go."

My knees went weak. My voice dropped.

"I would've stayed," I said. "For you. For us."

He shook his head. "I didn't want you to shrink. I thought if I held on, you'd fold into me instead of growing out of everything."

"I didn't grow. I combusted."

Silence.

Then he stepped back. Just slightly. Just enough to signal it was done.
But it wasn't.
Not for me.

Dorian

Dorian stood in the hallway.

He hadn't turned the porch light off yet. He didn't need to. The house was quiet, except for the soft creak of the floorboards as Liv walked the perimeter like a ghost not ready to settle.

He'd seen this before. In Malibu. In the Echo Park studio with the broken AC. In hotel rooms that cost more than her entire childhood home. The silence that came before she wrote.

Only this time, it felt different.

She passed him without a word. Their eyes met. He didn't ask.

But he saw the fire.

The kind that doesn't beg to be lit—it demands to be used.

Liv

We got home, and I couldn't sit still. Dorian offered tea. I shook my head.

My skin felt too tight. My throat too open.

I didn't know what to do with this heat in my chest except bleed it out.

So, I opened the notebook. The one Rey gave me, with the soft cover and the binding that creaks like it's holding in secrets.

I wrote. Scratched out the first two lines. Wrote again. Wrong chord. Wrong tone. Too angry. Too soft. Too desperate.

I kept going. Not because it felt good. But because it felt necessary.

I started to hum. Just under my breath. Notes I didn't recognize. A melody I didn't trust yet.

I wrote the chorus first. Then the second verse. Then the bridge.

I paced the kitchen. Opened the fridge. Closed it again. Stared at my reflection in the microwave.

I wasn't Libby. Wasn't Liv from the crick either.

I was someone new. Someone cracking open.

Back in the bedroom, I sat cross-legged on the floor and whispered the title.

"You Said Forever With Your Hands."

I wrote the first verse:

"You said forever with your hands
Pressed flat against my back like prayer
Told me soulmates weren't a myth
Just two kids dumb enough to think they'd be spared."

It felt like slicing something open. It felt like birth.

The night stretched out.

I moved from floor to desk to edge of the bed. Scribbled a new line on the back of an envelope. Whispered a chorus into my voice notes app with a trembling voice I didn't recognize as my own.

Somewhere near 3 a.m., I found my childhood guitar. Out of tune. Dusty.

I didn't tune it. Just held it. Let it press into my ribcage like it used to. The familiar shape of something that once made sense.

I picked three chords. Wrong ones. But I played them anyway.

When the melody came, it wasn't beautiful. But it was mine.

I wrote the third verse leaning against the bathroom sink. The mirror fogged with emotion, not steam.

"They all called it fame.
I called it hiding.
And every man I met since you,
Was just a softer kind of lying."

By morning, my fingers were raw. My eyes stung.

But the notebook was full.

The story had landed.

And for the first time in years, I had something that felt like mine.

A song.

Not for anyone else.

Just for the girl who still believed love should've been enough.

Chapter 20: The Ghost of Lacey Brenner

For a week, I pretended the night at the bar didn't exist. Like I wasn't torturing myself writing a song about Tucker. Letting him live rent-free in my head. Letting myself believe I still had the right. And then acting shocked when he stopped coming around the house. Apparently, I hit a nerve. We both did.

He didn't text Dorian. Didn't call. Didn't ask Marianne how I was, or swing by the barn like he used to. And I told myself that was fine. I told myself I didn't want to be seen. But the truth was— it gnawed. Not the silence. The absence. The knowing I pushed him away, and this time, he stayed gone.

I was antsy. I'd already wiped down the kitchen counters twice. Rearranged the spoons in the drawer. Rebraided the lavender stalks by the window.

The farm stand was only half a mile down the road. Dorian offered to go. So did Mom. Even Big Al half-muttered he'd "throw on pants and be back in ten."

But I needed air. Real air. Not lavender-candle smoke or ceiling fan breeze. I needed sun on my scalp, even if it had to press through the cheap auburn wig I found in Marianne's old costume bin from some forgotten Halloween.

I wore it with a trucker hat and oversized sunglasses that kept slipping down my nose every few steps. Add the flannel, and I looked like a very hungover librarian from 2008.

It was early enough for dew to still cling to the edges of things. The gravel crunched under my sneakers in a rhythm that almost felt like breathing.

There was a hush to mornings out here. A reverence. Even the wind made space for it. Birds didn't chirp so much as confess. The trees didn't rustle—they remembered.

The stand came into view, a painted wooden shack with a tin cash box and hand-lettered signs for duck eggs, honey sticks, and sweet corn.

I grabbed a carton. Tucked it under my arm like contraband.

Then I heard it:

"Oh my God. Liv?"

Just like that. No warm-up. No warning. Just an old voice that still knew where my soft parts lived.

I turned.

Lacey Brenner.

Hair too bright, smile too wide, sandals too expensive for a gravel road. She hadn't changed much, just polished the edges and sharpened the smile.

"Wow," she breathed, stepping closer like we were filming some low-rent reunion special. "I thought that was you. That walk, nobody forgets that sway."

I forced a smile. Tight. Libby-like. "Hey, Lacey."

Her eyes scanned me—wig, sunglasses, the egg carton clutched like a shield.

"God, it's been what, twenty years?" she said. "You look..." She let the sentence dangle like bait.

I didn't bite.

"Just picking up eggs," I said, starting to edge away.

She stepped with me. "You know, you could've called. I mean, Tucker's probably not gonna say it, but he was a mess when you left. We all were."

"Were you?"

She blinked. Not used to me biting back.

"We thought you'd forget us," she said. "Guess we were right."

"I didn't forget," I said. "I just couldn't afford to remember."

Her mouth curved into something I couldn't read—pity? Possession?

"Welcome back," she said. "You and your... hat."

I didn't answer. Just turned, the eggs pressed tight against my ribs, and walked faster.

But the truth was already cracking. Because she saw me. And if Lacey saw me, others would too.

The walk home stretched longer than the road should've allowed. Every few steps, I passed a marker. The ditch where Tucker and I used to light bottle rockets. The pine tree Dorian carved his name into with a house key. The bend in the road where Lacey tried to make herself part of us and never quite fit.

It wasn't that we were mean. We just knew what we were. Tucker, Dorian, me—we had gravity. A pull that didn't require permission. Lacey saw it. Wanted in. Tried too hard.

The night I finally agreed to a sleepover at her house, she cornered me in the basement with too many scented candles and a too-sweet wine cooler. Started asking questions that didn't feel like curiosity.

"You and Tucker ever hook up? Like, really? Or is it just a 'deep connection'?"

"Does Dorian sleep over? I mean, you guys always seem like a package deal. Like... a throuple or something."

"I think I'm gonna be famous too. I don't know how yet, but I feel it. We could be like, parallel lives."

That night, I wrapped myself in her scratchy guest blanket and counted the hours until morning. When I left, I knew something final had closed.

A week later, someone told me Lacey had introduced herself at a party as my best friend. Said we were inseparable. Claimed she'd inspired my first song.

I laughed so hard I cried. Or maybe it was the other way around.

And then there was the assembly. Sophomore year. She got up in front of the whole auditorium and read a poem "inspired by friendship." It was clearly about me. Except none of it was true. She used my name like a prop. Described a late-night heart-to-heart we never had. Claimed we pinky-swore to chase dreams together.

I remember Dorian looking at me across the rows. His expression was half-amused, half-murderous.

Later, I found a copy of the poem taped to my locker. In glitter pen. Signed, "Your forever friend."

It wasn't the lies that got me. It was the way she erased the truth and replaced it with something shinier. Something easier to digest.

What no one knew—what no one asked about—was the night before that assembly, when I sat between Tucker and Dorian in the old hayloft. We were high on nothing but late summer air and the thrill of harmonizing without trying. Tucker played a half-broken mandolin with no musical prowess. Dorian made up lyrics on the spot. And I laughed until I hiccuped.

That was friendship. That was truth.

The second I turned the bend past the cornfield, my breathing changed. It didn't falter—not yet—but it thinned. Like my lungs couldn't trust the air to hold them.

I walked faster. The gravel stung through the soles of my sneakers. Every crunch felt like a mistake I couldn't unsay.

What I should've said.

What I should've worn.

What I should've done with my hair.

Why the hell did I grab the auburn wig?

I wanted to claw the whole moment back and rewrite it. But Lacey's voice was already echoing in my ribcage, reshaping itself as guilt. It always did that—took up space like it paid rent.

I passed the old fence line and caught a splinter just above my wrist. It bled, barely. But it anchored me. At least something still stung in the real world.

She'd looked at me like a ghost, but it wasn't the haunting that lingered. It was the smirk. The self-certainty. Like she finally had proof that her version of me was the right one.

I wiped my hand on my flannel and kept moving. No music. No inner narration. Just me and the hum of shame growing louder with every step.

For a second, I imagined a red carpet. My old pose. Hand on hip, chin slightly tilted. The flashbulbs timed with my breath. The applause never quite matching the panic.

That was the trick Libby learned early: how to look composed while your heart crawled up your throat.

She was still in there. She always was.

But out here—under this sky, on this road—I felt her shivering. Stripped.

And Liv?

Liv felt like a raw nerve with legs.

By the time I got home, my hands were shaking. Not from withdrawal. Not exactly.

I set the eggs on the kitchen counter like they might detonate. Still in the wig. Still in the hat. Still hiding.

Marianne looked up from her notebook. She didn't ask. She just poured tea and slid it across the table.

I didn't touch it. Just stared at the wood grain like I was waiting for it to split open and swallow me whole.

"She saw me," I said finally. "Lacey."

Mom didn't flinch. "What did she say?"

I laughed. One note. Hollow. "She said Tucker was a mess when I left. Like she's the keeper of his secrets now."

"She's always wanted to be," she said softly. Not unkind.

I pulled off the glasses. Peeled back the wig. My scalp tingled in the open air.

"She looked at me like I was a ghost."

Marianne sipped her tea. "Then let her haunt herself with it. You don't owe anyone the living version of who they remember."

"I know," I whispered. "But it's not her I'm worried about."

Mom didn't press. She just waited.

"I looked her in the eye," I told Mom, "and for half a second, I felt like I was auditioning for my own redemption."

Marianne didn't look up. She was still scribbling something into the margins of her notebook, but I saw her mouth tighten. That barely-there line of recognition.

"Did you ever feel that?" I asked. "Like someone decided what your life was, and you just... inherited their version?"

She set the pen down gently, like it weighed more than ink.

"All the time," she said. "Especially after I married your father. I was 'the girl who gave up

New York.' The one who wrote poems in the margins but never quite made them public."

I blinked. "You wanted to live in New York?"

"For about five minutes," she said, smiling softly. "But I did want to teach abroad. Italy, maybe. Or Greece. I wanted to write a chapbook. Just one. No big release. No stage lights. Just a little spine on a shelf with my name on it."

She looked out the window like she could see the alternate version of herself still packing a suitcase.

"What happened?" I asked.

"You happened," she said, then caught herself. "I don't mean that as blame. Just... clarity. I chose this life. I chose you. But it doesn't mean the other one didn't ache sometimes."

I folded my hands in my lap.

"I think I lost my version before I even had a chance to choose," I said.

She nodded. "Because someone handed you a louder one first."

Silence settled in the kitchen again. This time, not empty. Full. A quiet that listened back.

"I still might write that chapbook," she said finally, picking up her pen.

"You should," I said. "Call it What I Didn't Give Away."

She laughed, sounding like old piano keys, slightly out of tune but beloved.

"And you?" she asked. "What would you write, if no one was watching?"

I didn't answer right away.

But I reached for my notebook.

And I wrote.

Later, I wandered into the barn. Not for chores. Just to move. To be in a space that didn't ask anything of me.

Near the loft ladder, half-tucked under a tarp, I found a cracked mirror that used to hang in my childhood bedroom. I pulled it free.

The crack ran right through the middle. Split my reflection in two. One side looked like Libby. The other looked like someone I used to know.

I pressed my fingers to the glass. "You're both real," I whispered.

I sat with it for a while. Cross-legged in the hay dust, the mirror propped against an old saddle bench. I watched the way the light caught my face and splintered it—how even when I stayed still, the pieces didn't quite align.

I didn't cry. That surprised me. But there was a heaviness in my chest, like I'd just been told a secret about myself I wasn't sure I wanted to know.

I whispered song fragments. Not full verses, just the ghost of lines. A chorus that hummed behind my teeth. Words I'd never say out loud, except maybe here—where no one was listening, and everything, finally, felt mine.

I ran my thumb over the glass crack. Not sharp, not dangerous. Just enough to remind me I wasn't seamless. Had never been.

For a long moment, I did nothing but breathe.

And then I stood, mirror in hand, and carried it back to the house like an artifact from a former life.

That night, I dreamed I was on stage—but there were two of me.

One stood at the mic in glitter heels and perfect lipstick. The other sat cross-legged in the wings, barefoot and bleeding from the palms.

The audience kept clapping, but no sound came out. The spotlight flickered. The barefoot version stood and walked into it, eyes fixed on the mic. The glittered one stepped back. They didn't speak. Just stared at each other until the light went out.

I woke up sweaty, heart pounding, the dream still humming behind my ribs.

I got up. Turned on the lamp. Grabbed the notebook.

Inside, between Tucker's verses and the chorus for Lacey. I found a folded page I didn't remember writing from when I was nineteen.

A journal entry. From years ago.

It read:

"I don't want to be known for the things that hurt me. I want to be known for the things I survived without anyone noticing. The quiet braveries. The hidden wars. The songs that almost didn't get sung."

I stared at it.

Then flipped the page and wrote:

"You never knew the war I waged,
To keep the softness in my rage.
You never asked what silence cost,
You only loved the girl I lost."

It wasn't a hook. Not yet. But it bled true.

Dorian knocked lightly a few minutes later. Didn't come in. Just said, "You good?"

I said, "Getting there."

He paused. "You're writing again."

"I'm trying."

"You don't have to try. You just have to tell the truth."

The hallway creaked as he walked away.

So I told the truth. In fragments. In lines. In the way my pen scratched like it was sharpening something old and sacred.

I hummed the bridge. Tried a harmony. Scratched it out. Wrote the hook again.

Some ghosts don't want closure. They want co-writing credits.

I let the ink bleed.

By midnight, I tiptoed down the stairs with the notebook tucked under my arm. The house was dark except for the blue flicker from the living room stereo. Dorian had loaded one of my demo files.

I pressed play.

It was raw. The melody wandered. My voice cracked in places I used to smooth.

But it was mine.

That night, I didn't dream. I just listened.

By morning, I had three full pages.

And a title:

"Not Yours to Tell."

Chapter 21: What They Don't Say Out Loud

"I don't want to hide," I said.

Rey blinked slowly. "Then don't."

Simple. And dangerous.

We sat cross-legged in the garden, late afternoon light pouring through bee-buzzed lavender. Rey wore a black tank and linen pants. I wore a mask that felt like skin.

"She saw me. Lacey."

"I figured." Their gaze flicked over me, thoughtfully. "You've got that haunted shimmer."

I let out a short, bitter laugh. "She said Tucker was a mess when I left."

"Does that matter to you?"

"I don't know."

Rey tilted their head, not unkind. "Sounds like it does."

Before I could unpack that, Dorian appeared with iced tea and a frown held too tightly in his jaw.

"You called?" he asked, settling beside me on the stone wall. His sunglasses dangled from his collar. His shoulders were too still.

"I needed a third voice," I said. "I need to talk about... what's next."

Rey leaned back on their hands. "She doesn't want to stay invisible forever."

"I didn't think she would," Dorian replied carefully.

"But she's not asking for a comeback rollout," Rey added, softer. "No campaign. No curated re-entry."

"I'm not planning one," Dorian said, too quickly.

Rey arched an eyebrow. "Aren't you?"

That landed sharper than it should have. My chest tightened.

"I called you both," I said. "So, we could talk. Not turn me into a project again."

"You asked for honesty," Dorian said. "The truth is, word's already moving. Lacey seeing you? That's enough. One careless post and the press will come sniffing. They love a resurrection."

"She's not Libby anymore," Rey murmured.

"And she's not anonymous," Dorian countered.

Silence.

Then Rey stood slowly, brushing dust from their palms. "If this turns into a strategy meeting again, Liv... you need to know now. Because healing's not halfway. You're either in your skin, or you're back in the wig."

Dorian looked at me. "Is this about control... or fear?"

I didn't answer. Couldn't.

Because the truth was, I was afraid.
Afraid of Lacey. Of Tucker. Of the weight in my chest every time I pictured him near her. Of how close I'd come to asking Dorian to stop for bourbon after the egg run.

Of the whisper I still couldn't shake, Libby's voice, soft and sugar-sweet:

"Just one drink, sweetheart. Just a little glitter to take the edge off."

Rey paced a slow loop. Dorian stared at his hands.

They weren't fighting over media plans.

They were circling a deeper question neither wanted to name.

Who gets to walk beside me now?

And I hated how much it echoed the boardrooms, the label meetings, the branding calls, every version of me that got designed instead of discovered.

"I need to think," I said, standing.

They both looked at me, Rey patient, Dorian tense.

I wasn't fragile. I wasn't furious. I was just... full.

Full of grief and hunger and dreams shaped like ruin.

"You keep asking what I want," I said. "I don't know yet. But I know what I don't want."

Rey's voice was quieter now. "And what's that?"

"To be handled."

They both nodded.

Neither apologized.

I walked into the house. Up the stairs. Into the sunlit room with the cracked mirror and the old guitar in the corner.

And I locked the door.

Because even if I wasn't ready to show the world I was here...

I needed to prove it to myself first.

As the latch clicked, my body sagged into the silence. I leaned against the wall, heart knocking into my ribs like it wanted out. My hand brushed the cracked mirror—Libby's last costume change still hanging in its reflection. She always knew how to pivot when the heat got too close.

But what if I stayed?

What if I didn't script my next step?

The question pulsed louder than the answer.

Memory: Liv

And like a film reel I didn't ask for, he came back.

Sterling Vale.

Polished teeth. City watch. That voice, warm enough to pass for safe. Sharp enough to cut before you noticed you were bleeding.

It was a Thursday night in Media.

I was nineteen.

Third Verse Café still smelled like burnt espresso and overshared poetry. The open mic chalkboard was full of dreamers, and I was somewhere near the bottom.

Tucker drove us there in his truck, parked two blocks away so I wouldn't panic about the crowd. He carried my guitar in like it was sacred.

"You want me up front?" he asked, that sideways grin tugging at his mouth.

"Always."

And he was, first row, center, arms on his knees, wearing that denim jacket I'd once stolen and returned with lyrics scribbled inside the pocket.

I sang something new.

A dusky ballad with corners. Too honest. A love song that knew fear.

It held both of us in it, me and him, in verses wrapped in wonder and doubt.

The kind of love where you plan futures in whispers but never say them aloud.

The kind that feels invincible because it hasn't yet been tested.

When I finished, the room clapped. A few whistles. A longer silence, like they were letting it land.

Tucker's eyes were glassy. Proud. Not possessive. Just present.

"You killed that," he said softly when I sat beside him, fingers still trembling. "Like you bled it out right there."

I kissed him behind the coffee bar.

I remember the taste of cinnamon and certainty.

What I didn't see was the man in the back.

Sterling Vale.

He wasn't even supposed to be there, cousin to the next act, visiting family in Chadds Ford.

Irritated to sit through amateurs.

Until he heard me.

He waited outside.

Light jacket. Pressed shirt. Smile like a trapdoor.

"You're the kind of voice people remember," he said. "The kind that could fill a theater and make it feel like a bedroom."

Tucker stepped forward, quiet, steady. "She just sings 'cause she needs to."

Sterling smiled wider. "That's the kind that sells."

He handed me a card. Simple. Clean. One name. One number. No promises.

"I'm not here to pressure," he said. "Just saying... if you ever want to be more than open mic, I can help."

Then, as he turned, he tossed it out like a joke, only it wasn't:

"You're not a singer. You're a commodity."

And something in me cracked open.

Not because I didn't believe Tucker when he said I was enough.

But because the lights whispered maybe. And Sterling knew how to echo the voice I hadn't learned to silence.

The one that said:

You're not just meant for him. You're meant for everyone.

I took the card.

Told myself it was just curiosity.

I didn't know it was a door.

And once I stepped through, Tucker couldn't follow.

The next morning, we had coffee on the porch outside my dorm. Tucker brought me a scone and wore his worry like a second layer.

"You okay?" he asked.

I smiled too wide. "Yeah. Just tired."

He handed me the scone, kissed the side of my head, but his eyes lingered. "You seemed different last night. After the show."

I shrugged. "Just nerves."

I didn't tell him about the card in my back pocket. I didn't tell him how my fingers kept brushing it like it was a prayer or a matchstick.

I told myself it was nothing.

But in my gut, I knew.

That was the moment everything started to shift.

The memory faded like smoke, but the ache stayed.

I blinked at the ceiling. My childhood ceiling. The one I used to stare at while dreaming of stadiums, soundchecks, headlines that read: Libby Morgan: A Star Is Born.

Now I stared at it like it owed me an apology.

My mouth was dry. My hands twitchy.

That hollow pull beneath my ribs again.

The one I used to fill with glitter. Or silence.

I stood too fast.

Paced the room like I could outwalk the past.

The guitar sat in the corner. The notebook waited on the bed.

But they felt rigged.

Every song I'd ever written had Sterling's fingerprints somewhere in the margins.

Even the love songs.

Especially the love songs.

I sat again. Pulled the blanket over my shoulders like armor.

You're not just meant for him. You're meant for everyone.

The whisper again.

But this time, I whispered back:

"I don't want everyone."

I didn't know who I wanted to be.

But I knew I couldn't be her again.

I curled up like I used to when I was twelve, knees to chest, forehead pressed to the wall. Outside, the wind rattled the hydrangeas. Inside, I held my breath and waited for the craving to pass.

And then I cracked.

Not loudly. Not all at once. But in the quiet way paper tears.

I stood and crossed the room.

Opened a drawer I hadn't dared since I came home.

Inside: old lyric sheets, yellowed and creased. A burned CD labeled "Libby's First Takes." A photograph of me on stage, grinning too wide, all teeth and spotlight.

I stared at it.

Then ripped it clean down the middle.

Not out of rage. But necessity.

I took the torn pieces, pressed them between notebook pages like wilting flowers. Evidence of a version I no longer answered to.

Then I picked up the pen.

And for the first time in months, I wrote without an audience in mind.

Not for Dorian. Not for the press. Not for redemption.

Just for me.

One line. Then another.

They didn't rhyme. They didn't need to.

It was enough to be true.

And that night, I didn't dream of stages or scripts.

I dreamed of dirt beneath my fingernails and a song with no name.

And when I woke up, I remembered every word.

Chapter 22: Not Everything Needs A Song

Liv

I sat at the edge of the bed, wrapped in my blanket, not sure when I'd last moved.

Lacey's voice was still threaded through my thoughts, like a needle catching on old seams.

I hated that she got in.

That she made me doubt what I knew.

That she smiled like she already owned the next chapter of my story.

The craving wasn't loud tonight. It never is when it's old.

It just hovered.

A soft invitation.

Like a room you used to live in, still furnished, still lit, still waiting.

I didn't want a drink.

I just wanted not to *feel*.

Not this particular blend—shame and sadness and that deep fatigue of trying to stay clean in a world that keeps tugging at the thread.

I thought about texting Dorian.

Or Rey.

But I didn't.

Because the feeling wasn't urgent. It was ancient.

And that scared me more.

I didn't plan to call him.

I just... did.

It was after midnight.

The kind of quiet that feels earned.

The house was asleep. My thoughts weren't.

I lay curled in the dark, staring at the wall, the craving not in my body, but in my mind.

That's worse, sometimes.

When the ache doesn't shout, it whispers.

I didn't drink. Didn't take anything.

But I thought about it.

That old reflex, rising.

That voice that says just one sip would smooth the edge.

Just one pill could mute the memory.

Just one.

That's when I reached for the phone.

Eli answered on the second ring.

No hello, just a low hum, like he'd already tuned in to whatever station I was on.

"Hey," I said.

"Hey, Little Star."

The nickname still disarmed me.

Not for what it meant, but because of who said it.

"You up?"

"I'm old," he said. "I nap in chapters now."

I smiled. A small one. Barely there.

"I didn't do anything," I said. "Didn't drink. Didn't use. But I wanted to."

"Wanting," he said gently, "is not the same as doing."

"I hate that it still lives in me," I whispered.

"No one hates the fire," he said. "They just forget how to sit beside it without getting burned."

I exhaled, shaky.

"I remembered Sterling," I said. "And I hated myself for not seeing him for what he was sooner."

Eli was quiet for a moment. The line hummed, soft and familiar.

"You were nineteen," he said. "And lonely. That's when we're most vulnerable. When applause sounds like love and predators sound like praise."

I swallowed. The lump in my throat wasn't new, just louder in the quiet.

"I thought being seen was enough."

"Being seen," Eli said, "is not the same as being known. And it sure as hell isn't the same as being loved."

I closed my eyes. Pressed the phone tighter to my ear, like his voice might steady the tremble in me.

"I miss singing," I whispered. "But not as her. Not in the glitter. Not in the cage."

"Then don't go back to the cage."

"What if the cage is all they want?"

He didn't answer right away. I could almost hear the creak of his old chair, the soft scrape of a record spinning in another room.

"They don't get to want you anymore," Eli said. Gentle. Certain. "Not them. Not Tucker. Not Lacey. Not even Dorian."

That last one made me flinch.

"I don't know how to stand without someone telling me where to put my feet."

"Then don't stand," he said. "Sit. Breathe. Let your voice come back to you before anyone else tries to borrow it."

It settled in, his words. Not like a command. More like a blanket pulled tight around a part of me I didn't know was still cold.

We sat in silence. Not empty. Not awkward. Just space.

"Do you remember," I said slowly, "that night in Chicago? When I was three drinks deep and started crying about whales?"

Eli chuckled. "You said you didn't understand how something that large could still feel alone."

"And you didn't laugh."

"I never laugh at grief disguised as wonder."

That made me smile. And ache.

"I'm proud of you," he said finally. "For calling. For not doing. For remembering what almost means."

"I didn't write anything tonight."

"Not everything needs a song."

Memory: Liv

And just like that, his voice sparked a memory.

Not of fame. Not of music. Not of Sterling or Tucker or even the cage I once gilded.

But of a folding chair in a windowless church basement.

The air had smelled like cheap coffee and paper plates.

I was thirty-nine. Hollowed out. Still bruised from the last night with Jax. The one with sirens. The one where the police didn't believe me until they saw the blood.

I hadn't been to a meeting in two years.

I thought I'd be judged. Whispered about. Greeted with side-eyes and side conversations.

But Eli didn't flinch.

He saw me walk in—makeup still smeared, sleeves tugged down over wrists—and he just nodded.

He didn't hug. Didn't hover.

He just pulled out the chair beside him and slid a Styrofoam cup my way.

And then he waited.

After the meeting, I couldn't talk. My throat locked up.

He handed me a peppermint and said, "You're still here. That's enough for today."

It wasn't magic. It didn't fix me.

But it steadied something. Anchored the place I thought was too shattered to patch.

Over time, we started walking after meetings. Around the block, sometimes in silence.

Then one night, he told me the story.

Not in detail. Not for effect. Just truth, plain and jagged.

He used to drink.

A lot.

One night, when he was 33, he got behind the wheel. Thought he was fine. Just buzzed. Just tired.

His wife and daughter were in the car.

He doesn't remember the impact. Just the aftermath. Metal folded like paper. A silence so sudden it rang in his ears.

His daughter was seven.

Her name was Lila.

His wife, Monique, died two days later.

He said the grief didn't come all at once. It oozed. It clung. It calcified.

And for a long time, he drank more—because what else do you do when your guilt outweighs your breath?

"I wanted to die every day," he told me. "But I didn't. So I figured the least I could do was try to matter to someone else."

That's how he ended up here. This town. These meetings.

Quiet. Present. A lighthouse with a broken bulb that still managed to shine.

I remember asking, "Do you ever forgive yourself?"

He didn't say yes.

He said, "I forgive the version of me who couldn't see another way."

Then he looked at me and added, "And I try to give the new version something to live for."

That's what Eli gave me.

Not lectures. Not pity.

Just space to be new.

Not clean. Not cured.

But alive.

[Journal – 1:36 a.m.]

Lacey smiled like she knew something I didn't.
That was the worst part.
Not her words.
Not even the implication.
But the certainty in her eyes.
Like my return was just another rumor in a small-town bingo game.
Like Tucker was a story she'd already claimed the ending to.
Like I was a ghost trying too hard to look alive.
And the truth? I let it get to me.
I let her decide what my absence meant. What my silence cost. What my history held.
I know she doesn't know him—not really—not the way I did. But maybe that's the cruelest part.
That I'm not sure I still do.
Then Dorian and Rey,
My lifelines. My family.
Still orbiting the idea that I need steering.
I know they love me.
But it still felt like management.
Like I couldn't just be, I had to be framed.
Had to be shaped into something legible again. Sellable, maybe. Even if they'd never admit it.
And then Eli's voice.
Still. Quiet. Steady.
He didn't tell me what to do.
Didn't strategize.
Didn't spin.
He just reminded me I didn't have to do anything tonight.
That I could sit.
Breathe.
Not disappear.
That wanting the silence doesn't mean I have to be afraid of it.
But silence is tricky.

It leaves room for other voices.

The press. The past. The Laceys of the world.

Even Libby.

She still whispers sometimes.

That glitter is easier than grief.

That praise is safer than truth.

That escape is just one swallow away.

Tonight, I didn't listen.

But I heard her.

I also heard Eli.

Telling me forgiveness doesn't come all at once.

That survival doesn't mean standing. It means staying.

That the new version of me deserves more than shame.

But even now, I can't shake the look in Lacey's eyes.

Like she'd already rewritten my ending.

Like Tucker belonged to the version of me I hadn't yet become.

And that maybe, in the time I was gone, she learned more about him than I ever did.

That part hurts.

More than I want to admit.

So no, I don't want a stage.

Or a spotlight.

But maybe I do want an answer.

Not for the press.

Not for Libby.

For me.

Maybe I need to know if the song still lives in me.

Maybe I need to know if he still does, too.

I closed the journal.

Set it gently on the windowsill, beside the cup of now-cold tea and the peppermint Eli gave me months ago that I still hadn't unwrapped.

And I walked to the guitar.

The same one I'd avoided all night.

Not to play.

Not yet.

Just to hold.

It was dusty.

A fine veil over the frets, like time itself had settled in to wait with me.

I curled around it on the bed like a talisman, forehead resting against the worn wood, the hum of old songs echoing in its hollow belly.

The scent of it—pine and memory—wrapped around me in ways I wasn't ready for.

My fingers brushed the strings.

One chord.

Soft. Tentative.

The kind of sound you make when you're not trying to be heard, just trying to remember.

It vibrated through me.

Low and fragile.

Like breath.

I didn't cry.

I didn't hum.

I just *listened*.

To the silence.

To the shape of absence.

To the question that lived in my hands, not yet a song but something seedling.

I let my fingers slide to the fretboard.

Not for melody.

For memory.

A G chord.

Then E minor.

My body knew it before I did.

I used to write in this room.

Before Libby.

Before hotels and handlers and hallways I couldn't breathe in.

Here, I could bleed and no one would ask me to rhyme it.

I strummed again.

Lighter.

Like coaxing a ghost into daylight.

Maybe the song hadn't left.

Maybe it was just hiding.

Like I had been.

I remembered what Eli said:

That not everything needs a song.

But maybe some things do.

Not for the charts.

Not for the comeback.

But for the reckoning.

The strings buzzed under my fingertips.

A little out of tune.

Like me.

But still intact.

Still capable of music.

I whispered to the guitar.

A soundless promise.

I'm not ready to sing.

But I'm ready to listen.

And maybe that was enough.

For now.

I let the final chord hang in the air.

Not closed.

Not resolved.

Just... suspended.

Then I held it to my chest.

Like a heartbeat.

Like a question.

And somewhere inside me, something shifted.

Not dramatically.

Not permanently.

But honestly.

Maybe the girl who used to write under this roof wasn't lost.

Maybe she'd just been waiting.

For me to sit still long enough to find her again.

Chapter 23: The Song That Broke Us

Liv

I woke to birdsong and the scent of coffee.
Not tea. Not chamomile comfort.
Coffee.
Black.
Bitter.
Bracing.
I poured a mug and stood at the window,
fingers tight around the heat.
The first sip burned, bitter and unforgiving.
I didn't add cream. Didn't sweeten it.
I needed the sting.
Outside, the garden glowed like something
from a memory I wasn't sure was mine anymore—
lavender trembling in the mist, sun breaking slow
over the hill. Inside, everything in me was taut.
Braced.
Like the day might ask too much.
I wasn't spiraling.
Not quite.
But I wasn't steady either.
Lacey's face still lived behind my eyes.
That knowing smile.
Like she'd seen something in Tucker I hadn't.
Or worse—something in me I didn't want to
reclaim.
I hadn't slept. Not really. Just floated in and
out of fragments—Eli's voice, the guitar's hum,
Sterling's card in my hand.
The craving had passed, but the ache stayed.
The decision to return to the crick wasn't
grand.
It didn't feel brave or cinematic.

It felt quiet. Heavy. A thread I was afraid to pull.

But I needed to know if the song still lived in me.

If *I* still lived in me.

The cup warmed my hands, but nothing inside me softened.

Not yet.

Downstairs creaked with the sound of morning.

A kettle hissed. A bird called once, then stopped.

And somewhere in that stillness, I felt the edge of something old and sacred turning back toward me.

I didn't know if I'd sing tonight.

But I'd listen.

That much, I could promise.

The morning light painted the garden gold, mist still clinging to the lavender like memory. But inside, I was steel.

Dorian found me like that.

Barefoot. Hoodie-wrapped. Eyes half-lidded but mind wide awake.

He didn't speak at first.

Just filled his own mug, moved to the opposite counter.

Watched me the way he always had, like he was checking for tremors only he could see.

"I wasn't trying to control you," he said softly.

I didn't answer. Not yet.

"I know it felt like that yesterday," he added. "But I need you to hear this, Liv. Keeping you safe... that hasn't been strategy. That's been survival. For me."

That pulled my eyes to his.

"I built a whole empire," he said, voice catching just slightly. "But none of it mattered when I thought I might lose you. Not the records. Not the Grammys. Not Jag."

He paused. His eyes didn't waver.

"You're not just my artist," he said. "You're my oldest friend. My home. The first person who ever made me feel like I could be exactly who I am, without apology."

A memory flared.

High school hallways. Lockers slamming. Laughter too sharp.

Dorian, sixteen, shoulders hunched from carrying silence.

Me and Tucker flanking him, walking him to class like bodyguards who couldn't punch but could stare someone into dust.

"You were the first person I ever came out to," he said, quiet. "And I'll never forget that day. You didn't flinch. You just said, 'Cool. Let's go write a song about it.' And then Tucker threatened to rearrange someone's jaw for looking at me sideways."

That made me smile.

Ache, too.

Those years, so much was uncertain.

Except us.

"You remember New Orleans?" I asked suddenly.

His smile curved, but didn't quite reach his eyes. "Café Beignet. Bourbon Street. You crying over beignets."

"I was crying because you looked at me that night like I was a stranger," I said. "Like Libby had swallowed me whole and you didn't know how to pull me out."

He nodded, quiet. "I was scared I lost you." His voice dropped lower. "I never want to feel that again."

"I know," I said. "I know you love me. And I love you right back. But I need space to figure out

137

what I look like now... without someone building walls around me. Even with the best intentions."

He nodded again, eyes damp but unashamed.

"You've always been the storm," he said. "Even when you didn't know it."

I took a sip of coffee. Let the bitterness anchor me.

"I heard Sadie's on the list tonight," I said.

He lifted a brow. "You want to go?"

"Not as me. Not yet. Just to listen."

"You wearing the trucker hat again?"

I smirked. "Worse. I found a paisley scarf in Mom's attic."

He groaned. "Now that's a disguise. Please tell me it's orange."

"Burnt sienna. With fringe."

"Oh God, Libby Morgan in fringe, now there's a headline."

I moved past him, tapped my mug gently against his.

"Thanks," I said.

"For what?"

"For still being the safest place I know, even when I don't want to be protected."

His voice dropped, barely a breath.

"Always, Liv. That's never changed."

Back upstairs, I took my time.

Not because I was unsure.

Because I wasn't.

The mirror didn't scare me today.

No wig. No heavy lashes. No glittered mask..

Just Liv.

The long bob brushed my collarbone now, no longer weighted by tape-ins or stress.

My real hair. Soft. Light.

The kind of hair you could tuck behind your ear without a stage manager screaming continuity.

I curled it slightly at the ends. Just a bend. Just enough.

The old me—the curated me—would've layered it with texturizing spray, worked the angles, chased perfection.

Now, I just let it fall.

My skin had changed, too. All that water. The clean food. The sleep.

It showed. In ways the camera would never quite capture, but I could feel it.

The puffiness was gone.

The sheen of exhaustion, replaced by something quieter.

Something earned.

I dotted a hint of tinted moisturizer on my cheeks.

Mascara, one coat.

A little glow on the bridge of my nose. Lip balm with a rose tint.

No contour. No highlighter. No illusion.

Just glow.

Just enough to feel like me, not hiding, not performing.

Choosing.

I opened the closet doors slowly, like I was expecting ghosts to waft out.

And maybe they did.

The gowns were gone.

The stage heels. The sparkle. The armor.

In their place: cotton dresses in soft florals and linen solids.

Flirty. Comfortable. Serene.

The racks held jeans and tanks, oversized knits, faded button-downs I forgot I owned.

Clothes that breathed. Clothes that forgave you for having a body.

And the shoes—God, the shoes.

Sandals, both casual and strappy. Soft leather boots.

Slouchy ones. Sleek ones.

Heels in neutral tones with just a whisper of glam.

Worn-in sneakers. Ballet flats.

Slippers that looked too pretty to walk on carpet.

I mostly preferred bare feet.

But I still loved my collection.

Each pair like a little memory, a whisper of who I'd been when I bought them.

Not Libby.

Not always.

Just a woman who loved beautiful things and needed something solid underfoot.

One pair of boots caught my eye—low-heeled, oxblood leather, scuffed just enough.

I wore them to my last real rehearsal before the tour.

Before everything fractured.

I let my fingers linger there, then pulled away.

The scarf was too much.

So was the hat.

I grabbed the hoodie instead.

Black. Clean lines. Stupidly expensive.

I remembered the stylist saying it was made from bamboo and seaweed.

I'd bought it without even looking at the price tag.

Now, I pulled it on like armor.

Underneath, a white tank. Crisp. Soft.

Jeans, dark denim, high-waisted, broken in like good memories.

Also designer. Also mine.

When I looked in the mirror again, I didn't look like a star.

I didn't look like a ghost, either.

I looked like someone coming home to herself.

The blue in my eyes was coming back.

The freckles across my nose hadn't been visible in years.

The fillers had faded, leaving something gentler in their place.

I looked thirty.

Maybe a hard thirty-five.

But not forty-one.

Not tonight.

I zipped the hoodie halfway and pulled the hood up, just enough to shadow the top of my face.

Still hidden.

But not erased.

"Ready?" Dorian called from downstairs.

I didn't move at first.

Not because I was frozen, but because I knew once I crossed the threshold, something would shift. Some spell would break. Some truth would rise. And I wasn't sure yet if I was ready to face the weight of it.

I sat at the edge of the bed, hoodie sleeves pulled over my hands, fingers tugging absentmindedly at the hem.

The mirror caught me again.

Just the edge of my reflection.

Soft jaw. Bare lashes. The ghost of glitter washed clean.

For so long, I'd been performing recovery as much as I'd performed fame. Smile at the right moments. Drink the right tea. Say no to the wrong things. Let people believe I was getting better simply because I wasn't falling apart in public.

But healing wasn't linear. It wasn't graceful. It didn't arrive in golden light and grateful tears.

Sometimes, it came like this.

Quiet. Uneven. Raw.

With the faint taste of yesterday still in your throat and the echo of an old name clinging to your skin.

Libby would've looked at this outfit—this whole morning—and laughed. She'd call it earnest. Underproduced. Forgettable.

But Liv?

Liv was learning that forgettable might mean free.

Downstairs, I could hear Dorian rinsing his mug. The clink of ceramic. The soft drag of his shoes on the tile.

He didn't rush me.

He never did.

I stood slowly, palms brushing the worn quilt on the bed. I didn't take anything with me. No purse. No lipstick. No phone.

Just me.

I passed the mirror without looking again.

Halfway down the stairs, I paused.

The light in the hallway was different now. Warmer. Stretching longer across the floor like it, too, had been waiting.

I remembered something Eli once said: *"The point of coming back isn't to pretend nothing happened. It's to decide what comes next, knowing exactly what did."*

At the bottom of the stairs, Dorian waited.

Not impatient. Not eager.

Just present.

He looked up when he saw me. Not down, not over. Not through.

His eyes held the kind of silence that said: I see you. As you are. And I'm still here.

I nodded once, small but steady.

Then we stepped out the door.

And the air met me like a song I hadn't sung in years.

Outside, the day had begun its slow exhale into evening.

The sky was bruised lavender and peach, colors bleeding into each other like old watercolors. Crickets had started their chorus early, and somewhere in the fields, a cicada hummed its solitary song.

Dorian opened the passenger door without comment.

We didn't speak for the first few miles.

The road curved like memory—familiar, worn in. Potholes patched with stories. Fences repaired with wire and hope. Fields that had seen too many seasons but still bloomed when it mattered.

I pressed my palm to the window. Let it cool my skin.

"You okay?" Dorian asked softly.

I nodded. "I think so. I just... it's like I've been underwater for years. And now I can finally hear my own breath again."

He didn't answer right away. Just let the hum of the engine fill the space.

"You always had that," he said eventually. "That kind of gravity. Even when you were unraveling. You made people believe in something. Even when you couldn't believe in yourself."

"That's a dangerous kind of magic," I murmured.

"Maybe," he said. "But maybe it's also the kind that saves people."

We turned off the main road, gravel crunching beneath the tires. Trees pressed closer, and the air thickened with green.

The Crick wasn't far now.

I could feel it in my ribs.

The tug of place. Of memory. Of the boy who taught me how to wade through water and silence and fear.

I adjusted the hood slightly.

Not to hide.

To soften.

To meet what was coming on my own terms.

Dorian slowed the car as we reached the familiar bend. The same turn where, once upon a summer, Tucker carved our initials into the back

of a willow tree and told me the stars were brighter
here.

He hadn't been wrong.

They always were.

And maybe tonight, if I sang again, I'd
remember why I ever started.

Chapter 24: The Crick, Again

We parked two blocks away again.

Some rituals you don't break.

The silence in the car wasn't tense. It was something softer. A breath held. A tide waiting. I watched the town roll past through the window. Same cracked sidewalks. Same corner deli with its sun-faded sandwich board. Same antique store that had somehow survived a recession, a pandemic, and three owners.

None of it had changed.

Except me.

My hands were tucked into my sleeves, but they still trembled.

I told myself it was the caffeine.

I told myself a lot of things.

Dorian didn't say much. Just adjusted the radio until it landed on something instrumental. Strings, slow and cinematic. It felt like the kind of music that plays when a character returns home after the third act has already broken them.

He glanced at me once, brow raised like a question.

I nodded.

The hoodie stayed up.

It wasn't shame. Not exactly. More like armor. A soft shell against a place that remembered everything.

As we turned onto Riverstone, my chest tightened.

This was the road.

The one Tucker and I used to fly down after shows. Windows open. Music too loud. My feet on the dash, his hand on the wheel and the world ours for a heartbeat.

This was the road where he once pulled over just to kiss me under the stars.

This was the road where I first told him I loved him.

And tonight, I wasn't Liv from back then.

I wasn't sure who I was.

Just someone trying not to unravel.

I pressed my forehead against the cool glass.

Watched the lights smear into gold and blur.

I told myself it didn't matter what I saw inside.

Didn't matter if she was touching him.

Didn't matter if he laughed.

But something in me knew.

If I saw it—if I really saw it—I wouldn't be able to pretend anymore.

Not about what I still felt.

Not about what I'd lost.

Not about who had stepped in while I'd been gone.

Inside, The Crick hadn't changed.

The golden dim still glowed from worn sconces.

Beer-stained stories clung to the walls.

Someone half-tuned a guitar too close to the mic.

A trivia board curled in the corner like it hadn't been updated since spring.

And the air—God, the air—was thick with hops, bleach, and old secrets.

It was familiar. Not safe. But known.

The bar reminded me of the ones we used to sneak into at seventeen. The kind that didn't care if your ID was fake, as long as you kept quiet and paid in cash.

Where I learned how to read a room. How to cover Janis and Jewel in the same set.

Where the stage was a palette and the applause was a shot of something warmer than whiskey.

I slipped onto a high-back stool near the back of the bar, shadowed by the angle of a crooked old mirror and a potted fern that had clearly survived more than one ownership change.

It was perfect.

From here, I could see the stage.

Could see Sadie.

And I could see him.

Tucker.

Behind the bar.

Wearing that soft navy tee like the one I used to sleep in.

Hair a little longer. Eyes still impossible to ignore.

He moved like the space was his. Like it bent to him.

And she was there.

Lacey Brenner.

Leaning over the bar like it was choreographed.

Laughing too loud.

Fingertips brushing his forearm when she handed him her card.

He didn't flinch.

Didn't pull away.

Didn't lean in, either.

He just smiled. Nodded. Moved on.

Same as he did for the guy next to her.

The older woman three stools down.

The two teens sharing a cider and a plate of fries.

But I couldn't see it clearly. Not through the fog.

All I saw was her hand on him. Her laugh. Her proximity.

And it cracked something in me.

I almost missed Sadie's name being called. She walked up to the mic with her usual bounce. Long brown hair in a loose braid, combat boots under a sundress, denim jacket tied around her waist like armor.

Eighteen.

Newly legal.

A senior next month.

Still light.

Still unburdened by the weight of stages and contracts and rooms that took more than they gave.

She strummed a soft chord. Adjusted the mic. Smiled nervously.

And began.

The song wasn't about heartbreak.

It wasn't about fame.

It was about summer.

Hope.

Crushed ice in plastic cups.

The boy who walked her home with his headphones split between them.

It was about *before*.

And she sang it with her whole heart.

A hush settled. You could hear the air move. Even the regulars at the bar turned to look.

There was something about Sadie when she sang—like she didn't know you were watching, but she hoped you were listening.

I tried to stay in it.

Tried to hold on to the pride rising in my chest, the quiet thrill of seeing someone I loved do it right.

Sadie had been slipping by the house for weeks.

Late afternoons on the porch, working through lyrics and chords and stories.

She texted me through Dorian at midnight with ideas.

Sent voice memos.

Left flowers once when I'd had a hard day.

She'd become essential.

The first person I'd let matter in over ten years.

But I couldn't stay in the joy.

Because Tucker laughed at something.

And Lacey touched his wrist again.

And suddenly the sound of Sadie's voice blurred behind the thud of my own heartbeat.

I hated myself for it.

For losing focus.

For letting jealousy drown out the one thing that should've mattered most.

Sadie was shining.

And I was hiding.

And it wouldn't be long before the two collided.

I wanted to be proud. Wanted to rise to meet her light with my own. But all I could feel was the slow unraveling of something I hadn't even realized was still knotted inside me.

This used to be my world.

The open mics. The nerves. The hush right before the first note. I used to fill these rooms without needing the glitter. Just a girl with a guitar and something to say.

Now, I was a ghost in a hoodie, watching the future unfold with someone else's voice.

And it terrified me.

Not because Sadie was better. She wasn't. She was beautiful in a way that didn't compare. She wasn't chasing fame. She didn't need validation. She just wanted to *sing*.

But maybe that's what cut deepest.

Because I didn't know how to do that anymore. Not without the lights. The labels. The armor of Libby Morgan.

And watching Sadie, whole and bright on that stage, I realized how long it had been since I felt honest.

I used to think I was irreplaceable.

I used to think the world would wait.

But it didn't.

It filled the silence I left with new names. New sounds. New stories.

And maybe that's how it's supposed to be. Maybe that's how the river keeps flowing. But it doesn't mean it doesn't ache—to see the water rise without you.

Sadie had a song. She had the crowd. She had *Tucker's attention,* even if just for a minute.

And what did I have?

An old name no one could quite say without a question mark at the end.

A legacy soaked in glitter and rumors.

A past tense.

I wrapped my arms tighter around myself. Tried to shake it. But the jealousy was venomous. Shame layered over it like gauze, but it didn't stop the sting.

She deserves this, I told myself.

You're not in competition, I told myself.

This is what healing looks like, I told myself.

But still, something dark curled at the base of my spine, whispering, *You're not the voice anymore.*

You're just the memory.

The almost.

The used to be.

And God, I hated that part of me. The one that couldn't just let the next generation shine without measuring the wattage.

But I also knew—I couldn't silence it by force.

Not yet.

I had to name it first.

I had to admit the fear:

That maybe there was no stage left that wanted me.

That maybe I'd trained so hard to survive, I'd forgotten how to sing.

The thought stirred another one. A memory. Older than Libby. Softer than shame.

It was a dive bar just off 113, the kind that didn't check IDs as long as you looked like you belonged.

Tucker always did. Even back then.

He had that easy confidence, like he'd been carved out of the wood-paneled walls. Knew exactly how to lean just enough on the jukebox, how to toss a wink at the bartender without it becoming a thing.

We were seventeen. Maybe eighteen.

I was nervous. Sweaty-palmed and shaking.

I had a guitar, a borrowed one, and a song I'd written about a boy who'd never know he made me cry. The bar was half-full. Pool tables clacked behind me. No one cared if I played.

But Tucker did.

He sat front row—if you could call a barstool and a sticky table that—and he watched me like I was already someone. Like he didn't hear the notes I missed, only the ones I meant.

And when I finished, he clapped like I'd filled Carnegie Hall.

Later that night, as we walked out into the cool dark, he took my hand and said, "You don't have to be perfect. You just have to be real."

I didn't know it then, but that was the first time anyone saw me without the shimmer.

That was before the wigs. Before the stylists. Before Sterling took my voice and turned it into something polished and hollow.

That night, it was just me.

And him.

And a song that cracked something open instead of sealing it shut.

I remembered the way his thumb brushed mine. The way his hoodie smelled like sawdust and cinnamon gum. The way he kissed my temple instead of my mouth, like he didn't want to steal the moment, only hold it.

And now, across the bar, he was smiling at someone else.

Lacey wasn't me. She wasn't Libby.

But she was *here.*

And I wasn't sure if that made her more dangerous or less.

My pulse thudded harder.

Because if I was honest, I didn't just want the stage back.

I wanted *him* to see me on it again.

Sadie's voice landed like a kiss on still water.

Soft applause followed.

Some claps louder than others.

A cheer from the corner where a cluster of high schoolers sat, probably friends.

She bowed a little. Grinned.

Tucked her braid behind her ear and walked off stage with that loose, bright bounce I knew by heart.

I stayed still.

Too still.

Another young guy got called up—blonde, college age, acoustic guitar with a looping pedal.

He was good. Nervous. Earnest.

I heard none of it.

My eyes were fixed on the bar.

Lacey was leaning in again.

And Tucker,

God.

He smiled.

Dorian leaned close.

"She's amazing," he said.

I didn't respond. Couldn't.

I just whispered, "Text her. Tell her she was wonderful."

He nodded, already reaching for his phone.

But my stomach churned.

My skin felt too tight.

My pulse was thudding in my throat.

The next act faded into the background, a blur of chords and well-meaning nerves.

But I wasn't watching the stage anymore.

I was watching the corner by the back hallway, where Sadie had just reappeared, clutching a glass of water and smiling so wide it almost broke me.

She walked toward the bar.

Toward *him*.

Tucker leaned over, said something I couldn't hear.

Sadie laughed. Tucked her braid behind her ear. Nodded like she was trying to be cool but couldn't quite hide the blush.

He grinned back. That crooked half-smile that used to make me drop things.

Then—God—he reached across the bar and squeezed her shoulder.

Just once.

A blink of a touch.

Friendly. Encouraging. Proud.

But it knocked the air out of me.

Sadie said something. He replied. She smiled again. Then turned and headed toward the hallway, back toward the greenroom space they used for performers.

And for a moment, just a moment, Tucker watched her go.

Not long.

Not hungrily.

But with something softer than I'd seen in a long time.

Something like admiration.

Or memory.

Or maybe I was just projecting everything I didn't want to feel onto a man who'd never promised me anything but truth.

Still, I couldn't stop the thought from forming.

That Sadie was light.

And I was shadow.

That maybe, when I was gone, she filled the space I used to occupy.

That maybe she didn't mean to.

But that didn't stop the ache from blooming.

Because she deserved his kindness.

She deserved every bit of praise he gave her.

But I wasn't sure I could survive watching him give it.

Especially when I wasn't the girl with songs still untouched by grief.

I gripped the edge of the bar. Tried to breathe through it.

But the thudding in my chest didn't slow.

Because this wasn't just about Tucker.

Or Sadie.

It was about the space between who I used to be and who I was trying to become.

And how terrifying it was to watch someone else step into the light you once called home.

Something was breaking.

Not all at once.

But like ice underfoot—hairline fractures no one sees until it's too late.

And I was slipping.

Dorian noticed.

Of course he did.

He always had a radar for my unraveling.

He leaned close, the press of his shoulder grounding me for a second longer than I expected.

"You okay?" he asked, voice low, like he didn't want the question to ripple too far.

I nodded, but it was a lie. A small, instinctive one.

He didn't push.

Just slid his drink a little closer to me, the condensation leaving a ring on the table, something real to focus on.

"Want me to say something outrageous to distract you?" he asked gently, a hint of a smile ghosting his lips.

I managed a breath that might've passed for a laugh. "Like what?"

He scanned the room, eyes landing on a man with a handlebar mustache and a trucker hat that said "Jesus Saves—But I Spend."

"That man over there?" Dorian said, deadpan. "He's my style icon."

I smiled. Really smiled this time.

And then I almost cried.

Because I knew what he was doing.

Holding space.

Letting the storm pass without trying to fix the weather.

I gripped the edge of the stool tighter, grounding myself.

Sadie had been brilliant.

And I had almost missed it.

Because jealousy—no, grief—had wormed its way into my chest and made itself at home.

It wasn't even about Lacey.

Not really.

It was about the ache of not knowing where I fit anymore. Of seeing Tucker look relaxed in a world I used to occupy. Of wondering if I'd ever be able to sit in a bar like this and just feel joy without it getting tangled in memory.

Dorian's hand brushed mine under the table.

Not a grip. Not a plea.

Just a tether.

"Do you want to go up?" he asked.

That stopped my breath.

He wasn't talking about leaving.

He meant the stage.

The mic.

The part of me I'd buried so deep it pulsed under my skin like a second heartbeat.

"I don't know," I whispered.

"That's okay," he said. "But if you do... I'll be right here."

Chapter 25: Every Version of Goodbye

I don't know when or how it happened.

One moment I was frozen, paralyzed by the dizzying pull of fight or flight.

The threat of the press finding me.

Of Sterling finding me.

Of Libby clawing her way back to save us the only way she knew how—by becoming someone we were not.

I didn't even realize I'd stopped referring to her as someone else.

Libby. Me. Not me.

Both.

None.

But I was beginning to feel like Liv again.

Not just the wreckage.

Not just the girl who burned her life down.

But the woman who once curated a whole world and called it art.

Still, none of that mattered.

Because I saw red.

A flare of heat behind my eyes.

A noise behind my ribs.

Pain so old it had calluses.

And when I looked at Tucker—smiling, nodding, as if nothing had ever broken—something snapped.

He had to know.

Had to feel what I'd carried.

What I still carried.

How damaged I became.

How deep the wound ran.

How much I'd lost because he had to "work on himself."

I didn't know when I stood.

I didn't want to move.

Not because I couldn't.

Because if I did, I might never come back.

The glass in my hand was warm now, water long since gone.

Dorian's fingers brushed mine under the table again.

Not pressing. Just anchoring.

But it wasn't enough to stop the slide.

My pulse thundered in my ears.

My skin felt like it belonged to someone else.

The sounds around me warped—Sadie's laughter from the hallway, the reverb of a mic check, the mutter of the next performer tuning—none of it quite real.

I could still taste the jealousy.

Sharp. Metallic. Shameful.

I knew I had no right to feel it.

Not toward Sadie. Not even toward Lacey.

But it sat in me like sediment.

And I hated it.

Because this wasn't who I wanted to be.

Not anymore.

Not the ghost. Not the girl chasing old applause.

Not the woman drowning in a love she never learned to let go of.

My eyes locked on Tucker again.

And that was it.

That was the match.

He looked happy.

Maybe not blissfully so—but content. Present. Like he belonged here in a way I never had.

And it broke me open.

All the therapy. All the clean days.

All the journals and breathwork and boundaries.

None of it protected me from this:

The reminder that sometimes healing isn't enough to win someone back.

It just makes losing them clearer.

I didn't feel the hoodie fall from my shoulders. Didn't hear Dorian whisper my name or see his hand reaching for my wrist.

I just moved.

The climb to the stage was short. Unnoticed, at first.

The kid who'd played before me was unplugging cables.

A tech adjusted a mic stand.

The piano sat center stage.

Like it had been waiting for me.

No band.

No DJ.

No track.

Just a girl.

Just a piano.

Just a past too heavy to hold quiet anymore.

The bar had already begun to buzz.

Whispers.

Flashes of phones.

People nudging each other, blinking at me like ghosts don't bleed.

Dorian stood rooted in the corner.

Shock on his face.

Horror in his eyes.

But I wasn't looking at him.

I was looking at Tucker.

I sat down.

Played a single note.

And the room—every voice, every breath, every heartbeat—went still.

I looked up. Not at the crowd.

At him.

Tucker.

Then I leaned into the mic.

My voice low. Even. Unshaking.

"My name is Liv."

A pause. A breath that held its own gravity.
"This one's for the boy who said he was letting me go—for my sake."

She looks out at the silent room, voice flat. "But what he really did was disappear before I could choose him back."

A beat. Then softer—

"He didn't just leave. He broke the part of me that believed I was lovable *without* the spotlight."

Gasps.

Chairs shifted.

Glasses stilled.

And every eye turned to him.

Tucker

He didn't notice the stage at first.

He noticed the hoodie.

Black. Familiar. Folded and left at the corner high-top where someone had been sitting.

Where she had been sitting.

And then he looked up—and there she was.

On stage.

No armor. No mask.

Her hair catching the light. Her face bare except for truth.

Liv.

Not the Libby from posters. Not the voice from records.

Her.

His stomach dropped.

Then she touched the piano.

Soft. Certain. Like it remembered her. Like it was part of her still.

She leaned into the mic.

Voice low, cut from glass.

"My name is Liv," she said.

A pause. The kind that held its own gravity.

"This one's for the boy who said he was letting me go—for my sake."

Another beat. Measured. Lethal.

"But what he really did was disappear before I could choose him back."

Her voice softened—just barely.

"He didn't just leave. He broke the part of me that believed I was lovable *without* the spotlight."

The room collapsed into silence.

Then every head turned.

To him.

Tucker didn't move. Didn't flinch.
Just stood there, heart tight in his chest like a fist that wouldn't unclench.

She'd said it like a prayer. Or a wound. Or maybe both.

And every word had landed exactly where she'd aimed.

It was like someone had reached into his chest and gripped his ribs from the inside.

She didn't even look at him.

Just placed her fingers on the keys.

Breathed.

And sang.

"You said forever with your hands,
Pressed flat against my back like prayer."

Tucker's breath caught. That summer night by the crick. Her skin sun-warm. His hands shaking. He'd meant it. God, he meant it.

"Told me soulmates weren't a myth,
Just two kids dumb enough to think they'd be spared."

His jaw clenched.

They had been dumb. But not wrong. Not completely.

"You promised me a landing spot,
But I never saw the fall."

He blinked hard.

Because he could still see her in the passenger seat of his truck, not understanding why he was ending it.

"'Til you said you needed fixing,
And left me shattered through it all."

His stomach turned.

He thought he'd been protecting her.

He hadn't even realized he'd broken her open.

"You weren't ready,
You were scared.
You said love like mine deserved more than Delaware air."

His throat burned.

He remembered the exact words. He'd practiced them. Believed them. They sounded so noble back then.

"But I would've lived on scraped knees and second shifts.
If it meant your arms were still where I existed."

That line.

That one knocked the breath from his lungs. Because she would have. He knew that now. Too late.

"You turned my soul dark,
Lit matches in my chest."

She was crying now. Not with tears, but with voice. With rage woven in melody.

"I chased chaos, swallowed silence,
Built a shrine from my regrets."

And he was in every line. Every damn lyric.

"They all called it fame,
I called it hiding.
And every man I met since you,
Was just a softer kind of lying."

Tucker's hands twitched at his sides.

He wanted to stop the song, pull her away from the edge—but he was the edge.

"You broke my heart,

Then my body,
Then the part of me that sang,
And I held the blame like melody.
A chord I couldn't change..."

By the time the final note faded, Tucker could hear his own heartbeat in his ears.

The silence wasn't quiet. It was thunder.

He didn't know whether to run to her or run from himself.

She stood from the piano slowly.

Shoulders squared. Chin high.

But he saw it— the way her jaw trembled. The glass behind her eyes.

She was holding herself together by muscle memory alone.

Then:

"Seriously?"

Lacey's voice.

Sharp. Stupid. Cruel.

Tucker's head whipped toward her, eyes blazing.

"Real classy. Trashy, actually. But hey, if the crown fits..."

He was on his feet before she finished.

But Dorian got to Liv first.

Wrapped her in an arm.

Whispered something that made her finally let go, just enough to lean into him.

They slipped out the side door.

Tucker didn't move.

Not right away.

His heart was a bomb he hadn't heard ticking until it went off.

Because this—this wasn't just about a song.

It was about the damage he'd left behind, convinced it was mercy.

And now he was the ghost in her lyrics.

The man she survived.

And still, even now, he loved her so much it hurt to breathe.

So, he left the bar.

Didn't look at Lacey.

Didn't speak to anyone.

Just walked out into the night.
Into the ache.

Because if she was going to bleed like that, he had to face it.

He had to face her.

Liv

The moment the final note faded, I froze.

My hands hovered above the keys, but they didn't feel like mine. Nothing did. Not the piano beneath my fingers, not the weight of my bones, not the silence folding over the room like a second skin.

I heard a glass clink. A whisper. The buzz of a phone too loud in the stillness. Somewhere, someone was recording. I could feel it. That strange electricity of being watched—admired or dissected, I couldn't tell. Maybe both.

My breath came sharp, shallow.

Not stage fright.

Exposure.

I had cracked open in front of them, not with glamour, but with truth—and truth didn't glitter. It bled. It left stains. And I was standing in them now, barefoot and blinking under lights that suddenly felt too white.

I pushed back from the bench. Stumbled once—just a half step—but enough to notice the tremor in my knees. Someone gasped. Not loud. Just close. Maybe a girl near the front. Maybe Sadie.

I didn't look at her. Couldn't. If I saw her eyes—soft, proud, unbruised—it might undo me.

164

The exit pulsed like a heartbeat at the edge of my vision. I could vanish. Slip out into the night and let this moment become myth. Let them argue about whether it was real. Whether I meant it.

But then—

"Liv."

My name. Small. Steady. From somewhere behind the speakers.

Dorian.

Just that one word. Not a command. Not even a plea.

A tether.

And I stayed.

Not for the audience. Not for the aftermath.

But for the part of me that had finally remembered how to feel without flinching.

Chapter 26: What We Never Said

I didn't remember the ride home.

Not the back door slamming behind us.

Not Dorian's voice, low and steady, guiding me down the alley like he had so many times before.

Not the car.

Not the turns.

Not the porch light flicking on like an accusation as we pulled up.

Only the silence.

And the weight of it now.

I stood in the kitchen, hoodie back on, hair damp from the light rain that had started. I hadn't dried it. Hadn't even realized I was wet until Dorian pressed a towel into my hands and murmured, "You're freezing."

The tea in my hands, untouched. The steam long gone. My fingers trembled against the ceramic like the cup might shatter from memory alone.

"I did it," I whispered. Mostly to myself.

Dorian leaned against the counter, arms crossed, expression softened. He looked like he wanted to hold the pieces of me together—but knew better than to try. Knew what it meant to witness a collapse without interrupting it.

"I outed myself," I said louder. "To everyone. Just, like that."

"You told the truth, "He said gently.

"Yeah? At what cost?"

I laughed, but it fractured halfway up my throat. Sharp. Unstable.

"Sadie's night is gone. That place will be flooded by morning. Press. Fans. Sterling."

"Liv—"

"I felt it coming," I cut him off. "I knew I was spiraling, and I still did it. I stood up and I let her out. I let Libby out."

"No." He stepped closer. "You let Liv speak."

I blinked.

"She's... you've never spoken like that before," he said, voice low and sure. "Not once. Not even in the songs. Tonight wasn't Libby. It was you."

The tears hit before I could brace.

Hot, unstoppable waves.

"I didn't want everyone to hear me," I whispered. "Not yet. Not like that."

I set the mug down. My hands were shaking too hard to hold it steady. Something about the clink of ceramic on tile made my stomach turn. Everything felt fragile now. Breakable. And I was tired of breaking.

"I should've left. I should've waited. What if that song gets out?"

"It will," he said calmly. "That's not the question."

"Then what is?"

He moved closer. Not to comfort—just to be close enough to catch me if I fell.

"The question is—do you regret it?"

I didn't answer right away.

Because I didn't know.

Not really.

I felt cracked open. Exposed. Like every scar I'd hidden behind sequins and stage lights had just been laid bare. But there was something else, too.

Something I couldn't quite name.

I shook my head. "I don't know. I think I might be proud of her."

His brow lifted gently. "Again, it was not Libby. You should be proud of yourself, Liv. That was you."

The kitchen felt impossibly still.

A beat.

Then another.
And then—
A knock.
Hard.
Three quick pounds.
Then silence.
We froze.
I didn't need to ask.
I already knew.
The knock came again.
And I opened the door.

Tucker stood there, shoulders squared, jaw tight.

That same storm in his eyes from when we were kids and he couldn't protect Dorian fast enough.

But now it was aimed at me.
And maybe at himself.
I didn't say a word.
Didn't invite him in.
I walked past him.
Down the porch steps.
Gravel biting beneath my soles.
Past the tomato vines curling in on themselves.

Past the garage where Big Al's wrench hung like a rusted memory.

Past the shed where I used to hide from the noise and write lyrics no one would ever hear.

The Crick came into view.
A shimmer of memory and consequence.
Behind me, his boots crunching leaves.
"Tucker," I said, lifting a finger, voice shaking.
"Not yet."

He stopped. Breath caught like a song stuck in his throat.

I turned toward the water.

"I need to say something," I said. "And you need to let me say it before you try to fix it. Or spin it. Or make it yours."

The quiet behind me was a scream. The wind skimmed the creek in slow spirals, like it was listening too. My pulse thudded in my ears, like an old metronome I couldn't turn off.

"I'm barely holding it together," I continued. "Like, barely. My whole body is screaming for something to shut it all down. Pills. A bottle. A goddamn freight train. I'd drink every drop of alcohol in this county if it meant I didn't have to feel this."

A sob crept up. I strangled it. My throat burned. I was trying to stay whole, but I felt the seams fray with every word.

My voice hardened.

"So, if you came here to make me feel worse? Don't. You can't. I promise you, no one could possibly feel worse than I do right now."

He moved. Just one step.

It shattered something in me.

"Don't you dare," I turned, voice rising. "Don't you fucking dare look at me like I'm the one who broke us."

His face twisted—grief, guilt, fury all rising like floodwater. His hands opened and closed like they didn't know where to go. I could see it on him— every unspoken apology, every silent night he let me fall alone.

"You left," I said, hands shaking now. "You said I deserved more. But what I needed was you. To believe in me when I couldn't."

Tears slid freely. I didn't wipe them away. Let them paint me. Maybe they'd finally say what I couldn't.

"You left when it started, when Sterling was circling, when I didn't know what was safe or real. And you just... vanished."

He tried. "Liv, I—"

"No."

I cut him off.

"You don't get to comfort me out of this. This is yours too."

He flinched at that. And I saw it. That unspoken hurt—the way good men still cause damage when they walk away. That truth sank between us like stone.

"You said love like mine was too much. But I would've lived off diner coffee and broken strings if it meant waking up next to you."

He winced. Real. Full-body. Like the truth hit bone.

"I chased all of it because you weren't there to hold me still. When the lights got too bright. When the pills came. When I disappeared into her."

My voice cracked. The wind stopped. Even the trees seemed to still.

"You weren't there, Tucker. And maybe I would've broken anyway. But you were the beginning of it."

I crumbled to the ground. Knees in the dirt. Hands buried like I was trying to dig my way back to something pure. Something before.

"And I'm so fucking tired of carrying it alone."

He didn't speak. Just stood there, hands balled, breath ragged.

Then, slowly, he sat. Not beside me. Near. Like he knew touching me might break the last thread holding me up.

"I didn't leave because I stopped loving you," he said finally. "I left because I loved you more than anything in this entire fucking universe."

I turned slightly. Needing air more than answers.

"I got hurt. I couldn't play. I had no purpose. And you, Liv, you were becoming more. You were about to be more than both of us ever dreamed.

And I didn't want to be the reason you ever looked back in regret."

He paused. Voice tightening.

"I built the bar. Learned business. Worked with Big Al. Because I needed something real. Something rooted. So that if you came back, you would have a place that felt like home."

He looked at me, bare. Wrecked.

"I did it all for the version of us I thought would survive."

I stood. Breathing hard. Fists tight. A storm trembled beneath my skin.

"But I never came back."

"No," he said, voice breaking. "You didn't. And I watched you disappear into men who didn't deserve you. Watched you smile through headlines that felt like grief."

He stepped closer.

"You moved on like I was just a memory."

My body tensed.

"You think I wanted that?" I snapped. "You think I chose men who broke me? Who branded me? Who silenced everything I used to love?"

He opened his mouth—then closed it. Like the truth in my voice burned hotter than any answer.

There was a beat. The kind that changes everything.

And then I moved. Without thinking. Toward the garage. Toward the bottle I knew was there. Toward the ache I understood better than I understood love.

Each step was a fight against gravity. Against memory.

The smell of cut grass. The way his hands felt on my back that night we parked by the quarry. My mouth on his collarbone. The way he held my face like it was breakable.

I was unraveling and knew it. But I didn't stop. I couldn't. Not when the ache felt honest. Not when silence felt safer than his sorry.

He didn't call after me. Not yet.

But I felt him behind me. Still.

Maybe ready. Maybe not.

I reached the door to the garage. My hand hovered near the knob. There was a bottle in there.

And if I turned it just right, the cap would sigh open like an old friend.

I wanted it more than I wanted air.

Behind me, the floor creaked.

And Tucker's voice, low and rough, broke the silence.

"I still keep your guitar pick in my glove box."

I froze.

"The one you dropped after your first show at that dive in Harrisburg. It's cracked down the middle now. But I still look at it sometimes when the bar's too quiet. My soul still feeling tethered to you with that piece of plastic."

Tears prickled at my eyes.

I didn't turn.

Didn't speak.

But the match in my hand trembled.

He didn't say another word.

And I didn't open the door.

Yet.

But something shifted. Not a full step. Not forgiveness.

Just enough to make staying present a choice instead of a punishment.

Shaking. Fractured.

And a match in my hand.

I walked through the door.

Chapter 27: Where the Fire Starts

Tucker

He followed her in silence.

Didn't dare say her name again.

Didn't dare reach for her.

Liv stormed into the garage like she could outrun the ache in her bones. Like the flood inside her needed somewhere physical to land.

She wasn't crying. She wasn't screaming. But she was coming undone.

He stood at the threshold, heart pounding, hands trembling—not with fear of her, but for her.

The air hit him like a memory: turpentine, paint, dust, old gas. The scent of Big Al's projects. The past preserved in chemical sharpness.

Liv moved like she didn't even feel her body. Like she was made of wires shorting out.

She yanked open drawers. Slammed cabinet doors. Knocked over a box of spark plugs without noticing.

There were no words. No rhythm. Just chaos.

Her hands were shaking, too fast, too erratic to be anything but desperation.

Tucker took a step in. The floor creaked.

She didn't turn around. Didn't speak. Just kept digging.

And then—

She found it.

Back corner. Hidden behind an old can of primer and a cracked plastic funnel.

The bottle.

A thick, dust-covered fifth of whiskey. Still sealed.

Her fingers gripped the neck. Tight.

He saw the breath leave her body, like something sacred had returned.

And he couldn't move. Couldn't blink. Couldn't breathe.

She was seconds away from ending it all.

Not her life, maybe. But her recovery. Her clarity. Her progress.

And he didn't know if anything he said would matter anymore.

He wanted to run to her. To snatch the bottle. To shake her until she screamed and remembered and shattered into pieces he could finally gather.

But he stayed. Still. Breathing shallow. Watching her choose.

He wanted to believe love could fix it. Wanted to believe his being there could be enough. That showing up could rewrite the years of absence.

But he knew better.

He remembered the sound of her laugh when they were seventeen. The way she fell asleep on his shoulder in his dad's truck. The poems she wrote in margins. The way she sang when no one was listening.

He remembered the last look she gave him the day he left—full of betrayal and belief.

Like he was her compass.

And he'd pointed her off a cliff.

Tucker swallowed hard. His voice lodged behind too many years of silence.

He looked at her—the girl he loved, the woman she became, the ruins she was trying to climb out of.

And all he could think was: *Don't let me be another weight she has to carry.*

He stepped forward. One slow step. And waited for her to break.

Liv

The cap hit the floor with a soft, traitorous clink.

My hands were shaking so hard I had to steady the bottle against my chest.

The glass was cold.

But the scent was warmth. Spice. Earth and fire and forgetting.

God, it was beautiful. Delightful sweetness. Caramel and oak. A whisper of smoke.

I could taste the numb just by breathing it in.

One sip. That's all it would take.

Just one. And everything would hush.

The grief. The rage. The ache of Tucker's voice saying he built it all for me. That he waited.

But also, Sadie's eyes when I sang. The way the crowd watched her. And me, stealing it back.

The shame. The weight. The unbearable heat of feeling again.

I didn't want to be Liv anymore.

Liv felt too much.

Liv cracked open at the worst times.

Liv believed in forever and look where that got her.

But Libby?

Libby could handle it.

Libby smiled when her body was breaking.

Libby danced on glass in stilettos and made it look like a runway.

Libby pulled the wool over the world's eyes and wrapped it like velvet around her lies.

I'd been too hard on her.

Libby was the strong one.

The smart one.

The one who showed up when Liv disappeared.

Libby finished what Liv couldn't.

And maybe, just maybe, if there was no more Liv... Libby could finally be free.

I raised the bottle to my lips.

And then, it was gone.

Tucker's hand shot out, slapped it from my grip.

It shattered.

Whiskey bled across the concrete like a funeral.

The scent surged, a final cruel exhale.

My legs gave out. I dropped to the floor, crumpled in the ruins of what could've been escape.

The glass shards glittered like stars beneath me, but none of them burned bright enough to pull me back.

I was lost in the storm. Drenched. Hollowed. Bare.

"No," he said, grabbing me by the shoulders.

His voice didn't shout. It quaked.

"Look at me."

I couldn't.

"Liv. Look. At. Me."

He held my face in his hands, rough and firm and real.

I blinked through tears.

"I'm here," he said. "I've always been here. Even when you shut every door. Even when you pushed Dorian away. Even when you tried to convince yourself that nobody loved you enough to stay."

I tried to turn away.

He wouldn't let me.

"Think about who's carried you," he said. "Dorian, canceling shows, working from the goddamn kitchen table to protect you. Your parents, finally getting to be the ones to take care of you again."

His eyes burned.

"Ari. Pax. Eli. The family you found even when you were too lost to know it."

I sobbed, full-body, gasping.

"And me," he said. "Don't you dare forget me. I never moved on. I never loved anyone the way I love you."

His voice cracked.

"You're wrapped around my soul, Liv. Stitched into it. I breathe with it. And if you go down, if you let this thing take you, I swear to God we'll both drown."

He held me so tightly I could feel the quake in his chest.

"No one is letting you disappear again. Not ever."

And that's when I broke.

Not in rage. Not in defiance. But in surrender.

I didn't speak. Didn't scream. Didn't sob.

Just let the numb settle. Heavy and slow.

But deeper now, like maybe it wasn't numbness, but softness.

Flickers of something else stirring beneath it, something like surrender. Something like change. Something like a flickering pilot light under all the ash.

Tucker

Her body folded into mine like it remembered the shape of us.

Like every fight, every silence, every year apart hadn't broken the blueprint.

She didn't fight it. Didn't resist.

Still, I carried her like she might fall apart with any jolt.

Every stair creaked like a warning. My boots felt too loud. The air too thick.

She was weightless and heavy all at once.

She buried her face in my shirt. I felt the wetness of her tears, the soft puff of her breath.

I didn't breathe right until we cleared the hallway.

Dorian stood like a statue, eyes rimmed with grief, love, fear. I nodded. He didn't speak. Just stepped back, giving us the world.

As I passed him, he reached out—just one hand, ghosting over Liv's back like a prayer. Then let it fall.

Big Al met me on the landing. Marianne at his side. His arms around her. Her face pale. His nod a kind of blessing.

She whispered, "Thank you."

I opened her door like it was sacred. Because it was.

Liv

He placed me in my bed like I was made of glass.

The sheets were soft. Familiar. But the room wasn't. Not anymore.

It held ghosts. Teenage Liv. Hopeful Liv. The Liv who wrote lyrics in spiral notebooks and fell asleep dreaming of stages.

I stared at the ceiling, and it stared back. Like it knew all the versions of me that had passed through. The ones I'd buried. The ones I missed.

The pillow held my scent. Not Libby's perfume or makeup residue or hairspray. Just me. Lavender shampoo. Salt from old tears. Skin.

Tucker climbed in behind me. Wrapped his arms around my shaking body. Not possessively. But protectively. Like a shelter. A vow. A whisper that I was not alone.

His breath matched mine until mine steadied. His heartbeat thudded against my back, a metronome for a life I wasn't sure I still had.

He didn't speak. Didn't offer anything but presence.

And for the first time in what felt like years, I let it in. All of it. The fear. The exhaustion. The wreckage. The miracle of still breathing.

In the darkness, I let my fingers curl into the blanket. Just enough to feel something solid.

And in that moment, with Tucker's breath on my neck, I felt it:

Not peace. Not yet. But possibility.

The tiniest flicker of something resembling hope.

And maybe, just maybe, that was enough.

Tucker

I waited until I felt her settle. Not sleep, not yet. But something like it.

Her breath slowed, her hands relaxed.

And gently, I slipped out from behind her.

Every movement was careful, like I was disarming a bomb.

I padded down the hall, socks soft against the hardwood, and knocked once on the guest room door where Dorian had set up camp.

He called out, "Yeah?"

I cracked the door. He was lit by the glow of his laptop, headphones in, editing something, maybe audio from a concert. His brow was furrowed, fingers flying over the keys.

"Hey," I whispered.

He looked up, saw me, blinked. "She okay?"

I nodded. "Sleeping. I just... don't want to get into bed next to her smelling like bourbon and fear. Can I borrow... clothes?"

He gestured to the corner without pausing. "Drawer. Left side. There's new packs in there. Take what you want."

I opened the drawer, careful not to disturb anything. A few neat piles, and one unopened pack of what looked like designer underwear. I didn't check the label. Just grabbed a pair and a t-shirt and slipped into the hall.

Ten minutes later I stood in the bathroom, steam fogging the mirror, hot water rushing over my back.

I scrubbed the scent of the garage, of whiskey, of ghosts, from my skin.

I looked at myself in the mirror. Older. Worn. But still here.

Still fighting.

I thought of her. In bed. Alive.

And I made myself a promise.

No more distance. No more silence. No more letting her drown alone.

Whatever it took—whoever I had to become— I'd carry her out of this.

And I wouldn't let go again.

Not ever.

Chapter 28: The Morning After the Fire

Liv

I woke to heat.

Not sunlight, body heat.

A warm wall pressed against my back, the rise and fall of steady breath ghosting the nape of my neck.

I didn't move at first. Just breathed. Let my body remember what safety felt like. Let my eyes memorize the way his chest rose and fell behind me—slow, steady, like the tide.

He was still asleep.

I tilted my head, just enough to glimpse his face. The soft slack of his mouth. The faint crease between his brows, even in sleep. His hair had flattened on one side, tufted at the crown. One hand lay open on the pillow beside me, calloused and quiet. The same hand that had caught mine a hundred times. The same hand that caught the bottle before I could destroy myself.

I let my gaze trace him.

He was older now. Worn in places. But stronger, too. More rooted. Less boy, more anchor.

And still, the way he curled around me, unconsciously, like some primal instinct told his body I needed protection—it undid me.

He used to hold me like this in the back of his dad's truck, windows fogged, limbs tangled. I'd fall asleep to the hum of cicadas and his heartbeat in my ear.

Now we were here. On the other side of everything.

And somehow, he was still the only place I ever felt completely known.

My tank top clung to my skin. I was in my underwear. Which we will come back to later. My throat was dry, and my body felt hollowed out, like someone had scooped me out with a silver spoon and left the shell behind.

I blinked into the soft gray morning.

He was still here.

Tucker.

Still in my bed.

Still wrapped around me like he was anchoring me to this world.

I shifted, just enough to glance back.

He was shirtless.

And wearing boxers that sparkled faintly in the morning light.

I blinked again.

"Are those... Dorian's?" I croaked.

His voice, low and sheepish, rumbled behind me. "Apparently, he only wears a new pair every day. Fancy-ass perk of being rich."

I stared at the shimmer. "Why are they shiny?"

He sighed. "Don't know. Some designer thing. I smelled like beer and chicken wings. Figured you didn't want to wake up and immediately crave buffalo sauce."

I snorted.

He grinned, then quickly sobered. "I didn't look," he added gently. "I promise. You passed out and I just... I stayed."

I looked down at the stretch of him in my bed.

Massive. Solid. Grown in every way. His legs hung over the edge. His shoulders too broad for the pillow. His presence somehow filling the entire room and yet not crowding me at all.

"Jesus," I muttered. "You're like a human barn door."

"Is that a compliment?"

I shrugged. "Depends on if you take it shirtless or not."

We both laughed, quiet, cautious.

Because something had shifted.

I wasn't shattered anymore.

But I wasn't whole.

I felt broken in places I didn't know could break.

And I could feel it in him, too.

He held me like I was made of fire and glass.

Like one wrong move could set everything ablaze again.

But he stayed.

That was the point.

He stayed.

And we slept. Again.

I didn't move for a while.

Just lay there.

Staring at the way the morning light turned his skin golden.

His lashes were long. Dark.

There were faint lines near his eyes now.

He breathed deeply, arm slung over the edge of the bed like a man who had nothing left to fight for except the woman next to him.

I memorized him.

The curve of his shoulder. The quiet hum of his breath.

I tucked a strand of hair behind my ear and let my fingers brush his.

Soft.

Safe.

Mine, even if just for this morning.

Eventually, I slid out of bed as gently as I could.

Tucker murmured something incoherent, one arm flopping across the mattress like he was still holding onto me in his sleep.

I padded down the hallway, each step echoing like I was moving through someone else's house.

The cold tile bit at the soles of my feet, a sharp little reminder I was still here. Still breathing. Still breakable.

The light in the bathroom was too honest.

I flicked it on and froze.

The woman in the mirror stared back at me— eyes swollen, lashes stuck together, hair twisted in wild, saltwater knots. My tank top had twisted sideways. My collarbone jutted like punctuation under skin that looked too pale, too thin, too unfinished.

I barely recognized myself.

But not because of the damage.

Because I wasn't hiding from it.

Something burned quietly behind my ribs. Not rage. Not grief. Something else. Something almost holy. Like I had walked through fire and found the tiniest ember still glowing.

I reached for my toothbrush with fingers steadier than they should've been. Squeezed on the mint paste. Brushed like it was a ritual. Like reclaiming my mouth meant reclaiming my voice. My power. The part of me that still knew how to sing.

Because no matter how broken I felt, I was still a woman.

Still breathing.

Still capable of curling my lashes, brushing my hair, and choosing to walk back into that room with my chin held high.

I reached for the linen cabinet like I'd done a thousand times before, but everything felt new. The soft shorts I grabbed were worn and cottony, a faint lavender scent still clinging to the fabric. I stepped into them like armor, tugging them up over hips that once starved under stage lights.

Swiped on deodorant with a calm that felt earned.

Then reached for my perfume—an old favorite with notes of amber and fig, something Marianne once called "dangerously feminine." I sprayed just beneath my collarbone, then again at the pulse point on my neck.

Not for him.

For me.

Because I needed to remember what it felt like to tend to myself. To scent the air with something that wasn't survival. To mark my skin with something intentional instead of damage.

I brushed my hair back with my fingers, glanced once more at the mirror. I wasn't flawless. I wasn't fixed. But I was choosing to re-enter the day with softness.

With strength.

And maybe that was enough.

And yes, I was now sharing a bed with a man who once wrecked me and was somehow the only person I could unravel in front of.

But I was also Liv.

And Liv didn't vanish after the spiral.

She came back.

I slid into bed, legs brushing his.

He shifted, awake now, blinking at me. "You smell... expensive."

I smirked. "You smell like a man who borrowed designer underwear."

He chuckled. "You want me to put on pants?"

"No," I said too quickly. Then added, "Just, don't stand up too fast. Those boxers reflect light like a disco ball."

He laughed again, and something in me warmed.

His fingers brushed mine. Lazy. Familiar.

His eyes dropped to my hip. "That scar's new."

I followed his gaze.

Small, pale, just above the curve of my waistband. "Hospital. Two years ago. Ulcer from stress and diet pills."

His fingers lingered near it, gentle. "Still beautiful, and tragic."

I rolled my eyes, but my cheeks flushed.

He turned onto his side. "Remember when we used to make out in the back of your dad's truck, parked at the drive-in, thinking we were being so subtle?"

I snorted. "We steamed up the windows so bad Big Al thought someone had broken in and hot-boxed it."

We both laughed.

He reached for my arm first, fingers feathering over the small burn just above my elbow.

"Still got this," he said softly. "From lighting your scarf on fire in the chem lab."

"That scarf was ugly."

"You wore it every day."

I smirked. "So? Still ugly."

He turned my wrist, brushing the scar there. Thin. Faint. "What's this?"

"Sterling's apartment. Glass frame. I was trying to leave. He wasn't ready for me to go."

His jaw tensed, but he didn't speak.

Then I lifted his arm, tracing the long line of pink across his bicep.

"Motorcycle?"

"Bar fight."

I raised an eyebrow.

"With a door. I was drunk and mad and took it personally."

I laughed softly. "Still a bad boy, huh?"

His smile faltered when I shifted closer, lifting the hem of my tank slightly to show the jagged scar on my ribs.

"This one..." I hesitated. "This one's from Jax."

His body stiffened beneath me.

His hands gripped my waist, firm, possessive.

And when he looked up, his eyes weren't soft anymore.

They were dangerous. Brown, but burning, amber threaded with gold and hints of red. Like fire behind glass. Like he could set the world ablaze for me if I asked.

His fingers slid across the mark like he could erase it.

"I should've been there," he whispered.

"You weren't."

"But I would've been. If you'd told me. "

"I didn't want you to see me like that."

"You think there's any version of you I wouldn't fight for?"

I couldn't answer.

I couldn't breathe.

And then,

Knock. Knock. Knock.

Dorian's voice filtered through the door as he entered my room.

"Twelve hours. You broke the internet."

Tucker didn't move.

Neither did I.

But the air between us was charged, like static waiting to snap.

Dorian cleared his throat dramatically.

"Also, Tucker, I swear if those are my Versace boxers you're defiling, we are having words."

He walked back out.

But I didn't laugh.

Not right away.

I turned back to Tucker.

His thumb brushed my knuckles.

And in that stillness, I realized:

There was no going back.

Not to the girl I was.

Not to the pain I lived in.

Not even to the version of us that once was.

187

Whatever came next—
It would be new.
Real.
Ours.

I rested my head against his chest, felt the steady beat of a heart that had always known mine. For once, there was no fear. No pretending. Just the hush of a morning that didn't ask for anything but truth. My fingers curled into his. Our breath found the same rhythm.

And I was ready.

Chapter 29: Reckonings in Real Time

Liv

The war room was the kitchen table.
Coffee cups. Crumbs. iPads. Phones buzzing.
Dorian's MacBook open like a presidential
command center.

Tucker sat beside me like it was the most
natural thing in the world. Same jeans from the
night before, hair damp from a lightning-fast
shower, and Dorian's Versace tee clinging to his
chest like it had never met that much muscle. The
neckline sagged a little, revealing the hollow of his
collarbone and a smudge of aftershave that
smelled like cedar and resolve.

I was trying to focus.

I really was.

But my hormones—quiet for the last three
years—had staged a full symphonic return.
Pirouettes, percussion, and a trumpet solo, all
aimed at the man seated precisely one inch too
close.

He reached for his coffee, and the hem of his
sleeve tugged back just enough to show the curve
of the tattoo on his bicep. The one I traced once,
back when we were seventeen, lying under stars
and talking about forever like it was something
you could catch.

I looked away fast.

Focus, Liv.

No time for lust.

But his knee bumped mine.

And suddenly, I was aware of everything.
The warmth of his skin. The sound of his breath.
The way he smelled nothing like whiskey anymore.

The world might be collapsing, but my body hadn't gotten the memo.

Dorian sat at the head of the table like he was hosting a crisis response briefing at the Pentagon. Black hoodie zipped up to his chin, face carved into focus. His laptop glowed like a runway light in the pre-dawn haze. In his hand?

My phone.

He hadn't turned it on since I collapsed. It had been sitting in a drawer, dead to the world, like I had been.

Now it pulsed like a live wire, a hive of chaos vibrating in his palm.

"Thousands of unread texts from June through August," he said, flicking his thumb so fast it blurred. "Group chats, label execs, press agents, Sadie's mother. One message just says *'You bitch'* in all caps, no context."

He paused. "And as of this morning, over eight million notifications. Trending across multiple platforms. Fan art. Fan edits. Breakdowns of your lyrics with color-coded emotional arcs. And at least four slow-mo 'Liv crying' GIFs with cinematic filters and Billie Eilish overlays."

My stomach dropped.

"Conspiracy theories?" I asked weakly.

"Buckle up," Rey muttered.

Dorian didn't blink. "One thread has 40k upvotes claiming you died in 2019 and were replaced with a lookalike. Another insists you're hiding in a cult in Vermont. A third thinks Sterling Vale brainwashed you and planted false memories."

Marianne gasped softly behind me. She hadn't even sat down. Just kept pacing the tile like she was walking off a panic attack.

"And Sadie?" I whispered.

Dorian held up the phone again. "Split right down the middle. Half of her fans are furious on

190

her behalf. The other half think you're her misunderstood mentor and are already shipping your dynamic as #Ladie."

Rey's mouth twitched.

I couldn't breathe.

"And the media?" I croaked.

He turned the iPad toward me. Headlines scrolled like ticker tape.

LIBBY'S BREAKDOWN: ICON OR LIABILITY?

TOO RAW, TOO SOON: WHAT LIV'S COMEBACK SAYS ABOUT ART & TRAUMA

VALE MANAGEMENT RESPONDS TO CRISIS—BUT IS IT ENOUGH?

I pressed my fingers to my temples. My pulse was sprinting.

"It's not all bad," Dorian said gently. "Some people saw you. The real you. And they didn't look away."

"So... they found her," Marianne said, voice quiet but trembling with everything unspoken. She was still standing, still in her robe, still gripping her mug like it was the only thing holding her together.

"No," Dorian corrected gently. "She revealed herself."

He didn't mean it as praise.

He meant it like a storm.

"Now it's a full-blown media landslide," he continued. "The coverage is coming in from every direction—TMZ, NPR, Vogue, even *Billboard*. All at once: adoration, speculation, concern, and a few strategically placed hit pieces meant to shake the narrative before it can settle."

He turned the iPad toward me, scrolling with two fingers.

A flood of posts flickered by:

@music4liv: "Liv Morgan Reed just sang her whole life on stage. Could this BE more real? 💧 #LivReborn"

@libbyfandom: "If Libby's in PA, who's paying the rent in the chateau in Switzerland? #PRFail"

@gossipdrip: "Somebody check on T. Hayes, he just watched her tear herself apart in real time."

@valeofficial: "Libby Morgan is currently dedicating time to wellness and recovery with family. Vale Management fully supports her creative journey and mental health. We stand by her always."

@realari: "Reminder: recovery is not linear. Fame doesn't equal immunity. Nobody owns her story."

Dorian paused to tap on a headline, then read aloud:

"'LIBBY'S NEW SOUND TOO EDGY? INSIDERS SAY RISKY FOR MILLIONS.'"

My stomach turned.

"Because God forbid a woman goes off-script," I muttered.

Big Al grunted his agreement.

Dorian set the iPad down and looked directly at me.

"They're primed to spin the narrative," he said, calm and razor-sharp. "But this time, they're not the authors."

He reached into the folder next to his laptop and slid a thick document across the table.

"Every original track recorded under Liv Morgan Reed—especially those released under Jag—belongs to you."

My breath caught.

I stared at the folder like it might vanish if I blinked. My name. My songs. My story. Not leased. Not borrowed. Not stolen. For the first time in years, I wasn't a product. I was a person. And maybe that meant I could finally create something that belonged to me.

Rey leaned in. "So if you want to record again, you can. Without Vale. Without permission."

"I don't know if I want to," I said honestly.

Dorian nodded. "That's okay. You don't have to decide that right now."

Then he leaned closer, voice gentle but firm.

"But maybe, Liv... maybe you should decide who you want to be tomorrow."

The table went quiet.

No one reached for their mugs. No one moved. The weight of that sentence settled over us like fog—thick, dense, full of everything we hadn't said.

I looked at my hands.

They weren't shaking.

They had, for so long. On stage, backstage, in planes, in rooms I couldn't name. My fingers had trembled through interviews, through signings, through nights I couldn't sleep and mornings I couldn't wake. But right now?

Still.

I touched the document in front of me. Ran my fingertip over the edge like it might slice me open.

It didn't.

It grounded me.

"Do I have to be anything?" I asked. "Tomorrow?"

"No," Dorian said. "You just can't pretend anymore."

I glanced at Tucker. He was quiet, gaze steady, like he was holding vigil beside me. Not pushing. Not pulling. Just there. Present.

His hand rested near mine on the table, not touching, just close enough to remind me I wasn't alone. He didn't speak, but his silence was a vow. No more leaving. No more running. Just here.

Marianne finally sat down. She didn't say anything, just slid her hand across the table until it rested atop mine. Her skin was warm. Familiar. Unbreakable in that mom way that somehow made me feel twelve and invincible all at once.

Big Al cleared his throat, rough as gravel. "Whatever you choose, kid, we got you."

Rey nodded, chin lifted like they were daring anyone to say otherwise.

I closed my eyes for one breath.

Just one.

Then opened them to the mess of cables and coffee rings and crumbs—proof that this wasn't a press room. This was home. This was life.

And maybe it didn't have to be war.

Maybe it could be a beginning.

The kitchen eventually emptied—Rey to their studio, Big Al to his truck, Marianne to her garden. Tucker lingered long enough to refill my coffee, then slipped outside, giving me space.

I found Dorian on the porch swing, legs crossed, hoodie pulled low over his eyes like armor against the world.

I sat beside him.

He didn't look at me right away. Just passed me one of the donuts Big Al had left behind and said, "I always pictured us ending up in a recording studio, not a farmhouse kitchen war room."

I took a bite. Powdered sugar clouded my breath.

"Me too," I said. "Though this place has better snacks."

We rocked in silence, the swing creaking with its usual stubborn rhythm. Beyond the porch, the yard was alive with cicadas and the shimmer of heat off the grass.

"I don't know how to do this," I whispered.

Dorian finally turned to me. "Do what?"

"Be her. Or not be her. Figure out where Liv ends and Libby starts. Or if they've always been the same person, just shaped by different hands."

He reached for my hand, threading our fingers loosely. "Maybe you don't figure it out all at once. Maybe you just live. One choice at a time."

I looked down at our joined hands.

Then up at him.

"You brought me back from the dead," I said, voice quieter than I meant. "And I didn't even see it at first. I thought you were just saving my life. But... you weren't just pulling me out of the dark. You were pointing me toward something. This. All of this."

His throat bobbed, but he didn't speak.

"I'm not sure I ever thanked you," I went on. "Not really. Not for staying. Not for dragging me out of that penthouse. Not for holding the pieces when I didn't know what shape I even used to be."

He blinked, and for a second, his eyes shined too bright.

"I'd do it all again," he said. "Even if you never came back. Even if you hated me for it."

"I did," I whispered.

"I know."

We rocked a little longer, letting the truth settle.

"You were the first person who saw I was drowning," I said. "And instead of just throwing a rope... you dove in."

He squeezed my hand, then let go.

"Go," he said, nodding toward the yard. "Before Tucker combusts from trying not to ask you to."

Chapter 30: The Bubble

Liv

We slipped out the back. No announcement. No shoes. Just bare feet on dew-slick grass, the hush of morning wrapping around us like a secret.

Down the hill. Past the garden where the tomatoes had gone wild. Through the stretch of trees that once felt like the edge of the world. The old path was still there, soft and worn and dappled with sunlight, the dirt giving just slightly beneath our steps like it remembered us.

Tucker carried the blanket. I carried his hand. And for a while, we let the silence speak.

A squirrel darted up a tree trunk. A butterfly spiraled low, brushing my knee before lifting away. The sun blinked through branches like it couldn't decide if it wanted to commit to the day.

Everything felt quieter. Sharper. Like my senses had been turned all the way up—sight, sound, scent, skin. I was present in a way I hadn't been in years.

I glanced at Tucker—his jaw shadowed with stubble, his profile etched in gold.

And I thought, *If the world spins out after today, at least I had this.*

This moment. This man. This feeling that maybe, just maybe, I was allowed to want something soft again.

When we reached the bend where the trees opened and the water sang, we stopped.

The creek still moved with its own rhythm. Not fast. Not loud. Just constant.

We stood there for a breath too long, just listening. The air smelled like wet moss and morning. A bird called somewhere nearby, sharp and insistent, like it had something urgent to say.

I let go of his hand and stepped forward, toes sinking into the cool earth at the edge of the bank.

There used to be a rope swing here. It was long gone now, the tree limb still bowed from where it had hung.

"I used to come here when I needed to think," I murmured, barely above a whisper. "Sometimes I didn't even know what I was thinking about. I just... needed to feel the world still turning."

Tucker didn't respond right away. He moved beside me, laid the blanket down with quiet hands, like the ground deserved gentleness.

Then he held his arm out, an unspoken invitation.

And I went.

Sat between his legs, back to his chest, his arms wrapping around me like they'd always known the shape of my body. Like they'd missed it.

And for a while, we just listened.

To birdsong.

To wind through leaves.

To water over stone.

No phones. No pings. No headlines.

Just this.

A piece of peace we didn't have to earn.

The sun felt different today.

Warmer, maybe. Or maybe I was different.

Maybe surviving meant learning to feel the heat on your skin again without thinking about burning.

I leaned back against him, head on his shoulder, and closed my eyes.

"I used to come here when I needed to think," I murmured.

"I know," he said, voice low against my neck.

"You followed me once."

"I followed you a lot," he admitted. "You just didn't always notice."

I smiled, but it didn't reach all the way. Because the real world still existed.

Still waited.

And it was loud.

He leaned forward slightly, chin on my shoulder.

"We have to talk about it," he said gently.

I didn't move.

"The media thing," he continued. "The coverage, the attention, the... everything."

"I don't want to."

"I know. But Liv, this is tri-state level now. Philly's already buzzing. DC and New York are watching. Paparazzi are posted at the road. Dorian said someone from TMZ offered a bribe to a pizza delivery guy just to confirm the address."

I exhaled sharply.

"I hate this," I said.

"I know."

"I didn't mean to come back like this."

"But you did."

"And I don't regret singing. I don't regret feeling. I just... I didn't want to do this again."

"You didn't come back to do Libby," he said. "But Liv, the one who tells the truth with her voice? She's still allowed to make choices."

I let my head fall back against his chest.

He was warm. Strong. Steady.

"Choices come with consequences," I whispered.

"They always did."

A hawk cried high overhead.

I closed my eyes.

"What do I do?"

"You let us help," he said. "You trust Dorian. Rey. Your parents. Me."

He paused.

"And then... we come up with a plan."

I turned, twisting in the hollow of his body until I was facing him.

His arms shifted to cradle my hips.

And for a second, I couldn't speak.

Because those amber eyes, flecked with fire and something ancient, were looking at me like I was the first thing he'd ever seen.

"I'm sorry," I said, quiet but clear.

"For what?"

"For the circus. For Libby. For dragging you into all of this."

"You didn't drag me anywhere."

"But it's chaos. I'm chaos. And you... you had a life. A quiet one. A good one. I would understand if you wanted to walk away. From all of this. From me."

He didn't answer right away.

He just looked at me.

Really looked.

And then he spoke, voice low and steady like the earth itself:

"There's no version of this life I want to live that doesn't include you."

He gripped my waist like he was anchoring me.

"I don't care if you're Liv or Libby or something in between. I know you've tried to split them into two, but there's going to come a day where you see what I see, that it's all you. The art. The rage. The joy. The fear. The ache."

His voice cracked.

"I'm not nineteen anymore, running scared from the size of your light. I'm a grown-ass man. I've built a life I'm proud of. And yeah, it's quiet. But it was built with you in mind."

I swallowed.

He wasn't finished.

"I let you go once. I own that. I helped break you. But I'm not letting go of the person you're becoming. I'll stand next to you, behind you, in front of you, whatever you need. Because I believe in you, Liv. In us. Whether that means we're together or just two people healing side by side."

My heart exploded inside my chest.

Something unshackled.

And before I could second-guess, I moved.

Straddled him.

Fingers in his hair.

And I kissed him.

Like the moon had tipped over and poured its glow into my mouth.

Like every star in the sky had been waiting for this breath.

Like I was finally allowed to exhale after a decade of drowning.

It wasn't perfect.

It wasn't clean.

It was real.

And in that kiss, I forgave him.

I forgave me.

And I was.

Just... was.

We didn't speak right away.

Didn't move.

The wind rustled through the leaves like applause from the earth itself, soft and reverent.

My forehead rested against his.

Our breaths mingled.

And for the first time in what felt like forever, I didn't feel like I was performing intimacy. I was living it. Letting it settle into my bones, my skin, my breath.

My fingertips still tingled from his hair.

My lips tasted like his name.

I wanted to remember this. Not in a dreamy, fragile way. But with clarity. I wanted to recall the warmth of his hands on my hips. The steady thrum of his heart under my palms. The way his mouth had mapped the shape of my grief and kissed it tender.

He didn't ask for more.

Didn't push.

Just let me hold him like he was the anchor and the sky all at once.

I knew it wouldn't always feel this easy. The world would come back. The noise. The past. The press.

But for now, I let the silence stretch.

And in that quiet, I started to believe we could build something new.

Not from scratch.

From truth.

Tucker

It felt like the Phillies, Eagles, Sixers, and Flyers all won the championship. On the same damn day.

And even that didn't come close.

Because Olivia Reed, my Liv, was in my arms, on top of me, kissing me like the universe had stopped spinning just for us.

Her fingers tangled in my hair.

My hands fisted in hers.

And every ounce of control I'd built over the past decade cracked like cheap glass.

She kissed like salvation.

Like surrender.

Like we had never been broken, just paused.

My body reacted before my brain could catch up. It wasn't just the rush of being wanted—it was the jolt of being seen. Fully. Stripped of the years. The grief. The guilt. All the quiet stories I'd told myself about how I didn't deserve her anymore.

I wanted her.

But not the way boys want trophies.

The way men want truth.

Hard. Rougher. Needy in a way that scared the hell out of me because this wasn't just lust.

This was remembering how to want without shame.

This was years of silence.

Of loving her from across time zones and Instagram filters and goddamn tabloids.

Of driving past her billboards with my jaw clenched and my heart cracked open like a goddamn peach.

Of seeing her light up rooms I wasn't in—and pretending that didn't burn.

Of swallowing the ache every time I saw her with someone who wasn't me and telling myself I was the one who let her go.

In my arms.

On top of me.

Like we had always been.

I pulled her tighter, groaning into her mouth as her hips shifted just enough to make me forget how to breathe.

She gasped.

I kissed her deeper, slower, like maybe if I did it right, I could rewrite everything we got wrong.

We tangled.

Limbs. Breath. Memories.

And for a second, I felt the volcano crack.

All of it, rage, grief, joy, want, it threatened to swallow us whole.

But she pulled back.

Just a little.

Enough to look at me.

And I saw it.

Not fear.

Not regret.

But choice.

She chose not to let it go further.

And I chose to respect it.

So I kissed her forehead.

Let her press her hand to my chest.
And together, we breathed.
This was something new.
Something bigger than us both.
Not a return.
A beginning.
We didn't say much as we stood.
Just lingered in the quiet.

Her hand brushed my jaw as she climbed off me, a soft, instinctive touch that felt like a benediction. My heart hadn't stopped pounding. Not just from the kiss—but from what it meant. The permission. The promise.

I shook out the blanket slowly, watching her shake the leaves from her hair. She looked lighter somehow. Not untouched—but unburdened.

The light filtered differently through the trees now. Warmer. Like the world was rooting for us.

She turned and offered her hand.
I didn't hesitate.
I held tight.
Like a promise.
Like I'd never let go again.
And we walked back up the hill.
To the house.
To the noise.

To the plans and press and pieces of our old lives waiting to be rebuilt.

But we walked back as something more than what we'd been.

We walked back as a team.
As a unit.
As a family.
And whatever came next?
We'd face it together.

Chapter 31: The Plan

Liv

They came back for me.

Not the press. Not the vultures with lenses longer than limbs.

My people.

Ari and Pax arrived first, suitcase in one hand, sourdough starter in the other, like they were just popping in for a week at the lake.

Eli flew in next. Quiet as always, wrapped in linen and peace. He hugged me with both arms and his whole spirit, and I nearly collapsed into him.

Dorian's team followed. A few trusted PR strategists. One manager who looked like he'd handled crises involving royalty and rogue billionaires.

Notably, no one from Libby's camp.

I corrected myself immediately.

Not Libby's.

Mine.

Because Tucker was right.

There was no Libby without Liv.

And there's no Liv without Libby.

I was the one who stood on stage in Berlin, belting out the anthem that became the soundtrack to a generation.

I was the one who poured whiskey tears into lyrics that went platinum four times over.

I wrote the music.

I bled the songs.

I signed the contracts.

I showed up.

Libby was never a separate entity.

Libby was my armor.

My costume.

My business card.

But *I* built the brand.

I owned the empire.

And for the first time in years, I saw it for what it was.

Not just headlines and heartbreak.

But twenty-two years of undeniable work.

Blockbusters.

Stadiums.

Broadway.

Global licensing.

Equity stakes.

Real estate portfolios.

Intellectual property.

Dorian passed me a folder later, when it was just the three of us. My best friends.

I flipped through.

And I froze.

Because in black and white, on legal letterhead and official filings, was a simple truth I had somehow forgotten:

Olivia Morgan Reed was a billionaire.

Not just famous.

Powerful.

But it wasn't the number that undid me.

It was the math behind it.

Every streaming royalty. Every sold-out tour. Every perfume ad, Broadway cameo, tech investment. Every negotiation I barely survived and every contract I walked into bleeding and came out with ink on my hands.

It was there.

All of it.

I saw the outlines of years I didn't remember living.

I saw the price tags on trauma I hadn't even named.

How many nights had I traded sleep for strategy? How many heartbreaks turned into headlining slots? How many times had I dressed up my own undoing, smiled for cameras, and told the world I was just *so grateful*?

I didn't just survive the machine.

I built it.

With trembling hands, mascara tears, and a voice hoarse from chasing perfection in a soundproof room.

I set the folder down.

Silence rippled through the room.

Dorian was the first to speak.
"Well, shit."

I laughed.

It broke something in the tension.

"I forgot," I said softly. "I really... forgot."

He looked at me with wide eyes, blinking slowly like his brain was rebooting. "You forgot that you're richer than Beyoncé?"

"I forgot *why*," I said.

Tucker stayed quiet.

He stood by the window, arms crossed, jaw working through something he hadn't found words for yet.

But I saw it.

The flicker of awe. The knot of doubt. The way his eyes didn't settle.

He was proud. But he was also recalibrating—measured, masculine, the kind of man who'd rather dig ditches than talk about money.

"Say it," I prompted.

He looked at me, then at Dorian, then back again.

"It's not the number," he said. "It's what it means. You did all of this. You made all of this. And I've been over here wondering if I could afford a second location for the bar."

He didn't say it with bitterness.

Just... honesty.

A quiet reckoning.

Like he was coming to terms with how wide the gap had grown—not between us, but between the lives we'd been living.

Dorian snorted. "I own a record label and still do my own taxes. Let's not make this weird."

Tucker gave a half-smile. But his eyes didn't move.

"I'm not intimidated," he said after a beat. "I'm not running. I'm just... trying to wrap my head around the scale."

Dorian clapped a hand on his shoulder. "Welcome to the penthouse, baby."

I smiled, but it didn't reach all the way. I walked to the table, palms flat against the folder.

"I was always scared of what it meant if I took credit," I said. "Like it made me responsible for the fallout too."

"You were always responsible," Dorian said gently. "But not for the abuse. Or the press. Or the pressure. Just the brilliance. The work. That's yours."

Tucker crossed the room.

He stood beside me, his presence warm and steady.

"You're not alone in it anymore," he said. "Not in the pain. Not in the glory. And not in what comes next."

I looked between the two of them, my twin flames in different colors.

This was my family.

This was the fire.

They gathered around the table like a war council, each of them an anchor from a different part of my life.

It hit me all at once—how rare this was.

To be seen.

Not just by fans or press, but by people who knew every version of me. Who had watched the rise, the spiral, the silence. Who stayed anyway.

Ari, leaning back with their signature black lipstick, legs crossed like royalty, a notebook full of impossible ideas and the confidence to make them real.

Pax, already color-coding timelines, murmuring about rollout phases, their focus razor-sharp beneath soft eyes.

Eli, hands folded in his lap, every breath a sermon, presence like a lighthouse—constant, unwavering.

My parents, weathered and wild in their own way. Big Al stood with arms crossed like a bouncer outside a club, while Marianne sat still and soft, her gaze threaded with quiet magic.

Tucker stayed close. One hand resting on the edge of the table, eyes scanning every face like he was memorizing the moment. Like he couldn't believe he was here but wasn't going to miss a single second of it.

And Dorian—my anchor, my mirror—sat beside me. Not speaking yet, but his energy alone kept me from floating away.

The PR manager, a clean-cut woman named Micah with smart glasses and a sharper tongue, clicked on a presentation slide from her tablet and started in.

"There are three approaches," she said. "Full retraction and rehab angle, which most expect. Media-friendly, low-impact. Libby disappears for a while; you resurface with a sanitized statement and new management."

I cringed.

Micah noticed.

"Option two," she continued, "is the 'reinvention' play, pivoting the narrative to focus on your healing, your truth, and your art. You play the comeback queen. Controlled press rollout. A few key interviews. Maybe Oprah."

Someone coughed. It might've been Tucker.

Micah's eyes scanned the room. "And option three?"

She tapped again.

"Burn it all down. A full reset. Liv Morgan, artist. New label. New voice. You write the story, drop the music, and own the chaos."

I didn't breathe.

"Option three is riskier," Pax noted. "But it's pure."

"It means lawsuits," added Rey, who had been quietly scrolling through projected buyout clauses. Yeah, they were more than a therapist. "And headlines. And backlash."

"It also means freedom," Dorian said quietly.

Everyone looked at him.

He slid his hand over mine, grounding me.

"This time, you get to choose," he said. "How to do it. What to say. Who to be."

I stared at our hands.

I'd spent so long being handled, steered, muted.

I closed my eyes.

Saw the stage.

Felt the piano beneath my fingers.

Remembered the silence that came after the last note, the kind that listened back.

"I want to record an album," I said. "No label interference. Just me. At Jag. Like we used to do it."

A beat.

Then Ari smirked.

"Girl, you're richer than dirt. Any fees you eat from brand pullouts, you'll make back in one day off interest. Let 'em come."

I laughed. A real one. From the gut.

"This started with a girl," I said. "A book of lyrics. Two best friends. A piano. A guitar. That's the music I want to make again. The kind that breaks something open."

Marianne touched her heart.

Big Al wiped something from his eye.

"We'll need to phase out Libby Morgan carefully," Micah said. "Control the death narrative. Let the world mourn her while you rise."

"Not just rise," Dorian said.

He looked at me, then around the room.

"She's going to burn the whole damn sky down."

Ari raised a brow. "Phoenix?"

Tucker added, "Phoenix. Has to be."

Everyone turned to me.

I stood.

Slowly. Deliberately.

Not for drama. For gravity.

Because this wasn't just a moment—it was the moment.

The hinge between the life I'd survived and the one I was choosing.

"Then let it be known," I said, voice low but unshakable, "Libby Morgan is dead."

No one moved.

No one breathed.

"I carried her," I continued. "Her heartbreak. Her ambition. Her armor. I loved her, and I also nearly died trying to be her. But it's over now."

I looked at each of them. My council. My circle.

"And Olivia. Morgan. Fucking. Reed..."

I paused. Let the weight of it land.

"...is reborn."

For a second, the world went still.

Then someone clapped.

Then everyone did.

And for the first time in my life, the sound didn't feel like pressure.
It felt like home.

Chapter 32: Blueprints and Burn Notices

It started with a burner phone.

Not sleek. Not flashy. Just matte black with a barely-there buzz and no history. A reset in plastic and pixels.

A new number. A new name in the system. A quiet rebellion against the empire I once ran.

Only nine people in the world had it.

My parents.

Tucker.

Ari.

Eli.

Pax.

Dorian.

Rey.

And Sadie—because I didn't want to miss a single lyric she texted at 3 a.m. that might crack my heart open.

That was it.

Everything else was noise. And I was done listening to noise.

The old number, tied to Libby's life like an umbilical cord of obligation, was handed off to Dorian's crisis manager. It still buzzed and blinked and begged for attention with a desperation I didn't have the bandwidth—or the interest—to acknowledge.

Emails. Voicemails. Press inquiries. Death threats. Marriage proposals. A fruit basket from Harry Styles.

And a handwritten letter from Sterling Vale, wrapped in thousand-dollar stationery, begging me to "return home and let us fix this."

He still didn't get it.

That was never his home to begin with.

"You're seriously doing this?" Dorian asked, staring at the blueprints on the foldout table like they were written in hieroglyphics. He tipped his head, squinting. "You're turning our vintage carpet warehouse into a Scandinavian fever dream."

Sadie twirled a paint swatch between her fingers like a baton. "I like it. The nooks? The blankets? It's giving ethereal insomnia."

"I'm going for soul sanctuary meets functional acoustics," I said, pointing to the mock-up of the studio floor. "Hardwood for warmth. Warm white walls for reflection. Skylights for actual sun. Draped corners for soundproofing. Writing nests with pillows and plug-ins for guitars and grief. It should feel like a song you want to crawl into and never leave."

"Don't forget the espresso machine," Pax added, flipping through the vendor list like a seasoned producer scanning a setlist.

"Top of the line," I promised. "Bean to cup. With single-origin roasts from Costa Rica, Ethiopia, and Sumatra. Hand-frothed oat milk for the divas."

Sadie practically bounced. "I could die in this building."

I handed her a reusable bottle from the hydration bar mock-up. "Stunts your growth."

She rolled her eyes. "No, it stunted your growth. I'm 5'10", built for the stage, and already getting offered campaigns I can't say yes to yet because I'm 'still in high school'."

Dorian groaned, dropping his forehead to the table. "You spoil her."

"I mentor her," I corrected. "With good coffee and better boundaries."

Through it all, Tucker floated around the space like a calm tide. He wasn't directing, just observing. Occasionally he'd brush against me—a hand on my back, a kiss to the top of my head, fingers finding mine in passing. Small reassurances that said: I'm here. I see you. We're okay.

We existed in the margins.

Together.

And in the middle of the blueprint chaos, espresso debates, and flooring samples, one truth rang louder than the rest:

We were dismantling Libby Morgan.

Her product lines.

Her perfume contracts.

Her photo licensing, streaming deals, and signature shades of lipstick.

Piece by piece, we were deconstructing a pop persona that had once eclipsed everything I was. They thought they owned her.

But they never owned me.

We were sitting around the back table at Jag.

The energy was strangely calm—too calm, maybe—like the moment before a thunderstorm when even the birds stop singing.

Dorian had his phone in hand, scrolling with practiced detachment. Sadie was half-curled in a giant reading chair, laptop open, hoodie pulled over her head like armor. Tucker was crouched near the espresso bar, fixing a squeaky stool with a screwdriver and a look that said this is chaos, but I'm letting you have it.

The social team's final text buzzed in:

"Ten minutes to blackout. Platforms syncing. Watch for lag."

This wasn't a tantrum.

This was tactical.

A year's worth of branding was about to vanish in under five minutes. Dorian's team had coordinated the full digital scrubbing—images, bios, auto-play loops, product placement—across every platform. Nothing left to interpret. Just silence and space.

I took a breath and sipped my lemon water, the kind of citrus-clear stillness that made you feel holy, and watched the monitor Dorian had installed above the couch.

A countdown began in the corner of the screen:

"Phase One: Scrub in Progress."

Spotify visuals blinked dark.

Instagram archived a decade in milliseconds.

TikTok pinned one last Libby Morgan clip—me at Berlin, then static.

Even the ancient Facebook page I hadn't touched since 2014 collapsed under the algorithm's eraser.

"God, it's like watching someone die in real time," Sadie muttered, not looking up.

"It's like watching a shell molt," Pax said from the floor, flipping through the backup analytics.

Dorian tapped the monitor to the next sequence:

"Phase Two: Identity Shift."

Every major handle transitioned in clean, quiet succession.

@LibbyMorgan → @LivMorganReed

@libbyworldtour → @livwritesmusic

@officiallibbybeauty → deactivated

The silence in the room was sacred.

Then the final countdown began in the top corner of the screen.

Ten seconds.

Nine.

"Bet you five bucks Twitter implodes," Sadie said.

"It's called X now," Dorian corrected.

She flipped him off without missing a beat.

Three.

Two.

One.
The screen blinked to black.
Every platform.
And then, almost like breath returning to a chest, they lit up again. But not with her. Not with Libby.
With me.
The new profile banners glowed in subtle gold and gray.
A single line pulsed across them all:
"The truth sounds different."
My new phone buzzed in Dorian's hand. He turned it toward me.
Notifications flooding in.
Comments multiplying by the second.
Trending hashtags firing like flares in the dark:
#WhoIsLiv
#LibbyMorganIsDead
#LivMorganReed
#PhoenixDrop
Rey looked up from their laptop. "Sterling's office just issued a statement. They're 'shocked and dismayed' by the branding changes. But our cease-and-desist holds up. Licensing clause from 2012. They didn't read the fine print."
"Of course they didn't," Dorian muttered. "They were too busy building a cage."
I exhaled.
Long. Deep. Like blowing out a decade of fog.
"They should be afraid."
Sadie spun her screen toward me. "Comments are bonkers. Some fans are mourning. Some are making memes. This one says, 'Libby wore masks. Liv lit them on fire.'"
I smiled. "I like that one."
"Same," Dorian said, sliding closer. His fingers found mine, anchoring me.

"This is your story now," he said. "You say when. You say how."

Across the room, Tucker looked up from the stool, wiping his hands on a towel.

"I'd say you just told them."

We all turned back to the screen.

One final update ticked across the top:

"Coming Soon: The Truth Sounds Different."

The silence that followed wasn't awkward.

It was reverent.

Then Sadie stood, stretching like a cat. "Okay," she said. "Now that you've burned the internet to the ground... can we please circle back to this bougie hydration station you promised?"

Later, after everyone had drifted to their corners—Sadie off to doodle lyrics in her room, Dorian buried in final press strategy, Pax and Rey debating fonts—I slipped outside.

The air was warm. Still. Like the world hadn't quite caught up to what just happened.

I sat on the back steps of Jag and closed my eyes.

Somewhere far away, the internet was losing its mind. Think pieces were being drafted. Group chats exploded. Sterling was probably already pacing like a general who realized his army had defected mid-battle.

But here?

It was quiet.

Birdsong. Wind. The soft hum of a life I was finally allowed to live.

I tilted my head back and let the sunlight kiss my face.

I didn't feel scared.

I didn't feel small.

For the first time in years, I felt like myself.

Whole.

Real.
Reclaimed.

Chapter 33: The Man Behind the Curtain

Sterling

The email came through at 6:14 a.m.

Cease and desist. Termination. Non-negotiable.

Final.

He read it three times.

Then, calmly, he closed the laptop.

His reflection stared back at him in the glass. Still sharp. Still immaculate. The razor part in his dark hair held steady. Button-down crisp. The silver Cartier cufflinks glinting like talismans against the rising L.A. sun.

To anyone else, he looked like a man in control.

To Sterling Vale, control was a mirror you only needed to glance at to restore.

He stood, stretched his back with the precision of someone who did Pilates three mornings a week, and reminded himself of a simple truth:

She would come back.

Libby always came back.

He didn't panic. That wasn't in his lexicon.

He adjusted.

He strategized.

He recalibrated.

Because that's what visionaries did.

And he was nothing if not visionary.

The entertainment world was made of glass and smoke, and Sterling Vale had mastered both. He'd watched titans crumble because they couldn't adapt—couldn't anticipate. He was already thinking five moves ahead.

If Libby wanted to play rebrand, fine. He could pivot too.

A "lost artist finds herself" arc always sold. Maybe a docuseries. Maybe a ghostwritten memoir with just enough scandal to trend. Maybe he'd even leak a few photos of their old sessions—the vulnerable ones. The ones where her eyes were glassy, but the angles were perfect.

Control wasn't about brute force.
It was about narrative.

The assistant didn't meet his eyes when she brought in his espresso.

That was new.

She placed the espresso down with a clink and pulled her hand back too fast. A tremor, almost imperceptible—but Sterling caught it. And noted it.

He let the espresso sit, untouched.

Warmth was a luxury.

Today required clarity.

Sterling tapped his thumb against the oak desk, slow and even, scanning the folder his PI had delivered last night. Aerial shots of a farmhouse. A grainy image of him, that boy, that nobody, his arms around her in the backyard.

Tucker.

Even the name was pathetic. It sounded like a truck. Or a bark.

Sterling laughed once, short and hollow. He flipped the photo facedown.

Libby Morgan was supposed to be resting. That was the arrangement. Everyone knew it.

When she unraveled, which she did, spectacularly, every few years, he gave her time. A sabbatical. A cleanse. Maybe even a fake rehab stint if it helped the optics. And then?

She came home.

He kissed her forehead. Called her his muse. Booked a shoot. Lined up an endorsement. She'd blink, smile, and Libby would return, lip-glossed and glittered, camera-ready.

So the cease-and-desists?

Unexpected.

And the fact that she'd changed the handles, the branding, the music rights?

Unforgivable.

"Does she really think she built this alone?" he muttered.

He stood and paced the length of the room.

Ten steps. Turn. Ten steps back.

A loop of fury under the skin.

"She was crying over some redneck buck in Pennsylvania when I found her. She was nothing."

The memory came sharp and bitter: Libby on the hotel floor, mascara smeared, curled around a bottle of NyQuil.

He'd taken the phone from her hand, read the texts from "Tucker," and deleted the thread.

She'd needed something stronger than love.

And Sterling had given it to her.

Pills. Praise. Press. Power.

And now? Now she wanted to pretend it wasn't his name that got her into those rooms? Into that stadium?

That it wasn't his calls that landed the Disney deal, the Grammy, the *Vogue* cover?

Ungrateful little bitch.

He walked to the window.

The city glittered, unaware of his ruin.

"She's scared," he told himself. "That's all." She was always scared.

That was what made her great.

What made her need him.

"She just needs to hear my voice. She needs to remember."

His phone buzzed. A text from his lawyer asking for a statement draft.

Sterling deleted it.

He didn't need lawyers.

He needed her.

He turned back to the folder. One more photo. Libby—no, Liv—in jeans and a hoodie, ducking behind some bar in a town that looked like it barely had indoor plumbing.

She had never looked so normal.

And she was glowing.

Sterling stared at the photo for a long time. It shouldn't have mattered. Jeans. Hoodie. That cursed small-town smile. It was pedestrian.

Forgettable.

But she looked alive.

And worse—like she didn't need him.

He exhaled slowly, the breath more animal than man.

If she wasn't going to come back willingly, he'd find another way.

Reputation. Leverage. History.

He had enough footage in the vault to ruin her, to remind the world how unstable she was. What she owed. How much of her story was curated—by him.

One push, and he could change the narrative again.

Because no one left Sterling Vale.

Not for long.

He straightened his cuffs. Walked to the mirror.

"You'll come home," he said to the glass. "You always do."

His reflection didn't blink.

Neither did he.

Chapter 34: The House on the Hill

Tucker

It wasn't a grand plan. Just a thought that turned into a text. A question, really. Simple. Direct.

Dinner? My place?

Liv didn't answer right away, but when she did, it was just three words: *I'd like that*.

And so, it began.

Tucker Hayes wasn't a man who chased chaos. He'd lived through his share of it, sure dreams crushed by torn ligaments, heartbreak left rusting like an engine he never quite finished fixing. But he'd built this house to be different. Quiet. Clean. Predictable in the ways the world wasn't.

Ten acres out in Westtown, high up on a ridge where the wind smelled like pine and freedom. He'd bought the property when he was thirty-one, half on a whim, half out of stubbornness. The house had been gutted. Rotting porch. Mold in the basement. Nothing but bones. And maybe that was what drew him to it. Bones could be rebuilt.

Now, the house stood like a calm exhale. Oak cabinets. White quartz countertops. Open shelving with simple ceramic plates he *actually* used. No show, no flash. Just function. The accordion doors folded wide to the deck and the hill beyond, sloping toward trees and sky and nothing else.

He cleaned for hours that morning, even though the place was already spotless. Ran to the market for fresh garlic and ginger. Picked up bok choy, snap peas, a perfect cut of flank steak. Jasmine rice. Lime and mint for mocktails. He didn't overthink it. He just cooked.

And when she arrived, tucked in the back of a distributor truck, thanks to a good friend, *and hindsight not the best idea for a recovering addict,* hair pulled back and eyes flickering with mischief, Tucker felt something in his chest shift. Like maybe he could finally breathe again.

She wore a dress the color of honey at dusk. Amber, really. Soft and clinging in all the right ways. Shoes in her hand the second she touched grass. Always barefoot. And for a flicker of a second, when the light caught her just right, he thought: *That dress matches my eyes.*

He wore a fitted tee, a blue button-up left unfastened and sleeves rolled up, jeans that weren't bar-stained. He was barefoot too. Unintentional symmetry.

"Nice place," she said, stepping inside, fingers brushing the edge of the island. "Very...you."

"Clean?"

"Calm," she corrected, smiling. "Like you built a place where the world has to take its shoes off."

He laughed, low and grateful. "Well, you made it in. That says something."

They stood in the kitchen, the soft sizzle of steak hitting the wok filling the space. The air smelled of garlic and soy and something grounding.

"Mocktails coming up," he said, sliding her a glass. Lime. Mint. Something fizzy. Cool against her palm.

She leaned against the counter, watching him work. Not the way people watch chefs on TV, but the way someone watches something sacred. Like she couldn't quite believe this was real.

"You always this domestic?" she asked.

"Only on Tuesdays and when pop stars sneak out of hiding in beer trucks."

She laughed. Really laughed. And the sound was balm.

They ate on the deck. Candles flickering. Sky bleeding into stars. Plates scraped clean and seconds offered without pretense.

He didn't touch her. Not yet. But he looked. God, he looked.

He'd seen her at her biggest—on jumbotrons, on red carpets, on a billboard above I-76. He'd seen her at her worst, too. Pale and shaking in a hospital gown. But nothing compared to this. To her—barefoot, candlelit, chasing stray rice grains with her chopsticks on his deck. She was a song no one had written yet. And for the first time, he was afraid he didn't have the right chords."

Because this wasn't Libby. This was Liv. Stronger now. Still cracked. Still tender. But alive in a way that made the hair on his arms rise.

And for the first time in years, he let himself believe:

Maybe healing could be quiet.

Maybe love didn't need fanfare.

Just stir fry. Bare feet. And the kind of silence that held space instead of weight.

Tomorrow, the world might come knocking.

Tonight, she was his guest.

And he was home.

Liv

I insisted on helping clean up.

Because that's what you do when someone makes you a five-star meal on a Thursday. Because standing up felt better than the uncertainty of what sitting close to Tucker did to my body. Because I needed to feel useful, like I wasn't just some rescued relic he was trying to preserve.

So, of course, I ruined the system.

I loaded the dishwasher all wrong. Didn't rinse the plates. Dropped a fork into the disposal with a clatter loud enough to make him flinch. And maybe, just maybe, I stood over the skillet eating extra steak with my fingers, like a feral thing who once lived off Nobu and minibar espresso shots.

Tucker watched, one hand gripping a dish towel like it was a white flag.

"Liv..." he started.

"What?" I said around a mouthful of steak. "You like a mess, remember?"

"I said I liked *your* mess," he murmured.

I turned. Leaned back against the counter, toes bare against cool tile, dress fluttering around my thighs. The amber fabric clung in the warm light, one of those reckless, impulsive purchases that felt like nothing in LA but felt like *something* when he looked at me.

I lifted a finger, dragged it slow across his bottom lip. He didn't move.

"I forgot," I whispered, "Tucker Hayes doesn't like a mess if he can't control it."

His eyes darkened. His body went completely still.

Then: "That's not true," he said, voice low and even. "I just like the kind of chaos that lets me breathe."

"And what kind is that?"

"This," he said.

And kissed me.

Not like the tentative, careful kisses we'd been trading in the quiet of borrowed moments.

This one had weight.

Heat.

History.

His hands found my hips as mine gripped the edges of his shirt. The kiss deepened. Grew.

He backed me into the counter, lifted me in one motion, like muscle memory, like prayer, and I wrapped my legs around his waist without hesitation.

We kissed like grown-ups who had broken things and healed them badly. Like people who'd wanted and waited and weren't sure how long they had.

His hands slid beneath my dress, not demanding, just reverent. My fingers tangled in his hair, his beard, his shirt.

He felt broader than I remembered. Harder in the chest and arms. But he still smelled like grass and firewood and some cologne he never named. And I?

I was softer now.

Curvier.

Fleshy in places I'd once fought to sculpt into camera angles.

But he touched me like I was everything.

Like this was everything.

"Are you sure?" he asked, breath ragged against my neck.

"Yes," I whispered.

He held me tighter.

And then, without letting go, he carried me down the hall into the master bedroom.

It was darker than I expected.

I hesitated for a moment at the door, not because I wasn't sure, but because something sacred lived in this threshold. Every bedroom I'd been in before had felt like a contract, a camera, a performance. But this one? This was quiet. Whole. It didn't ask me to be anyone but Liv

Cool.

Romantic.

A space not for show, but for retreat.

Clean lines. Deep blues. Wood and linen. No posters. No noise. Just intention.

Like him.

It turned me on more than I wanted to admit.

And for the first time in a very, very long time...

I didn't feel like I had to perform.

I watched him.

Drank him in.

The dark hair. The suntanned skin. The lines carved from work and age and time. And the veins, oh God, the veins, like they were drawn on for cinematic effect.

He shrugged out of the button-up, then tugged the tee over his head in one clean motion.

I was paralyzed.

Just... stared.

Wait. Was that drool?

He caught me looking. His smirk turned wolfish.

"You okay?" he asked, head tilted, eyes burning.

"Oh, I so am," I breathed.

I reached for the strap of my dress, started to slide it down.

He stopped me with one step forward, one hand against mine.

"Let me," he said.

And he did.

Painfully slow.

Fingertips tracing skin like memory.

The dress pooled at my feet.

The lingerie was a reckless thank-you to Les Corset in Woodland Hills, barely there, sheer, lace, struggling to contain the breasts that had absolutely grown since coming home. And the underwear? Equally insubstantial.

"I swear to God, I think you're about to take those off with your teeth," I blurted, eyes locked on his mouth.

His laugh was low, full of heat.

Color rose up my neck, flushing across my chest.

He stepped in, cupping my hips, towering over me like he was made to block out every distraction the world had ever hurled my way.

"I'm going to worship every inch of your body," he murmured, voice rougher now. "More than once."

I whimpered, not dramatic, not showy. Just... desperate.

But then I remembered who I was.

I wasn't afraid of this man. No.

He was complex.

He was stunning.

And I was done waiting for permission.

My fingers found his waistband, made quick work of the button, the zipper.

Slid his jeans down his legs, deliberate and slow.

I leaned in, mouth grazing his. "Get rid of them," I whispered.

We stared at each other, suspended in something thick and quiet. Not fear. Not even hesitation. Just the weight of knowing what this would mean.

Then we crashed.

Back into each other. Into the bed. All limbs and breath and memory until he flipped me gently, reverently, onto my back.

His mouth found my neck. Then lower.

The swell of my breast, caught in lace.

His teeth dragged the fabric aside, found my nipple, and worked it with a kind of aching devotion. Then the other. Again. Until I was gasping, arched, wrecked.

His nose, his mouth, hot and slow and focused, slid down my stomach, peppering kisses like tiny detonations.

And then, with the kind of quiet arrogance only he could pull off, his teeth grasped the edge of my thong and dragged it down to my toes.

He didn't look up.
He just wrapped my legs around his shoulders.
And devoured me.

Chapter 35: Morning Light

The light was different here.

Not filtered through blackout curtains or penthouse windows or sterile hospital blinds. It spilled through Tucker's wide, open windows like it belonged there. Like it was invited.

He was still asleep, bare-chested and golden in the early light. One arm thrown above his head, the other resting just close enough that I could feel his warmth. The sheets tangled low on his hips, and I stared like a thief. Like someone who'd snuck in and stolen something sacred.

And maybe I had.

Because last night wasn't just sex. It wasn't just bodies and hunger and sweat.

It was... more.

He had me. Over and over again. In ways I didn't think I could still feel. He made me scream, really scream. Cry out. Not because it hurt, not because I needed to be seen, but because my soul was on fire and I didn't know where else to put the flame.

I'd had lovers.

I'd enjoyed sex. Often. Unapologetically.

But this?

This was something else.

It was communion. Worship. Homecoming.

There were no words between us. Just hands and mouths and breath and the kind of silence that held so much meaning it didn't need filling.

I'd sent Dorian a frantic text when Tucker got up to get us water, my fingers trembling: *Sleeping at Tucker's. Don't panic. Let everyone know.*

Dorian hadn't replied, but Ari did almost immediately: *Spill. Everything.*

Then silence.

Because I'd tossed the phone aside and dove back into him.

I wasn't tired.

I felt alive.

More alive than I had in years. Maybe ever.

And, God, I felt peace. That elusive, slippery thing I had chased through city lights and stadium screams and magazine covers. Here it was. In this house. In this bed.

In him.

I didn't know if it was love yet. Maybe it was. Maybe it had always been. But whatever this was, it was holy.

My trauma still lived in me, coiled and quiet. It always would. But last night, I tried to meet him there. In the dark. With every inch of my body and every sliver of trust I had left.

I hoped it was enough.

I hoped he felt it.

Because I did.

With every kiss. Every touch. Every whispered yes.

This felt like the beginning.

Of something real.

We were at the kitchen nook an hour later, yes, he had a nook, eating chocolate chip pancakes with whipped cream like I was twelve again. I wore his old Phillies t-shirt, baggy and soft, brushing mid-thigh. He was shirtless, which felt borderline illegal, in nothing but a pair of sleep shorts, and I wanted to keep him like that forever.

Our hair was an absolute mess. My curls wild. His spiked in every direction from my hands.

We were licking whipped cream off each other's noses. Ridiculous. Cutesy. Perfect.

Tucker made me laugh so hard I nearly snorted coffee, and he grinned like a man who'd just stolen the sun and tucked it in his back pocket.

Then he reached across the table, brushed a crumb from the corner of my mouth, and just looked at me. Not the kind of look people give on red carpets or in interviews. The kind that sees everything. That holds you still.

"I don't know how I got this lucky," he said, soft, almost to himself.

"You made pancakes," I offered, my voice lighter than I felt.

"No," he said, setting his coffee down. "I mean it."

I froze. Because he meant it. Because I could feel it in my throat.

"I thought I lost you," he said. "Not just the girl I loved. But the version of you that laughed like this. That wore my old shirt and licked syrup off my fork like it was holy."

I swallowed hard, reached for his hand. "You didn't lose me. I just forgot where I was."

"You remember now?"

I nodded, my eyes full. "It's all back now," I whispered. "Every part of me."

And for a second, the world stayed quiet.

But real life doesn't wait long.

The showcase was a week away. Songs had been recorded, or at least drafted. Recording wasn't required, but the music had to exist. Sadie, Dorian, and I were the only Jag artists in the region, so we'd planned a stripped-down set. A few songs each.

Sadie would open. I would close.

And we were doing it here. Not just in Pennsylvania, but at The Crick.

A tent and tables were being added for overflow. Security was tight, thanks to the new team I'd quietly hired.

Yeah. I had people now.

And they were ready. Even for Sterling.

He hadn't reached me directly. But I could feel his shadow moving closer. His brand of control didn't die easy. And part of me waited for the punchline.

Then, like a spell breaking, my phone pinged.

A photo.

It was old. Glossy. Libby Morgan on a red carpet in heels too high and a smile too bright, being kissed on the cheek by Sterling Vale himself.

No caption.

Just... the reminder.

Libby still lived—in the mind of the one man who refused to let her die.

Back at my parents' house, the crew had gathered.

My phone sat on the table like a live wire. I hadn't changed my number until recently. Only the most trusted people had it now. So how the hell did that photo find me?

"There's no way anyone outside this room has the number," Dorian said, pacing.

Ari sat cross-legged on the couch, arms folded, lips tight. "Unless someone gave it to them."

"No one did," I said. "We're not doing that. We're not doubting each other."

But the air felt taut.

We ran through every scenario. Every possible breach.

Then Tucker blew out a breath and slammed his palm on the table. "Fuck."

All eyes turned.

He ran his hand down his face. "The other night. At the bar. I left my phone on the counter for a minute... Lacey was there. Eating dinner. Going on about something I wasn't listening to. She was digging for dirt."

Big Al leaned back in his chair, brow furrowed. "That girl's been watching you enter your passcode in the mirror behind the bar for years. Wouldn't be the first time she's gone through your phone."

I hadn't even looked at Tucker. Not really. We'd never talked about Lacey. Never defined whatever tension might have existed between them.

"I never led her on," Tucker said, voice low but certain. "Never touched her. But I played nice. She knows everyone in town, being a realtor and all. It paid off for the bar."

Big Al snorted. "Girl's been fame-hungry since high school. And jealous of Liv ever since."

Something in me shifted.

I didn't spiral.

I didn't retreat.

Instead, I preened.

Because he said it out loud.

Because he saw me.

And that validation was something Libby never got.

But Liv? She was getting it now.

We changed my number. Again.

Tucker locked his phone down tight, face recognition, pin verification, the works.

He would do anything to protect me.

But that only meant one thing.

Sterling had gotten his hooks into Lacey.

The thought made my stomach turn, not with jealousy—but with recognition. I knew what it felt like to be useful to him. To be shaped, used, discarded. If he'd sunk his teeth into her, it wouldn't be long before she lost track of what was hers and what was his. And I wouldn't let her become another version of me.

Chapter 36: Ballads and Blueberries

Money works fast.

And at Jag Records, it works like lightning.

But this time, it wasn't just the money that moved fast. It was the will. The vision. The quiet urgency of people who had nearly lost something sacred—and refused to lose it again.

The studio sat in two old warehouses off Temple Road, one a gutted-out carpet distributor from the seventies, still showing traces of its industrial bones, and the other a sleek, modern shell with clean lines and natural light. Somehow, the contrast worked. It was part memory, part manifesto. Like someone had fused nostalgia with intention and dared it to become a cathedral for sound.

The transformation hadn't been cosmetic. It was spiritual. The kind of restoration that only happens when someone pours love into every corner. The floors were polished reclaimed pine, rich with knots and history. The walls lined with warm, textured sound panels—custom-built by someone who understood that acoustics weren't just science, but soul. Vintage posters hung in floating frames like holy relics: Prince at the Troubadour, a cracked Stevie Nicks print, Nina Simone staring straight into your bones.

The air smelled like cedar and ambition. And somewhere beneath that—honeysuckle. Someone had left the back door open to the garden Ari had insisted on planting. Dorian said it was a nod to Bethel. To the old house. To me.

I knew that wasn't just sentiment. It was strategy. I could feel the psychology of it in my skin. The way the light hit the floor. The curve of the couch that was always there for me to sink into. The weight of silence calibrated just right so the music could breathe.

Dorian hadn't missed a single detail. Of course he hadn't. He'd stolen a few design decisions from me, sure—patterns I once sketched on a cocktail napkin in Montauk, fragments of conversations we had at 3 a.m. during the Libby years, when dreams were currency and everything felt possible if you said it out loud enough times. He remembered it all. Filed it away. Not because he was planning this—but because he believed I might live to need it.

If this was going to be the cradle of a new era for Jag, it needed to reflect not just recovery, but reinvention. Something rooted. Something wild. A place where truth could be recorded without apology.

Sadie had claimed one of the new nooks by the window, curled up like she'd always belonged there. Her ever-present guitar balanced on her knee, a notepad smudged with lyrics resting against her thigh, and a green juice in hand that looked more like a science experiment than a beverage. Ari had made it, obviously. Sadie sipped it with the same defiance she brought to her chord changes—uncertain, but willing.

She looked like a fever dream of Gen Z brilliance and small-town sparkle. Braids half-undone, chipped black nail polish, eyeliner like war paint and a tiny crescent moon drawn beneath her left eye. A walking contradiction. Gorgeous in the way wildfire is—uncontrollable, bright, and built to remake the landscape.

"Okay, but hear me out," she said, plucking a dissonant harmony from the guitar like it owed her something. "What if I opened with the ballad, then flipped it into the pop-punk chorus right after the second verse? Not the bridge. The verse. Like, derail the whole structure on purpose."

"Babe," Dorian said, not even looking up from his laptop, "you're eighteen. You can do whatever the hell you want. You're chaos incarnate."

Sadie grinned, unbothered by the chaos part. "I aspire to that."

I sat across from them, barefoot and cross-legged on the worn velvet couch that had survived three coasts, two floods, and too many recording sessions to count. A steaming mug of chamomile rested on one knee. A bowl of blueberries sat beside me, half-eaten and sun-warmed. The kind of snack you don't think about unless someone loves you enough to remember you forget to eat.

I didn't say much. I didn't need to. This wasn't a room for performance—it was a room for presence.

And I felt... whole.

Not unscarred. Not fully returned.

But luminous in the way people are when they've found their breath again.

"You closing with *Ashes* or *Air*?" Dorian asked, still typing but tuned into me like always.

"Thinking about it," I said softly. "Might add something new, too. Something raw. Not polished. Just... true."

Ari appeared then, drifting in from the back lounge like a couture ghost, draped in an oversized cardigan that could've come from a thrift store or the Met Gala. You never really knew with Ari. Their style was part oracle, part revolution.

They dropped onto the rug beside Sadie and took a long, skeptical sip of the green juice.

"This tastes like lawn clippings and regret," they muttered. "Perfect for your brand, Sadie."

We all laughed—big, body-shaking laughter that cracked open something in the room.

It didn't matter that the showcase was a week away.

That Sterling Vale's specter hovered just outside the frame.

That the press would come, and cameras would roll, and voices would sharpen to judge.

Here, in this space?

We were just artists.

Building. Plotting. Becoming.

Together.

Tucker

The bar was quieter than usual for a Friday afternoon. Sunlight filtered through the front windows, glinting off the bottles behind the counter. Tucker liked it that way. Clean. Predictable. Just enough buzz to keep the lights on and the regulars happy.

Then she walked in.

Lacey.

Hair done. Lipstick a little too perfect. That realtor smile polished to a knife's edge. Perfume too loud for daytime, trailing behind her like entitlement. Tucker clocked her the moment she stepped in, already bristling. The way she moved, all confident curves and curated charm, like she owned a piece of this place just because she'd lingered near its heartbeat once.

"Didn't expect to see you," he said flatly, wiping down the counter without looking up.

Lacey shrugged, sliding onto her usual stool. "It's still a public bar, isn't it?"

He finally met her eyes. "Not for long."

She arched a brow, but he saw it—the twitch in her jaw. The guilt masked as pride. She knew.

"I was a friend to you," she said, voice dipped in performative sorrow.

"No," Tucker interrupted, voice sharp. "You were an acquaintance. We talked. You drank. That's it."

She scoffed, leaning forward like she still had something to sell. "Funny. You didn't mind the attention when you weren't riding Liv's coattails."

Tucker's jaw flexed.

Big Al, restocking glassware nearby, paused just slightly.

"You want to say that again?" Tucker asked.

The air shifted. His voice dropped low, steady. Dangerous.

Lacey didn't flinch. "I told Sterling. About the showcase. He deserved to know. I invited him."

The room went still.

Tucker blinked. Once.

Then he stepped forward, slow. Controlled.

"How the hell did you even know?" he asked, his voice barely above a whisper—but somehow louder than any shout.

She smiled, sweet and cruel. "A little birdie. Or maybe a little phone."

The towel hit the bar with a sharp *slap*. Tucker's eyes burned.

"We had a plan. One post. One quiet drop. Just a date. Just a time. No big promo. No press release. Just enough for the right people to find it—and not enough time for vultures to swarm." He shook his head, the fury in him rising like a storm tide. "You stole that from us."

She rolled her eyes, arms crossed like a teenager caught sneaking out. "It's not like you all don't want the attention. She lives for that stage."

"No," he growled. "She nearly *died* on that stage."

Lacey blinked, caught off guard.

"You think this is about some comeback tour?" Tucker took a step closer. His voice cracked—raw, exposed. "She's rebuilding her life one breath at a time. Every second she stays clean is a goddamn miracle. And you—" he jabbed a finger toward her—"you decided *you* knew better. *You* put her at risk."

Big Al stepped out from behind the bar. "Tuck—"

"No," Tucker snapped, not taking his eyes off Lacey. "She went through my phone, Al. Read messages. Found dates. She used me. Put Liv in danger."

Lacey stood abruptly, the mask slipping. "You're overreacting. It's a showcase, not a secret operation."

"She's not *your* story to tell," he hissed. "Not yours to sabotage. You don't get to play puppet master because you're bored or bitter or still pissed I didn't fall for your late-night flirtation and bad karaoke."

Her lips curled. "You'll regret this."

"I already do," he said. "I regret ever letting you near any part of my life."

He turned to his staff, voice cold, decisive. "No one serves this woman again. She's banned. For life."

Lacey's face flushed, whether from fury or humiliation, he didn't care. She pivoted on her heel and stalked out, the door slamming hard behind her.

But the damage had been done.

Tucker stepped into his office and slammed the door harder than he meant to. The sound echoed off the old wood paneling like a gunshot. Bottles rattled on the shelf. A photo of his dad tipped slightly in its frame.

He leaned against the door, jaw clenched, chest rising and falling in sharp bursts.

For a moment, he just stood there. Still. Burning.

The kind of anger that didn't yell—it carved. It licked the edges of his ribs and whispered every line he should've seen, every red flag he ignored, every way he had failed to protect her.

He ran both hands through his hair, gripping the back of his neck like it might anchor him. His heart pounded. Not from fear. From fury. From shame.

He saw it too clearly now—Lacey grinning like she'd done something noble, like she'd gifted the world a spectacle. Like Liv wasn't a person, just a headline waiting to happen again.

He should've changed his password. Should've seen her motives unraveling the minute she lingered too long near the stage, asking questions she had no business asking. He'd let her in, even a little. And now this.

He kicked the leg of his desk hard enough to send a tremor through the floor. A pen cup toppled. Papers shifted. Nothing shattered, but something inside him did.

He reached for his phone.

Stared at her name.

Paused.

Then tapped *Call*.

She answered on the second ring, breathless and smiling. "Hey."

He closed his eyes at the sound of her voice. There was music in the background—live, low, human. A mug clinking against a table. Laughter. Warmth. She sounded light. Lighter than he'd heard her in years.

"You alone?" he asked.

"I can be," she replied, and he heard the shift—something quieting around her. "What's wrong?"

He dropped into his chair, leaning forward, elbows on knees.

"It's Lacey," he said. "She showed up at the bar. Ran her mouth. Told me she's the one who tipped off Sterling. Invited him to the showcase."

Silence.

Not the kind that panics. Not sharp or shattering.

Just a breath. Soft. Full.

"Liv?"

She answered, voice calm. Steady. "Let him come."

Tucker blinked. "What?"

"Let him come," she repeated, firmer now. "He won't like what I have to say. Or sing."

He ran a hand over his face. "You sure?"

A laugh, gentle but electric. "I've never been surer. I'm safe here. I'm ready."

He didn't respond right away. Just breathed.

And thought:

God help Sterling Vale.

Because Liv wasn't just ready to be seen—

She was ready to be *heard*.

Chapter 37: The Girl and the Piano

Liv

The lights were low in the writing room. Not dark, but warm. Like dusk caught in a jar. The old upright piano, refinished but familiar, waited in the corner, half-lit by the amber-glow sconces Dorian had insisted on.

"Mood matters," he'd said.

He wasn't wrong.

There was something sacred about this space—like it had been designed not just for sound, but for confession. The walls didn't just hold echoes; they held truths. Ones I wasn't brave enough to say aloud unless a melody made them safer.

I sat in front of the keys barefoot, spine curved, shoulders soft, a blanket over my lap even though the room wasn't cold. A notebook lay open beside me, its pages smeared with ink. Not lyrics, not yet. Not polished enough for that. Just raw thoughts. Scrawled fragments of pain and reclamation.

The call with Tucker still echoed in me. Not the anger—that had shaken me, sure—but more than that, it was his instinct to protect. Always that. Even after everything. Even now. And it made me want to be worthy of that protection. Of him. Of myself.

So I played.

Simple chords. Minor and patient. Like a heartbeat underwater. The kind of sound you could only make when you weren't performing—just surviving. Just feeling.

And I sang. Quietly at first, as if testing the room. Then louder, until my voice filled the rafters. The words weren't perfect, but they didn't need to be. They just had to be true.

"You built me from ashes,
Then blamed me for the fire.
Carved a legend on my skin,
And sold me as desire..."

I didn't need to say his name.

He would know.

Everyone would.

This wasn't just a ballad. It was a reckoning. For every lie sold as guidance. Every pill handed over like candy. Every shoulder squeeze laced with manipulation. Every time he whispered that I owed him my life because he made Libby marketable.

But the legend? It was never mine.

The dream? It had teeth.

And the star? She only burned because someone lit her from underneath.

By the time I stopped playing, my fingers were trembling. My eyes were wet. My voice had cracked on the final line, but I let it. I let it all break.

And still—I smiled.

Let him come.

Let him hear.

Let the whole world know who broke the girl,

And who finally wrote her story.

A few days later...

There's something sacred about a house just before the chaos.

Tucker's place—clean, open, meticulous—had started to shift. Not in big, dramatic ways. In quiet ones. One drawer at a time. One toothbrush at a time. One silk camisole draped over the back of a dining chair because I hadn't folded laundry in a week.

245

My things had begun to settle. To claim corners. To make roots.

My lotions, creams, and serums now lived in his bathroom, cluttering the vanity with labels like "rejuvenate" and "restore," even though what I really needed was rest. My shoes—mostly boots and bare-boned flats—took up the floor of his entry closet. My sweaters—earth-toned, soft, lived-in—hung beside his flannels like they'd been invited.

No sequins. No glitter. No stage-ready silhouettes.

Just me.

We weren't making declarations. We didn't need to.

We were simply making space.

And tonight? Tonight was our exhale. The last inhale of normal before the air shifted again. The Crick would shut down starting Wednesday—tents, sound, security, the whole machine—and Saturday would be the reckoning.

But tonight was tomato pie and hoagie trays and caramel apples on skewers from the church fundraiser down the road. It was community. It was Delco. It was a little too loud, a little too warm, and just right.

The living room didn't look like his anymore. Not completely. I'd snuck in framed photos, scattered like breadcrumbs across the mantle and bookshelves: my parents holding hands outside the garden shed, Tuck's folks beaming in front of an old convertible, Dorian and his mom wrapped in rainbow flags at a Pride parade, a blurry shot of the three of us—me, Tuck, and Dorian—drunk on French fries and ocean air during senior week at the Jersey Shore.

Someone had put a Spotify playlist on loop—soul classics, mostly. Tucker's vinyl collection had been "borrowed" by Sadie, who insisted we digitize everything before it melted in the attic. She and her parents had arrived with a tray of soft pretzels the size of hubcaps and a ridiculous charcuterie board shaped like a guitar.

Ari floated between the kitchen and the back patio, wrapped in the world's softest sweater and holding court like a deity in exile. They barked lovingly at Rey to stop garnishing the cider mocktails with star anise, claiming it looked like cursed woodchips. Rey only cackled and added two more.

Dorian's mom brought homemade dumplings. Pax hugged everyone like he was afraid they might vanish. Eli came late, arms full of apple butter and a worn Polaroid camera he used to snap candid shots without warning.

I didn't cook. But I knew food. I knew what it meant. And this—this wasn't Hollywood cuisine. This was comfort. Home. Love on a tray.

And it felt good to give it to them.

Tucker leaned against the counter, watching me with that look he got when he didn't have words but still wanted me to know everything. His eyes said it all. That he noticed. That he felt it

That this—this mess, this crowd, this fusion of past and present—was what we had both been building toward, even when we thought we weren't building anything at all.

No one said it aloud. They didn't have to.

This was the calm before the storm.

And for the first time in my life, I wasn't afraid of the wind.

Later, after most of the plates were cleared and someone had started playing an old John Mayer record through the speakers, I stood.

Cider in hand. Heart in my throat.

My palms were sweating, ridiculous as that felt. These were my people. The ones who'd held my hair through detox, who'd seen me raw and crumbling. And yet—I was shaking.

"I, uh... I just want to say something," I began.

The room quieted instantly. Not out of obligation. Out of love. Every single face turned toward me. Some smiling. Some already glassy-eyed. All of them fully present.

"I wouldn't be here without you," I said. My voice cracked, but I didn't pull it back. "That's not drama. Or exaggeration. It's just the truth. You saved me. All of you. Whether you dragged me home or stood by me, whether you handed me a hoagie and didn't ask questions or stayed on the line while I sobbed in a bathtub—you rescued me."

I glanced around the room. Let my eyes land, one by one.

Tucker. Steady as ever, hands tucked in his back pockets, gaze burning with something old and unshakable.

Dorian. Already wiping beneath his glasses. No surprise.

My parents—Mom leaning into Dad, both holding each other like they didn't need words.

Ari, arms crossed over their chest, lower lip trembling.

Rey, blinking fast, jaw clenched.

Sadie, curled on the floor like a kid, eyes wide and wet.

"You gave up your peace. Your anonymity. Your time. You let me claw my way back, even when it would've been easier to let me sink. And I know that. I see that. I won't ever forget it."

I took a breath. A real one. Full and slow. Then I continued.

"And Libby..." I paused. Let the weight settle. "She got me this far. She kept me going. She protected me when I didn't know how to be real. She shined so bright I didn't have to feel."

My voice softened. But it didn't waver.

"But I do now. I feel *everything*. And I think it's time."

I lifted my glass higher.

"Libby, thank you. Thank you for carrying me when I was broken. For being my shield. For taking the hits. But I've got it from here."

I swallowed.

"You can rest now."

Silence followed. Heavy and holy.

Then, like the softest bell, the first clink. Tucker, tapping his glass gently against the counter. Then Dorian. Then Ari. Then the room.

No one rushed in to hug me. No one shouted cheers. They just... stood with me. Held the moment.

A quiet chorus of love.

It was the closest thing to peace I'd ever known.

And it was mine now.

Not because I earned it.

But because I was finally ready to keep it.

Later, when the dishes were stacked and the music turned down low, I slipped out the back door with my glass in hand.

The night air wrapped around me like linen— cool, clean, a little damp from the river nearby. Tucker's backyard was mostly shadow, the porch light casting a quiet circle across the old stone path and the edge of the garden bed he'd started last spring.

I didn't go far. Just enough to hear the silence. Just enough to let the sound of everyone I loved fall into the background.

I sat on the top step, glass between my palms, the wood cool against my thighs through the thin fabric of my dress.

It hit me then. Not in a tidal wave. Just a soft, slow tide pulling at my ankles.

Libby was really gone.

Not erased. Not hated. Just... finished.

Like an era that had served its time. Like a coat you finally hang up after a long, hard winter.

I let the stillness hold me.

A moment later, the door creaked. I didn't have to turn to know who it was.

Tucker sat down beside me, close enough to touch, but he didn't. Not yet.

"You okay?" he asked softly.

"I think so," I said. "I feel like I just laid someone to rest. Someone I loved. Someone I feared. Someone who nearly killed me."

He nodded, staring straight ahead. "She kept you alive."

"She did," I said. "And now I get to decide what living looks like."

The cicadas hummed. A wind stirred the trees.

Tucker reached over then, quietly, and slid his fingers between mine.

We didn't say another word.

We didn't need to.

Chapter 38: The Room We Made

We crawled into the bedroom just past midnight, the house still echoing with laughter and music. Leftovers were crammed into too-small containers in Tucker's fridge, foil lids half-torn, a precarious tower of casseroles and condiments he'd curse at in the morning.

My skin was warm from cider. My hair still carried the scent of Ari's bonfire sweater. My feet ached in the best way—like I'd been dancing barefoot through something holy. And Sadie's laugh still rang in my ears like a chorus I never wanted to stop singing.

I was halfway through pulling my hair into a loose braid when Tucker leaned in the doorway, arms folded, a slow smile creeping across his face.

"You know," he said, tilting his head, "if you're gonna keep secretly moving in, we might as well start calling this your place."

I grinned. "Secretly? Please. You built me a whole damn cabinet."

He stepped into the room, barefoot and steady, and sat beside me on the edge of the bed. The smirk softened into something slower. Truer.

"I didn't know I was doing it then," he said, voice low. "But yeah... I think I was."

We fell into the pillows like gravity was optional—flannel sheets wrapping around us, limbs finding the geometry of each other the way old lovers do. It wasn't new. It was remembered.

For a moment, it was quiet. Easy.

Then I felt it.

The shift.

The weight behind his silence.

"What is it?" I asked, my voice barely above a whisper, fingers resting on his chest.

He sighed, brushing my hair back from my face. "Sterling. I keep thinking about what you said. About him coming. About what he might try."

I nodded. I knew that fear. Had carried it inside my ribs like a second pulse.

"He doesn't scream," I said. "He smiles. He doesn't push—he whispers. He acts like he's the only one who's ever understood me. He'll say he's proud. That he misses me. That he believes in the work."

Tucker's jaw tensed beneath my hand. I felt it like thunder held at bay.

"He'll call me his girl," I continued. "He'll bring up the early days. Try to make me laugh. And when that doesn't work, he'll offer me something I used to want. A stage. A deal. A door back into the machine."

I looked him dead in the eyes, fingers tracing the scar near his collarbone.

"But it's not mine anymore. None of it is. And neither is he."

He didn't nod. Didn't rush to agree. He just looked at me like he was memorizing every inch of my face. Then he pulled me close, his forehead resting against mine, breath steady.

"You let me know when to punch him in the face," he whispered.

I laughed into his shoulder, the kind of laugh that came from knowing someone had your back, fully and without condition. "You'll be the second to know."

"And the first?"

"Me."

He kissed my temple like a promise. Then again, lower. Slower.

His arm wrapped around my waist like it belonged there. Like it had always belonged there.

Like we had more nights like this ahead of us.

And maybe—just maybe—we did.

Tucker

Morning sunlight stretched across the hardwood floors of the study, golden and slow. Tucker stood at the window, sipping coffee from a chipped mug he'd brought back from the Jersey Shore. It still had sand in the handle.

Or maybe that was just memory.

He heard Dorian before he saw him—boots soft on the floor, the familiar cadence of someone who never took space, only shared it. That was always Dorian. Never louder than the room, never smaller than it either.

"Liv's in the kitchen," Tucker said over his shoulder, eyes still on the window. "Raiding the leftover apple cider and trying to convince herself caramel apples count as breakfast."

Dorian laughed. "Sounds about right."

They stood there for a minute, not speaking, the quiet between them worn in and comfortable. Like the pause in a song before the beat drops. Not absence—anticipation.

"You sleep?" Dorian asked eventually, moving toward the chair in the corner without needing permission.

Tucker shook his head. "Barely."

"Yeah. Me neither."

Dorian sat. Didn't press. He never had to.

"You mind if I say something before you start?" he asked gently.

Tucker turned, surprised.

"You and I..." Dorian began, "...we don't talk enough. Not like this. But I need you to know, I never stopped thinking of you as my brother. Even when Liv was gone. Even when everything was fractured. You were still there."

Tucker blinked, throat tightening. "Yeah. Same."

"I kept tabs," Dorian said, smiling softly. "You probably knew that."

"I suspected," Tucker admitted, sitting across from him. "Figured some of those 'industry updates' you dropped in my inbox were really about her."

"They were," Dorian said. "Filtered. On purpose. I told you what I thought you could hold. Protected you from the worst of it. Didn't see the point in drowning you in the chaos when you couldn't reach her."

Tucker exhaled. "Thank you."

"I also... may have told her once or twice that you were dating someone new."

Tucker raised an eyebrow. "Were you trying to make her jealous?"

Dorian shrugged. "Trying to make her *feel* something. You were always the compass."

A pause. Then a chuckle from both of them.

"So yeah," Tucker said, leaning forward, voice lower now. "I need to talk about Sterling."

Dorian's face settled into something more still. Not surprised. Just ready.

"Liv told me what he's like. The manipulation. The seduction. The calculated softness. And man, I get it now. I get how easy it would be to mistake him for safety when you're spiraling."

He stared into his coffee like it might explain the world.

"I want to follow her lead. I really do. I want to trust that she can face him. But God, man..." he rubbed the back of his neck. "I want to break something. I want to punch him. Kick him out. Protect her."

"And maybe," he continued, voice rougher now, "maybe I'm scared. Not of him. Of what he represents. That life. That whole other version of her world. It's loud and big and full of glitter and ego and damage, and I keep thinking..."

He paused.

"What if it calls her back? What if I'm not enough to keep her here?"

Dorian didn't answer immediately.

When he did, his voice was soft but certain.

"Tuck, that life nearly killed her. It stripped her down to nothing and called it love. The only reason she came back from it is because this life—the one here, with you—is the only one that was ever real to her."

Tucker blinked. The words landed like balm on a bruise.

"You're not the backup. You're not the footnote. You're the peace she didn't know she could ask for."

Silence stretched again, but this time it was gentler. Like the quiet that follows good news.

Tucker looked up. "How do you know?"

Dorian smiled, no pretense in it. "Because for the first time in twenty years, she's writing songs that don't sound like they're trying to survive."

Tucker's grip tightened on his mug.

"You really think I can let her lead this?"

"You already are," Dorian said. "You're just scared because it matters."

Tucker let out a quiet laugh. "Goddamn. When did you get so wise?"

"Somewhere between therapy and tequila," Dorian grinned.

They chuckled, and for a moment, it felt like old times.

But deeper.

Better.

Grown.

Outside the door, they heard Liv laugh at something Ari said—bright, breathless, alive. The sound curled down the hallway like a thread pulling them both forward.

"Come on," Dorian said, rising. "Let's go make sure she didn't eat all the apples."

"She probably did," Tucker muttered, but his smile gave him away.

And they left the study side by side.

Just like always.

Chapter 39: The Sound Beneath the Water

Liv

By late morning, The Crick had started to shift.

Bar stools rearranged. Back patio cleared. Cords and crates stacked like promises waiting to be made. It wasn't chaos. It was momentum. It was music still in the making.

The floors had been swept twice already, but sawdust still clung to the corners. Someone had plugged in a portable PA and was testing vocal levels with a mix of shrieks and warmups. From the kitchen, the scent of cinnamon rolls mingled with lemon cleaner and old beer. Familiar. Forgiving.

I wasn't barefoot—this was still a Delco bar, and I'd learned better—but I moved like I belonged. Because maybe I finally did. Not because it held my memories, but because it held Tucker's. Because it held possibility.

I paused near the stage riser, watching Sadie and Pax move cables like veins across the floor. Someone adjusted a mic stand with a satisfying metal twist. Eli was setting tea on a back table, pouring slow like it was ritual. Dorian hovered near the back with his notebook, already plotting the mix.

It hit me then.

This wasn't about performance. It was about presence.

And here, on this stage, I'd once poured out the last notes of my heartbreak, and that had been the crack in the glass. The way the light got back in.

This wasn't my bar.

But it had become part of my becoming.

And now? I was a builder.

"No spotlights," I told the lighting crew, stepping lightly between stacks of amp cases. "No rigged strobes. I want soft pools of light. Natural, wherever we can. Let the string bulbs do the heavy lifting."

They nodded, adjusting angles and wires with quiet competence.

I wanted the showcase to feel like it had always belonged here. Like the sound had grown up with the wood. Like it wasn't added—it *emerged*.

No glitter. No screens. Just voices. Just truth.

A reel-to-reel sat perched in the corner like a relic, its reels still for now, but ready. Ari had insisted on analog backup, "for the nostalgia," they'd said. But I liked the symbolism: a machine that listened in a way most things no longer did.

I stepped to center stage.

Closed my eyes. Breathed in wood and dust and memory. And the room breathed back— steady, waiting, alive.

Sadie found me near the back patio, clutching a clipboard that looked too big in her hands. A pencil was tucked behind her ear, and her hoodie sleeves were smudged with sharpie and pink glitter. She looked like revolution and rehearsal all at once.

"We're low on battery packs for the floor monitors," she said, breathless. "But I already called Pax. He's on it."

I smiled. "Of course he is. You're killing it."

She shrugged, cheeks pink. "Trying."

We sat on the back steps, the door propped open, breeze brushing past like a lullaby. The wood beneath us was worn smooth—Tucker had sanded it himself after a summer storm warped the grain. It creaked slightly when we shifted, like it was listening.

"Can I ask you something?" Sadie said after a long pause.

I nodded.

"How do you... not explode? When people say awful things?"

My breath caught. "Someone said something?"

Her lip caught between her teeth. "Some boys at school. About you. About the overdose. They called you... things."

My chest tightened. A hot prickle at the base of my spine.

"I told them off," she added quickly, eyes flaring. "Got sent to the principal. Might've shoved one. Just a little."

I stared at her—this teenager with lightning in her chest and fire in her spine. My heart broke and swelled all at once.

"Sadie..."

"I'm not sorry," she said.

"I'm not asking you to be." I reached out, took her hand—cool and strong despite the tremble. "You were braver than I ever was at your age."

She laughed, a little teary. "You were famous. I'm just... weird."

"I was scared," I said. "All the time. But I covered it with glitter and heels and music so loud it drowned me out. And no one ever said what you did. No one told off the boys. No one made noise for me."

I rubbed my thumb across her knuckles.

"There will always be noise. Always someone ready to tear you down just to make their own voice louder. Part of being seen... is being judged."

She nodded, blinking quickly. Her eyes were her mother's, but there was something else there too. A kind of knowing that only comes from watching the world disappoint someone you love.

"But you?" I said. "You're going to be seen for exactly who you are. And when that spotlight hits you, I want you to remember—you don't have to stand there alone. You have people. You have me."

Her voice went small. "You think I'll make it?"

I looked at her. Really looked. Her scuffed boots. Her chipped nail polish. The courage it took to wear herself out loud.

"I know you will. And I just want you to make better choices than I did. Learn from them. That's what legacy means."

She leaned her head on my shoulder, just for a second. Just long enough to steady something in both of us.

The bar buzzed behind us—strings being tuned, lights checked, chairs scooted across floors. Movement everywhere. Momentum building.

And I knew.

Whatever came next, it would be honest.

It would be ours.

I was inside, double-checking light placement and noting a flickering Edison bulb when the front door creaked open.

The air changed.

A cologne I hadn't smelled in months slithered across the room—expensive, saccharine, calculated. Synthetic comfort. Masked control.

Sterling Vale.

He entered like the room owed him silence. Leather loafers too pristine for Delco floors. A tailored charcoal coat. Wrist heavy with a watch that probably cost more than Sadie's college fund. Behind him: flowers, champagne, a Cartier box tucked into the crook of a personal assistant's elbow like an afterthought. Diamonds. Of course.

Tucker stiffened behind the bar. I saw it in his hands first—how they stopped moving, how his fingers curled against the polished wood. His jaw twitched. But he stayed still.

"Liv," Sterling purred, voice dipped in old theater and false warmth. "You look... incredible."

He scanned the room like it was a set. A stage. Something he could still direct.

"This place, it's got a real vibe. I love it. Rustic chic. And the energy? Totally on-brand."

He stepped forward like he owned the floor. Like his presence was a gift.

"I brought a few things," he said, gesturing lazily to the champagne and glittering trappings. "Thought I'd celebrate you. It's good to see you. Really. We've missed you. The world has. And I was thinking..."

He smiled—slow, practiced. Salesman in silk.

"...maybe this new chapter, this Liv era? Maybe it could be our masterpiece."

I didn't move. Didn't blink.

He faltered—just slightly. A flicker of something in his eyes, like a magician realizing the trick wasn't landing.

"I'm not interested in reinvention," I said. "I'm interested in truth."

He shifted gears instantly. His body leaned in, his voice dropped low.

"You know what we were. I loved you," he said, softer now. "You used to say I was the only one who really saw you. Remember that open mic in Baltimore? You sang barefoot, shaking, and I told you the world wasn't ready, but I was."

His hand moved—slow, deliberate. Fingertips grazing my arm like he still had the right.

I stepped back.

"You don't get to touch me."

His mask cracked, barely, but enough.

"You think you're above this?" he hissed, barely audible. "That this isn't all a show? You need me. You always did."

Behind the bar, Tucker moved. A glass tipped. I raised a hand without looking—keeping my eyes locked on Sterling.

"No," I said. "I needed to survive. And I don't need that anymore."

He scoffed. His smile was gone now. The silk was shredded.

"You don't get to rewrite history just because you found a new audience," he sneered. "You're still here because of me."

"No," I said again, louder this time. "I'm here in spite of you."

He turned then, sharply. Already halfway to the door when I called out.

"Hey, Sterling."

He paused. Looked back. Hope flickering—like maybe I was chasing him again.

I smiled. Just enough to cut.

"See you at the show."

He nodded, clinging to some sliver of belief.

But this time, when Sterling turned to leave, he looked toward the gifts, then toward me.

"I'll leave them," he said. "Thought you might come to your senses."

He smiled, soft and cruel, as if the perfume and diamonds could rewire my spine.

Then he was gone.

But I didn't go after the gifts.

I didn't even touch them.

But he didn't know. That belief was bait.

And this time, the stage was mine.

Sadie

Everyone got weird after the man in the suit left.

I was adjusting the mic stand, pretending not to notice how Liv froze a little too long, how Tucker's fists stayed clenched even after the door shut, how Dorian's camera was still in his hands but not recording.

The air felt like static. Silent. Dangerous.

I swallowed it. Tried to shrink.

But Liv caught my eye. Just a nod.

That was enough.

I pulled my guitar from the rack and stepped onto the riser. The floor was dusty under my boots, and the mic smelled like lemon cleaner and old beer.

Home, I guessed. Not polished or pretty—but real. It smelled like mistakes and second chances.

"Whenever you're ready," Pax called from the booth.

I nodded. My fingers shook, but I strummed anyway. Adjusted. Took one breath too many and still cracked on the first note. But I recovered.

I always did.

The song wasn't perfect. It wasn't meant to be. It came from a thunderstorm and a quiet floor. From too many nights replaying conversations in my head and not enough mornings where I felt seen. It had no chorus, just a pulse. It didn't build—it *spilled*.

Halfway through, I forgot they were watching.

I saw Liv's face shift. Not just pride. Something softer. Like recognition.

Tucker leaned on a stool, arms folded, jaw loose now, nodding slow. Dorian pressed record, which meant he thought it mattered.

And it did.

When the last note faded, silence hovered— light and heavy all at once. Then applause. Not polite. Not automatic.

Real.

I grinned, breathless, blinking fast. My chest felt too full and too light all at once.

And maybe, for the first time, I didn't feel like a kid pretending.

I felt like a girl about to break through.

If Liv had found her voice again, then maybe mine mattered too.

I was winding cords when Liv came over. She crouched beside me, pressed something into my palm.

"Here," she whispered. "Advance on your first album. Or your car. Or whatever future you're about to claim."

I looked down.

The Cartier box.

My breath caught. "Liv, I can't—"

"You can," she said. "Because that man thought it would buy me back. But all it's buying is *you*. Freedom. Forward. Light."

She stood. Touched my shoulder gently.

"You've already got the voice. Now go build the life."

And just like that, she walked back toward the stage.

But I stayed frozen for a second longer, box clenched to my chest, heart wide open.

The showcase was coming.

And this time, I wouldn't be background noise.

I was ready. Not polished. Not perfect. But mine. And maybe that was enough to begin.

Chapter 40: The Showcase

Liv

The room was hushed, save for the soft tick of the old clock above the vanity. I lit a candle—one of Ari's, bergamot and sage, wrapped in handwritten labels and love—and placed it gently on the corner of the counter. Its flame flickered like a heartbeat, fragile but steady.

I didn't speak, not yet. Just sat, let the warmth brush my skin, and hummed.

It started quiet, instinctual—one of Libby's warm-ups, the old scales she used to run before a shoot or a show. Arpeggios that lifted and dipped like tides. My voice followed, high and breathy at first, then deeper, rounder. I let it stretch. Let it remember.

The melody curled around my ribs, familiar and foreign. I didn't even realize I'd closed my eyes until they fluttered open again.

Libby used to use that warm-up to unlock range—belting at the top, whispering at the bottom. A vocal tightrope. It felt strange to touch it now without the pressure, without the looming camera or Sterling's shadow watching from the wings. Just me. Just voice.

I reached for the mirror, touched its frame. Then, almost without thinking, I whispered—not to anyone in particular, but not quite to no one either.

"Whoever's listening... just keep me honest. Keep me real."

It wasn't a prayer. Not really. I didn't know if I believed in a god beyond Ari's lavender-laced mantras. But I believed in something now. In rhythm. In redemption. In fire that didn't just burn but warmed.

I closed my eyes again. Took one long breath.

The candle swayed slightly, its scent catching in my throat like memory.

Then I opened them, and there she was.

Libby. Perched in the mirror.

Not fully formed, not a ghost, not a hallucination. Just... presence. Perched behind my pupils like she always was—glossed, guarded, gleaming.

"You were never just a costume," I whispered. "I made you. I know that now."

The mirror stayed quiet. But her weight hummed through the glass, a frequency only I could feel.

"It was easier to pretend you were making the choices," I said, voice low. "Easier to blame the script than admit I kept following it. But you... you were my armor. And I needed armor. Especially after—"

I stopped. Swallowed.

"Especially after Tucker. The girl I used to be—barefoot, bursting with dreams—tried to make him the villain. It was simpler than owning the ache. Than admitting I let his fear become my exit route. That's when I let you take over, Libby. When it hurt too much to be me."

"But the truth is," I said, sitting up straighter, "you gave me chapters I wouldn't trade. Not anymore. You let me survive."

I touched the mirror. Not goodbye. Just... release.

"Now I get to live those chapters as me. You can rest, Libby. I've got this next part handled."

From down the hallway, the night began to stir—low voices, a guitar tuning, the shuffle of boots.

I stood. Smoothed the fabric of my dress. One more breath.

And walked out.

Tucker's office smelled like cedar and citrus oil, soft and grounding. A single salt lamp glowed on the shelf, and the lights overhead were warm—not showbiz hot, but golden-hour soft. Cozy. Real. The kind of lighting that didn't demand perfection. Just presence.

The inner circle was gathered: Dorian at the soundboard, sleeves rolled, notebook full of crossed-out set orders and gut feelings; Ari adjusting Sadie's collar with fierce tenderness; Sadie cradling her guitar like a talisman, not a weapon.

They looked up when I entered.

No applause. No gasps.

Just knowing smiles.

The kind that held history and forgiveness and forward motion.

"I wanted to say something," I began, voice low but steady, hands tucked into the folds of my dress to keep from trembling. "None of this—tonight, this version of me, this second act—happens without you."

Dorian nodded, eyes gentle. *Keep going.*

"So I had the team post something. Just an hour ago. No fanfare. Just a date, time, and place."

Ari raised an eyebrow, half teasing, half assessing. "That's not exactly *go viral* strategy."

"I'm not trying to go viral," I said, smiling softly. "I'm trying to go home."

Sadie's eyes lit up, full of wonder and understanding. Her fingers tightened slightly on the guitar, like she already knew what that kind of home could mean.

"And I made sure they tagged you," I continued, turning to Dorian and Sadie now. "You two. You've carried pieces of me for years. This isn't a rebrand. It's a reintroduction. To Jag Records. To the three of us. Artists. Together."

267

The room shifted—no cheers, no slogans. Just breath. Like they all exhaled at once.

"I want this night to outlive the platform. I want it to mean something more than a stream count."

Dorian smiled, small and sure. Sadie blinked, the full weight of belonging settling into her bones.

We didn't need a glam team. No velvet ropes. No handlers. Just light that knew how to wrap around the truth without distorting it.

We had a full band. But tonight, we were playing too.

Like we used to. In garages and basements and backyards with half-broken amps and dreams that barely fit in our mouths.

Except now, the world had cracked open just enough to let the real songs through.

This time, it was honest.

Sadie

I stepped up first.

Not because I had to.

Because I was ready.

The house lights dimmed to a soft hush of amber and indigo, casting long shadows across the floor. My boots echoed gently, not loud, just enough to remind me I was real. The stage felt both too big and exactly right.

I adjusted the strap on my guitar—worn and familiar. My fingers trembled for a second, but my breath didn't.

"I'm Sadie Bell," I said, voice steady. "And this one's for the weird girls."

Laughter rippled through the room—gentle, knowing.

I nodded once.

And began.

"I know what it's like to be loud in the wrong way..."

The first lyric landed like a stone dropped in water. I couldn't see their faces, but I felt the room shift. Eyes turned toward me, not in scrutiny, but in something softer. Willingness. Recognition.

"To wish for the mic but dread the fame..."

I wasn't performing. I was *telling the truth.* Every note was something I'd carried. Every lyric, a page from my journal no one was ever meant to read.

But I was ready now.

"I won't crop my edges to fit your screen..."

The strings beneath my fingertips hummed low, pulsing like breath. My voice wasn't perfect— but it was mine. Raw and right.

In the shadows, I saw Liv lift a hand to her cheek, dabbing beneath one eye. She didn't hide it. Didn't flinch.

It wasn't pain she felt.

It was recognition.

"But I'm not here to be sweet and tame / I'm not a brand, I'm not a name..."

I stood taller with every verse. Not because the room gave me permission.

Because I had stopped asking for it.

"They say I'm pretty enough to bleed for it..."

Everything stilled. The floor. The air. Even my own doubts.

I meant those words.

I meant all of them.

And in the last breath of the song, I let it go.

"No, I'm not your next machine..."

The quiet after that line didn't feel empty.

It felt sacred.

Then the applause rose. Not stadium-polished. Not rehearsed.

Just honest. Human.

I saw Liv lean into Dorian's shoulder, lips moving close.

"She's going to be better than us," she whispered.

He nodded, his eyes shining.

And it didn't sound like defeat.

It sounded like *relief*.

I didn't bow. Didn't need to.

I just let the moment land. Let it become part of me.

And then—I played two more.

I didn't say much between them. I let the music talk. The second was stripped-down, all fingerpicking and ache. The third? A little louder. A little bolder. I closed my eyes during the final chorus and let myself mean every word.

The applause after the last song wasn't louder than before. But it lasted longer. And that felt better.

I opened my eyes. Smiled—not the stage smile.

The real one.

Crooked. Bright. Proud.

"Thank you," I said.

Soft. Sure.

I handed my guitar to a waiting tech and stepped off the riser as the applause faded into reverence.

Liv caught my hand in passing. Her touch was light. Grounding.

I saw you.

I nodded once.

I know.

And then, Dorian stepped into the light.

Dorian

They always said I was the steady one.

The scaffolding. The chord beneath the melody. Liv's safety net.

I never minded.

I never needed the limelight. Never reached for the center. I just wanted the music to land. To move. To matter.

But tonight, I get to be heard too.

Three songs. One stage. No gimmicks.

The first two are bright—groove-driven, pulsing. Old favorites reimagined. I let the rhythm move through my shoulders, let the audience move with me. I smile. Let the crowd respond. I don't flinch when they cheer.

I let myself feel good.

Really good.

Like remembering a language I used to speak fluently. Like coming home to a house I helped build but had never stayed in long enough to decorate.

By the end of the second song, my shirt sticks slightly to my back, and my pulse hums in time with the crowd's applause. I nod, take a drink of water, and settle in.

Because the third song?

That one's mine.

Not mine in the publishing sense.

Mine.

The lights dip to a warm, coppered hush. Like dusk on skin. Like memory.

I sit at the keyboard, fingers resting lightly, like they're remembering the weight of a world I used to carry.

I breathe in once.

"I light up rooms they tried to dim..."

The melody is simple. Just enough to hold the weight of the words. I let it rise slow. No frills.

Just truth.

*"Not your savior, not your shade,
I'm the song your silence made..."*

My voice doesn't shake. It soars and breaks and returns—but it doesn't hide.

I glance toward the wings. She's there.

Olivia.

No stage makeup. No flashbulb smile.

Watching me like I'm something holy.

And God, there were years I held back. For her. For myself. Because I didn't know what would unravel if I let it all spill.

"They want joy but not the weight..."

The crowd exhales. Feels it.

They've been there too.

Told to glow, but never grieve. To inspire, but never ache.

*"Smile. But not too loud.
Hurt. But not publicly..."*

I let the lyric breathe.

Then push forward.

"Built my voice with open hands..."

And it hits me—how true that line is.

Every harmony I sang behind Liv.

Every track I laid down to lift her up.

Every moment I buried my own story to build a world for hers.

I gave it away.

Hoping the echoes would bring her back to herself.

"Even scars can shimmer bold..."

The last note rings out like an exhale.

And I close my eyes—not because I need to, but because I want to.

I want to *feel* it in the dark.

The silence after isn't hollow.

It's sacred.

Then the applause.

Not polite. Not preprogrammed.

Real.

Raw.

When I stand, I don't need to bow. I just let the moment settle into me.

And when I step offstage, she's there.

No persona. No pretense.

Just Olivia.

She wraps her arms around me. Tight. Honest. No words at first.

Just gratitude.

Not for the song.

For *everything* before and beyond it.

"Thank you," she whispers.

And I know she doesn't mean for the show.

She means for the years.

For the nights I sat in silence just so she wouldn't have to.

For the chords I played so she could speak without shaking.

For the fact that I never asked her to be anything but herself.

And in that moment, I believe—

it wasn't just the music that saved her.

It was *us*.

Chapter 41: Just Liv

Liv

The lights aren't blinding. That's the first thing I notice. They're warm. Amber, low-hung. Tuck and Dorian spent hours adjusting them until they felt less like a concert and more like an invitation.

I step into the center of the stage. Boots planted. Guitar slung. Heart, steady enough. The crowd stretches wide, shoulder to shoulder, packed in tight. Locals. Familiar faces from gas stations and back porches. A few Libby fans, I can spot them by the makeup and merch turned subtle. And there, in the back near the bar, flanked by two empty stools like he's holding court,

Sterling Vale. Cufflinks. Designer shirt too crisp for Delco. Smile like he never lost a bet. He doesn't belong here. Not really. But he's here. And I am too.

I breathe in. Then speak. "Thank you for coming. My name's Olivia Reed, but you can call me Liv," I say with a crooked smile. "Some of you knew my name before tonight. Some didn't. Either way, I'm honored."

A pause. "And before I say anything else, I need to say this." I turn slightly, gesturing offstage. "To Sadie Bell, and to Dorian West. The two reasons I'm standing here as myself tonight."

Applause rises. Honest, sharp. Sadie peeks out with flushed cheeks and a grin that could power the grid. Dorian just nods, quiet and proud.

I smile. "I want them with me for this first one. Feels right." They step out, guitars slung, and we form a triangle. No frontwoman. No lead. Just... us.

I close my eyes for a beat and send a quiet prayer into the strings. Let this be truth. A memory flickers—the smell of stale beer, the crackle of old monitors, a room smaller than this but filled with the same kind of want. I used to tremble before the first note.

Now, I just breathe.

Then,

"*I used to chase the high, neon and numb Wrapped in the glitter, too scared to run...*"

The beat kicks in. The room vibrates. A few people whoop. Some just freeze, caught in the voltage.

"*But I burned the sequins, broke the spell I'm not your icon, I'm raising hell...*"

Sadie steps up for the harmony, our voices twining, "*Not a pill, not a crown, not your perfect scene This time, it's blood and strings and everything between...*"

The chorus rips loose. The crowd's swaying now. "*This time, it's me, no lights to blind I'm the fire you tried to find...*"

Sterling leans forward, arms crossed. Watching. But I'm not singing for him. I'm singing for every girl who cracked but didn't shatter. For every version of me.

The second verse shreds out, "*She took the stage, but left the chains Still got the scars, still sings through pain...*"

Sadie's bridge nearly breaks the room open, "*You wanted masks, we brought soul You wrote the script, we rewrote the role...*"

And then we hit the final chorus like a wildfire taking breath: "*This time, it's me, no veil, no shame...*"

My voice pushes through the noise, stronger than it's been in years. "*Not a starlet, not your scene Just a woman who dares to scream...*"

I drop to solo. Guitar fading beneath me. "*I don't need the high, I've got the song And this time, I've been me all along...*"

275

Silence. Not stunned. Not confused. Moved.

And when the applause comes, it isn't about fame. It's about truth finally having a voice. The last chord hangs like smoke. My fingers tremble slightly on the strings, not from fear. From release.

The crowd roars, but I don't move right away. I glance past the front row, scanning the faces lit amber by the stage lights. And there he is. Sterling. Leaning forward now. The crisp line of his shirt is creased. One button undone at the collar. His cufflinks, gold, unnecessary, catch the overheads like teeth. And is that... sweat? Good. Because there's no Libby here tonight. No gloss. No spectacle. No character bending herself into the fantasy he orchestrated. Just a woman. Raw. Breakable. And utterly unafraid to show it.

I turn my gaze. Tucker stands near the back wall, one arm around my mother's shoulders, my dad beside them, arms crossed but smiling that quiet way he does when he's proud and pretending not to be. Tuck's eyes are on me. Unmoving. Unshaken. Like I'm the only light in the room.

I nodded to Sadie and Dorian again, but this one's mine as they exit the stage. A little slower. A little deeper. A look back, but not to stay. Just to understand.

I strum. *"She was wild hair and paper dreams Writing songs where no one sees..."*

The first verse spills gently, like a diary entry whispered into a worn notebook. *"A voice too big for this small town..."*

I remember her. Nineteen. Hopeful. Soft-skinned and stubborn. Tucker and Dorian by my side, every harmony like oxygen. *"She only knew she wasn't scared..."*

I wasn't. Not then.

The tempo shifts slightly, brighter keys, more polished rhythm. *"Now the lights are loud, the dress is gold..."*

The Libby years. The illusion. I sing those words with a flicker of ache but no shame. "*Smile wide, eyes gone gray...*"

I don't look at Sterling now. He knows.

"*She traded soul for a name they'd say...*"

And I did. Willingly. Until I couldn't anymore. The chords strip down, sparser, lower.

The bridge comes quiet. "*Now she's silence in an old screen door Hands that shake, knees on the floor...*"

My throat tightens. But I don't break. "*Still me, somewhere, under stars...*"

Yes. Still me. Always me.

The outro fades like a prayer: "*So she sings, not to be seen, But to remember who she's been...*"

The final note is soft enough to hush the air. And in that hush, I know the next one will be the reckoning. The closer. The fire. But this? This was the memory. The reckoning of all the versions that built me.

And in the wings, the two who knew every version of this voice—Sadie and Dorian—watched without flinching.

Chapter 42: The Phoenix

The crowd is still. Still buzzing. Still breathless. But still.

I cross the stage slowly and sit at the upright piano. Not flashy. Not polished. The one Tuck had delivered last week because I said I needed wood under my fingers, not gloss.

I don't speak. I just breathe.

Then I look up. He's still here. Sterling. Table near the wall, eyes like he's trying not to blink. Shirt damp at the collar now. Something between fury and fear behind the gloss.

Good. He doesn't deserve this moment. But he's going to witness it.

I let my hands hover over the keys. And then I play.

The notes are haunting. Simple. Barely there. My voice cracks before the first word even forms.

"He lit the match, called it mercy,
Told me stars don't shine without scars.
Painted dreams in gold and chloroform,
Said I owed him every part.

I wore his silence like a diamond,
Learned to smile through the smoke.
Danced in gowns sewn from control,
Till the mirror finally broke.."

The chords are thin. My throat tight. I'm not performing. I'm remembering. Everything. The penthouse floor. The blackout. The pills. The silence. The smile I practiced in the mirror until my face forgot how to be mine.

"You built me from ashes,

Then blamed me for the fire.
Carved a legend on my skin,
And sold me as desire.

But I remember every line you fed me.
Every time you watched me fall.
I was never your creation...
Just the price behind it all."

The crowd is holding their breath. I can feel it.
Like they're afraid if they move, I'll break. And
maybe I will. But not yet.

"You taught me to be lovely,
As long as I was tame.
Fed me pills and praise in silence,
Then disappeared the shame.

Called it fame, called it devotion
But it felt like being owned
Every light you turned upon me
Was a lie I'd never known."

That's the line where something inside me
flips. Where the fire catches. My hands slam the
keys harder now.

"You built me from ashes,
Then blamed me for the fire.
Carved a legend on my skin,
And sold me as desire.

But I remember every line you fed me.
Every time you watched me fall.
I was never your creation...
Just the price behind it all."

I stop looking at him. Because he doesn't matter now. This is for me.

"I am not your ghost to keep,
Not your prize, not your song.
You thought you wrote my melody,
But I've been screaming all along.

You called me phoenix like it was praise,
But I was never yours to blaze.
I rose not from wonder—but your destruction.

You wore two faces: angel and king,
But you were the monster behind the pretty things.."

I take a deep breath and pause before my voice quivers at the end.

"You built me from ashes,
But now I hold the flame.
No more lines, no more whispers,
You won't ever know my name.
And when they ask who broke the silence,
I will rise, not bow or fall.
I am not your creation...
I was never yours at all."

The final note doesn't drift. It detonates.
The silence that follows isn't stunned. It's sacred.
And then the room erupts. Not for Libby. Not even for Liv. But for the woman who walked through fire and sang the truth from the ashes.
I don't bow. I just breathe. And somewhere inside me, something unlatches.
And I rise.

The applause doesn't echo the way it used to. It lands softer, like rain on the roof of a house that finally feels like home.

And for once, I don't chase it. Don't ache to be louder. Don't wonder who's watching.

I just stand there, heart thudding in my chest. Not from fear. But from something else.

The sound isn't a finish line. It's a threshold.

And I step through it barefoot, stripped of sequins and expectation. Not Libby. Not even a version of her.

Just the woman who survived.

Epilogue

What began as a quiet return home became wildfire. I hadn't expected the world to notice. But it did—loudly.

One blurry backstage photo. Two tagged names. A forty-minute set.

Four million streams. Seven exposés.

A producer's empire turned to ash.

I didn't set out to burn Sterling down. I only opened the window and let the light in. It was something I had to do—for myself.

But truth? Truth has teeth.

Within weeks, other artists came forward. Some famous. Some forgotten. Some just starting out. Their stories weren't all the same, but the patterns were:

Control.

Isolation.

The weight of someone holding on too tightly. Bruises no makeup could hide. Contracts no lawyer could undo. A noose, real or imagined, disguised as opportunity.

They called it another #MeToo moment. A reckoning. I didn't claim that. But I didn't deny it, either.

Hollywood being Hollywood, the headlines shifted. Forgotten was the documentary about my rise and ruin. Sterling took center stage. Thirty years of manipulation and quiet destruction finally laid bare.

I didn't want him to take up space in my story anymore. But I couldn't walk away from what I'd inadvertently started.

I said it plainly on a late-night podcast, Dorian's hand steady beneath the table:

"I should've spoken sooner. Louder. For them. For me. I won't go quiet again."

Something life-changing had happened—and I could no longer drown it out with champagne and pills. Recovery demanded I face it. Therapy demanded I name it. And healing meant I had to carry it.

It meant the quiet summer of home was ending. It meant my only plan couldn't be just making it through the day.

Even after the brand relaunch, after the careful reappearance online, I had to keep showing up.

Again and again.

Rey traveled with me. So did others—healers, friends, therapists—who helped me sit inside the pain each time I told the story. I was grateful for that support.

And I hated that not everyone had access to it.

That ache became Phoenix House.

A foundation not just for women, but for anyone silenced, manipulated, or bruised by power masquerading as love.

I refused to flatten the truth.

Abusers come in every gender. So do survivors.

The work became rhythm. Not performance. Not press. Just purpose.

Everyone in my orbit stood with me. Through every tide change.

My mom became my best friend—she helped build Phoenix House from the ground up. She launched writing programs to help members process grief through words.

Which means she finally wrote her chapbook.

More than one.

Poetic instructions, she called them—maps through grief, lit by poems that made others feel seen.

She and Rey became inseparable. Together, they made sure even the quiet ones—the ones hiding in the margins—found ways to speak.

And Dad?

Back at The Crick.

Still stubborn. Still revered.

Still kicking his "boss" out of the bar early.

The managers followed his lead. Pushed Tucker out often.

Told him to go live a little. Live his life.

With me.

That was the wildest part of all—

To love freely. Loudly.

No enablers. No handlers.

Just us.

We weren't the same Liv and Tuck who made promises by the creek. But we built something better. With Rey's help, we talked about the in-between. The missing years. The grief. The men.

The broken parts and beautiful ones.

We didn't know all our triggers. But we stayed curious.

We stayed safe.

We built a future that felt healthy. Real.

One of those sessions led me to Noah.

We'd been divorced nearly twenty years but always exchanged the occasional birthday text or holiday wish.

Tuck encouraged me—said it didn't have to be final, just honest.

I was terrified.

What if I fell into old patterns?

What if Libby came out to protect me?

Rey reminded me:

You don't have to hide from the past.

You just have to decide whether to carry it or lay it down.

One night, I sat in our office, phone in hand, unsure where to begin.

The woman known for her words couldn't type one damn sentence.

Eventually, I did.

"Hey, it's Liv. Let me know if you get a moment to talk."

Masterpiece, right?

I was tapping my nails against the oak table when FaceTime rang. Of course Noah wouldn't text back. He wanted to see my face.

I tapped *Join*.

There he was—smiling, settling into a porch chair.

"Hey, kiddo. Long time no talk."

"Hey Noah, how are you?"

"Great. Just talking to my beautiful ex-wife while watching my current wife have a garden tea party with our twins."

"Tw...Twins?? That woman deserves flowers every day and you on your knees worshiping her. You were a giant baby, your mom said."

"Two sets, Liv. Two girls, two boys. It's chaos. And it's heaven."

My chest ached—something unnamable. Like heartbreak, but not for Noah.

More like... something I'd lost. Or never had.

"I'm so happy for you," I said, meaning it. "It sounds perfect."

"It is. I'm a blessed man." He looked at me—really looked. "But that's not why you reached out, is it?"

I hesitated. "Not exactly. I mean... it's nice to see you. And I am happy for you. But—yeah. Tuck and I were talking, in therapy. We've got this no-secrets thing. Trying to build something honest. And Noah, I just..."

My throat closed. Tears welled.

"I am so fucking sorry for what I put you through."

Noah was quiet. Then smiled, eyes misting.

"Olivia Morgan. You have nothing to apologize for. We were young. Life was fast. I didn't know how to save you. I thought fame meant more than I did. But we've both learned a lot since then."

"What do you mean?"

"I wasn't your first or last love. But you were my first. I don't say that to guilt you. I say it because I needed to go through the story of us to get to where I am. I'm a better man, a better husband, because of you."

He glanced off-screen—toward the life he'd built.

"I wouldn't change a thing if it meant missing this."

I wiped my tears and laughed—soft and surprised—because I felt the same way. "I know what you mean."

"Tuck, eh?" Noah smirked, that familiar twinkle in his eye. "I always knew, deep down, you were saving your real self for him. You couldn't be fully you while trying to be Libby."

"What do you mean?"

"I mean," he said, pointing at the screen, "you could only carry one identity at a time. You let the best of yourself come through sometimes—but when it came to decisions, emotions, living? You put yourself on the backburner."

He leaned in, chuckling. "That was your first mistake. Because *you*, kiddo—the real you—that's the woman I saw on CNN. The one who saved herself. Who's saving others."

"I don't know about saving," I said, voice quieter now. "I had help. I still have help. But yeah... it's like the fog's finally lifting. And I want you to know... you were the best chapter in Libby Morgan's life. And I'll always be grateful."

He smiled, a gentle sadness behind it. "I wasn't in Libby's life, Liv. I was in yours. *You* were the one who made Libby the end-all, be-all. And I don't regret a single minute we had."

I looked at him—really looked—and for a second, the weight of our shared past felt like a blessing instead of a bruise.

Then I noticed Tuck standing in the doorway, arms crossed, a quiet pride softening his face. I had done something hard. And he knew it.

"I don't either," I said, eyes still on Noah. "But there's someone here I'd love you to meet."

"Oh yeah?" he grinned.

Tuck crossed the room and slid behind me, settling into the desk chair. I stood just long enough to sit on his lap and tilt the camera toward both of us.

"Noah," I said, "meet Tucker Hayes."

"Hey, Noah. Real nice to meet you."

Noah's face lit up. "Tucker Hayes. I feel like I already know everything about you. This one used to talk about you all the time. Nice to finally put a face to the name."

Tuck smirked, his hand resting at my waist. "Likewise. You're the only thing from her past that still comes with a smile."

Noah laughed—and then looked offscreen, waving someone over.

A moment later, a stunning brunette with soft green eyes and a smile full of sunlight settled onto his lap, adjusting the camera as naturally as if she'd always belonged there.

"Amelia," he said, wrapping an arm around her, "may I introduce you to the incomparable Olivia Morgan Reed—and the love of her life, Tucker Hayes."

Amelia's eyes widened at first recognition, maybe awe—but her expression softened into something warm and genuine.

"It's so nice to meet you both," she said, leaning in to plant a kiss on Noah's cheek. "Liv, I've heard so many wonderful things about you."

287

From that moment on, something shifted. Peace. Ease. Mutual forgiveness, unspoken but understood.

We chatted for a while—promises of visits, of stories shared over dinner, maybe even a meet-up someday.

And maybe it wouldn't happen. Maybe it would.

But for the first time in a long, long time...
I felt hope.
And I was grateful for that hope

Months passed.

Sadie Bell graduated in a white cap, boots under her gown, and eyeliner smudged from crying.

Valedictorian.

Her speech quoted Fleetwood Mac and thanked "the voices that didn't just teach me how to sing, but how to stay standing."

In the crowd sat a row of glorious misfits who'd flown in from all over the world to cheer for our girl.

Ari. Pax. Eli. My parents. Dorian. Tucker. And me.

I may have pulled a few strings to get those tickets. May have used a bit of celebrity leverage. But come on—my baby sister was graduating high school.

Yeah. She was mine. And I made sure everyone knew it.

I'd asked her once, if she could go anywhere in the world, where would she go?

She said, *everywhere.*

So, before she hit the studio, Dorian and I (plus a discreet but very alert security team) took her around the world.

We let her live without expectations. Eat street food. Drink sangria (where it was legal). Flirt and dance and stay up too late.

We wanted her to record her EP, sure—but more than that, we wanted her to see the world *as herself.*

Without a brand. Without pressure. Without performance.

Because I knew—without a single doubt—that Sadie Bell was going to be a global name. But before she gave the world her voice, she deserved to find her own life.

And selfishly? I wanted her to live a little longer. For herself. For the stories that would follow.

She was back in the studio by July.

Dorian called her a "bratty genius."

We let her lead. She let us guide.

The songs weren't perfect. But they were *honest.*

When her debut single dropped, it hit #3 on Spotify's *New Voices* playlist within a week.

I didn't cry then.

I cried when Sadie looked at me during playback and said:

"I want this to be the truth. Not just the story."

Speaking of crying—I'd been crying *a lot* lately.

During the trip, I felt... off. Exhausted in a way I couldn't quite name. Sadie and Dorian teased me about my constant naps, blaming it on "years of over-caffeinated insomnia finally catching up to you."

Maybe they were right.

Or maybe it was just that every time I was away from Tucker, I missed him with every cell in my body.

So, when Sadie said she was ready to go home, I almost wept with relief.

And home?

Home was slower now. Not quiet, I'd never be quiet—but slower.

Tucker's tools clashed against my scattered notebooks. His labeled pantry beside my chaotic spice drawer. A record always spinning. A window always open.

One September morning, I woke to find his hand curled around mine—his wedding ring glinting in the sunrise.

Mine beside it, heavier. Warmer. Perfect.

Yes—we got hitched.

The weekend after our Costa Rica stop, the last leg of our world tour.

No grand announcement. No designer dress. Just a backyard ceremony along the creek, at my parents' house.

The people we loved. The words we meant.

Dorian cried harder than my mother. He called it criminal that I reduced our wedding to "an overnight delivery dress and a thrifted veil."
I told him that was kind of the point.

We did let him marry us.

Which meant laughter through tears. A few inside jokes. And one poetic monologue that made even Big Al dab at his eyes.

I must've really enjoyed that wedding. And the trip.

Because suddenly... none of my clothes fit.

One afternoon in the studio, Sadie squinted at me and said, "Did you eat a *burrito baby* or something? You look *pregnant*."

Tucker had been off to the side, adjusting hydration filters. Our eyes met.

No.

Wait.

What?

When was the last time I had my period?

I'd skipped so often I'd stopped noticing. I always chalked it up to years of drug use. My cycle had never really returned.

Just that morning, Tucker had teased me for sobbing over a baby bunny in the yard—"our little bun bun," I'd insisted we rescue. We'd both laughed. But now?

We were frozen.

Sadie misread our silence, her face falling. "Oh god, I'm sorry. I didn't mean—girl power and all, I wasn't making a comment about your—"

We were already gone.

Tucker and I sprinted to the nearest store, grabbed a test, and raced back to the studio. We didn't wait to get home. We went straight to the bathroom.

Sadie kept nervously apologizing. Dorian was too deep in a mix to notice anything was wrong.

Thirty seconds later, that test blazed positive.

We screamed.

We cried.

We screamed some more.

And cried harder.

I burst out of the bathroom and covered Sadie's face in kisses. She tried to swat me off.

"Oh my *god*, are you on drugs again?" she shrieked.

Without thinking, I tossed the test at her (gross, I know).

She caught it midair and stared.

Dorian looked up—confused—then his eyes widened.

"Uncle Dori has a *nice* ring to it," Tucker said, sniffling.

Dorian broke.

Full tears. Full meltdown.

Laughing. Crying. Clutching my waist. Babbling about ponies, wills, stocks, bonds, and a trust fund.

Sadie still hadn't caught up.

Then, suddenly, she *did*.

She burst into laughter instead of tears.

"You're all *ridiculous* human beings."

I grinned, wrapped an arm around her waist. "You will be too, when you hold your niece or nephew in your arms."

Sadie, our cynic and comic, blinked once—tears threatening, then wiped them away and rolled her eyes.

But she held me a little tighter.

It became a core memory. One we'd talk about forever.

Now, on the fridge, a blurry black-and-white ultrasound hangs with a name scribbled on the back: **Bean**.

"Geriatric pregnancy," the doctor had said with a smirk.

I smirked right back.

"Try miraculous," I replied.

Some mornings, I still stand in front of the mirror and search for ghosts.

But they don't look back.

Libby's quiet now.

Not gone. Not erased.

Just... resting.

Like cooled ash beneath the soil.

I smile.

One hand on my belly. The other pressing gently to the piano keys.

And for the first time, I don't need a song to prove I'm alive.

But I sing anyway.

Something soft.

Something whole.

Something *new*.

Epilogue Part 2

I was 41 weeks pregnant, officially overdue, and completely over it.

People love to say pregnancy is a miracle. Those people aren't the ones waddling around with a human bowling ball pressing on their bladder and kicking their lungs like a punk band.

Everyone had turned our home into a "serene birthing environment"—whatever that means. Dorian installed dimmers and filled the room with lavender and lo-fi.

Ari kept swapping out hospital gowns I refused to wear for designer kimono robes and threatening to glitter-bomb the birthing tub.

Sadie, documenting the entire process on her phone (*"for the baby's memoir,"* she claimed), had recently made a montage of my pregnancy cravings set to Sade.

Even Big Al kept popping his head in with updates like, *"Backup generator's good to go in case she gives birth during an Eagles game."*

And Tucker?

Tucker was calm. Zen, even. Too zen.

Suspiciously zen. Like a man who knew the real chaos was coming and was saving his strength.

But the MVP?

That was Rey.

Turns out Rey—was dual-certified as a midwife.

"I do vibe checks and vaginal exams," they shrugged, sliding on gloves like it was a red carpet moment.

My OB had done something called a "membrane sweep" the day before, and Rey was

293

now giving me a 24-hour window before we'd "go in"—a phrase I did *not* want to unpack.

Apparently, the sweep was supposed to encourage labor naturally. So far, all it had encouraged was gas and rage.

Also, I smelled like clary sage and feet.

The birth tub was in our bedroom, right under the open window where wind caught the curtains like slow applause.

Tuck had built a playlist, laminated instructions, and prepped water temp charts.

There were cool cloths in the fridge.

Snacks on trays.

Herbal teas labeled by vibe: "Soothing," "Centering," and "Do Not Kill Your Partner."

Everyone kept whispering like I was a holy woman in labor, not a grumpy swamp witch who couldn't bend down to pick up her own socks.

Marianne was brewing bone broth. Dorian was misting eucalyptus. Pax was in the hallway meditating.

Amelia—yes, *that* Amelia, Noah's wife—was rolling a birthing ball across the living room like it was a beach toy.

After I found out I was pregnant, I'd called Noah to let him know I was joining the parent club. Then I asked if Amelia would talk to me. She did. She was honest. She told me about leaking boobs, cracked bones, and weird dreams about spiders in the bassinet. We laughed. Then we cried. Then we texted for three hours straight about the merits of adult diapers.

Now, she was part of the squad.

She was Team Bean.

Then it happened.

A contraction, sudden and deep, carved through me like a hot rope pulled tight. I inhaled sharply. Everyone paused.

I growled. Literally.

"Oh, it's happening!" Sadie squealed, then immediately backed out of the room as I gave her a look that could peel wallpaper.

Another one came. Then another.

"You are so strong," Amelia whispered, rubbing my back.

"Don't touch me."

"Of course."

"You're doing beautifully," Marianne said, placing a hand on my shoulder.

"WHERE IS MY MOM."

"You mean me?" she asked softly.

"YES YOU. I NEED MY MOMMY."

Rey checked my dilation mid-contraction, and I might've called them a traitor and tried to bite their arm.

"I'm gonna pretend you didn't just call me Satan," Rey said, checking their Apple Watch. "We're at 7 centimeters. Get in the tub."

Tucker helped me in. I nearly drowned him with one swipe of my arm.

Everyone was trying to keep me calm. To remind me to breathe. To moan. To vocalize. To *lean into the power of the feminine body*.

I screamed. Like a banshee on a warpath. "I AM NEVER HAVING SEX AGAIN."

Tucker nodded, wisely saying nothing.

"I CAN FEEL MY BONES."

"Good," Rey smiled. "That means it's working."

The world got smaller. Just hot water, tight space, the sound of my breath and everyone's awe and fear and laughter colliding in the corners of the room.

Every time I opened my mouth, someone tried to shove ice chips in it.

I launched them at Dorian. He caught them. In a cocktail glass. With garnish.

It was primal. It was chaos. It was beautiful and terrifying and sweaty and perfect.

And it wasn't done yet.

The next chapter would bring her earthside.

But for now, I am still in the storm.

And I was ready to meet the girl who'd made me waddle, sob, laugh, and fall in love with my body again.

Even if I'd probably yell at her on the way out.

And then—Rey snapped.

Like, **snapped**.

"EVERYONE OUT."

The command dropped like thunder. Sudden. Sharp. Absolute.

Pax dropped their singing bowl.

Sadie gasped.

Ari clutched pearls that didn't exist.

Even Dorian froze mid-spritz, lavender bottle hovering in midair.

Rey didn't raise their voice. They sliced it. Through the incense and the tension and the love—straight through all of us.

"This next part is sacred," they said, softer now. "And she doesn't need an audience. She needs space."

Marianne nodded first. Then Amelia. Then the rest of the holy chaos crew shuffled out in stunned silence, like reverent guests exiting a cathedral. I could hear Big Al mutter, *"Remind me never to piss that one off."*

The door clicked shut.

And then there were three.

Me. Tucker. Rey.

The world dimmed, but it wasn't dark. The light from the window caught the edge of the birthing tub just right—turning the water gold. Tucker knelt beside me, one hand resting on my back, the other gripping my hand like we were cliffside together, breathless and trusting.

Rey crouched down in front of me, calm again. Or maybe just fierce in the quiet way now.

"You're almost there," they whispered. "Let's bring her home."

The pain was tidal. The silence was thick. The air held its breath with me.

And still, somehow, I was laughing between pushes. At the absurdity of this. At the intimacy. At Tucker whispering *"you've got this, baby"* in a voice that cracked on every word. At Rey muttering *"this little Aries is dramatic already"* as they adjusted the mirror.

I pushed.

Once.

Twice.

Three times.

And then—her.

All at once and slowly, like thunder echoing backward, like the first note of a new song finding its pitch.

A silence followed that wasn't silence at all.

And then a cry. High, strong, clear.

Rey caught her with practiced grace, lifting her up into the dim gold light.

"Oh my God," Tucker breathed.

I couldn't speak. Could only watch. Could only reach.

Rey handed her to me, slippery and perfect and warm, still tethered to the body that made her.

"Hi," I whispered. "You're here."

In the hallway, the chaos resumed. Sadie was yelling something about missing it. Dorian was crying. Again. Pax was chanting. Someone— probably Big Al—was popping a bottle of beer meant for a christening.

But in this room?

Just us.

She was so small. And yet, she filled every corner of me.

We hadn't named her yet.

Not officially.

But we would.

And when we did, we'd whisper it into her hair.

Into the space between worlds.

Into the hush that comes after the storm.

**Scan to hear original music inspired by the book
and the characters you love.**
Available now on Spotify and other platforms.

While I may not be a musician, I write with my whole
heart. I'm deeply thankful to Suno AI Pro for helping bring
Liv, Sadie, and Dorian's voices to life—and for giving me a
way to share the music I've always heard in my head.

Acknowledgements

With Love and Gratitude

To my husband—thank you for rolling with the "I have a crazy idea" moment, and for loving me through every spiral that turned that idea into an obsession.

To my beautiful broke bestie—my seven-year-old—who went from "Mommy's writing a book?" to "When can we write our first one together?" Oh, we will.

To my left retina (yes, really), which detached in December and left me unable to see out of one eye for months. Turns out I'm not the biggest fan of audiobooks, which gave my mind permission to wander. And in that wandering, Liv found me. Or maybe she was always there. She just needed help coming to life.

To my brain—for moving like a cinematic masterpiece. I see in color and sound. Liv's world came through like a reel that wouldn't stop playing.

To the future authors out there who dream in images, soundscapes, and spiraling notes: I hope we're building a new kind of storytelling. One where books feel like films. Where stories move like songs. Where the page is just the beginning.

To my family and friends—thank you for letting me stay weird, for listening to my rambles, and for loving the parts of me that don't quite fit the mold.

And once again, to my dad, who passed away in 2020 and is watching over me and our family. I imagine him chillin' with our fur besties over the rainbow bridge—I miss you every day of my life and will always long for one more hug and one more laugh.

For Mom, we may drive each other crazy but I know without any doubt, you are my biggest fan.

And to the tech that helped me bring this world to life—ChatGPT, Suno, Starry AI, Canva—you didn't write the book (that voice, that mess, that magic? All mine), but you sure helped me get it into the world. You answered every question, filled every knowledge gap, and made the impossible feel doable. AI didn't replace the soul—it just helped carry it farther. Also, I said please. Always. Just in case.

This is for the real ones.

To Liv—I'm proud of you.

To Sadie—I don't think we've seen the last of you yet...

About the Author

Lauren Lee Mann is a lifelong resident of Delaware County, Pennsylvania, with roots that stretch just across the border into Delaware, where she spent much of her young adult life. She is married to the love of her life, August John, and is the proud mother of a vibrant red-haired daughter, Emma.

By day, Lauren has built a successful career in the corporate business world since the age of 21. She deeply values her work, her family, her friends, and long summer days at the beach.

Though raised in a dog-loving household, life had other plans, she is now a devoted cat mom to five: three beloved seniors, Blake, Carmie, and Muffin, and two mischievous youngsters, Gigi and Tiger.

The Life and Death of Libby Morgan is her debut novel.